A far different path

A Far Different Path

For information: www.afardifferentpath.com

ISBN#: 978-1-7326713-0-0

Printed in the United States of America

Cover Design: www.damonza.com

Interior Formatting: www.damonza.com

For Lucile

*"I ask not for any crown
but that which all may win;
nor try to conquer any world
except the one within."*

Louisa May Alcott

MICHAEL STONE

A far different path

A NOVEL

BASED ON A TRUE STORY

Chapter 1

1918

RIDING THERE IN the dark, gently rocking back and forth, I lost track of the order of stops before finally relenting to the exhaustion. I couldn't have been asleep for more than an hour when the train conductor slammed open the door at the rear of the car and raised the lights.

"Mackinaaawww City!" His voice was as booming and practiced as any vaudeville announcer's. "End of the line folks."

Blinded and squinting, I stole a quick glance at my watch—11:30 pm. Nearly thirteen hours had passed since leaving home that morning and at least six more remained between me and a proper bed. Unlike any of the previous stops on the Michigan Central line this one was still and deserted. Even the hissing steam engine fell silent for the first time since we'd boarded. The train sat at the northern most tip of the Lower Peninsula, facing the Straits of Mackinac head on. Part Lake Huron, part Lake Michigan, the five-mile stretch of dark, churning water left us completely cut off from our final destination. We had literally run out of track.

It never occurred to me that we would have to cross the Straits to get to the Upper Peninsula and make the connection to Munising. I was not normally so absent-minded, but the week that unfolded just prior to climbing aboard that train left me no time to contemplate the actual trip. It all started with a late-night knock on the door of my family's farmhouse. A full day of threshing left us in the fields until dark and we had just sat down in the parlor, resting for the first time since sunrise.

There was nothing timid or uncertain about the knock. My parents froze in their chairs, moving only their eyes to look at each other and then me as the same thought raced through our minds. We lived far enough from town that nighttime callers rarely brought good news and my fiancé Howard was overseas fighting on the Western Front. He'd been gone four months and even tiny Albion had lost several boys to the Germans by then. I jumped up from my chair, dropping the five-foot strand of lace I was tatting for my wedding dress back onto the seat.

"Let me see who that is," Father said, pushing himself up with some effort. He forced a smile my way and clucked his tongue two times, like he often did when he noticed me worrying. He opened the door, but paused first, steadying himself for whatever news was on the other side. Standing there on our porch was Mr. Riley, Albion's postmaster. Like a hawk soaring the skies for prey, I instantly spotted the envelope in his right hand.

"Good evening Elmer. I'm sorry to bother you so late," Mr. Riley said. He nodded at each of my parents, but his eyes came to rest on me. "Got a telegram here for Lucile."

I just stood there, not sure if I should lunge for the door

or run from the room. The dilemma must have registered on my face.

"I know I'm not supposed to say anything, but it's nothing to do with Howard, that's for sure. From a Mr. Abell, up in Munising." I felt a flush of relief emerge over the tops of my cheeks as the news allowed me to breathe again.

"Thank you, Mr. Riley," I said.

"Abell?" Father repeated, opening the door to accept the flimsy note. He inspected it closely in the porch light's dim glow, oblivious to an eclipse of moths flitting inside.

"I told the man no one likes to find me on their stoop this late," Mr. Riley said, with a shake of his head and a shrug. "You all have a nice evening now." He disappeared into the darkness hugging the bottom of the stairs.

"Thanks Tom," Father replied, still studying the envelope. He let the screen door go and without even looking caught it just before it slammed shut, guiding it to a gentle close instead. "Do you know what this is about Lucy?" he said, finally passing it to me.

"I think so."

Mother came and stood right next to me. "Who's Mr. Abell?" She looked barely able to keep herself from grabbing the telegram out of my hand.

"It's about a job," I said as casually as I could, but the words got caught on my tongue. She was already unhappy I hadn't accepted a teaching position at the local elementary school. I opened the envelope with a whisk of my finger.

"Miss Ball. Need qualified replacements for high school teachers drafted. Albion College President recommends you highly. $120 per month. Start next week."

"Next week!" Mother gasped.

"Desperate for help. Wire answer tomorrow. With sincere gratitude. Mr. Harold Abell, Superintendent of Schools. Munising, Michigan."

"It's out of the question," Mother said. She dropped into the creaky, straight-backed Victorian chair where she did her knitting each night. "A young woman has no business traveling so far from home." She gathered up the sweater she was making for my brother Elton and began to count stitches on one of the needles, as if an entire conversation had occurred and no longer required her attention.

"It is good money," Father said. Smiling. Proud. The salary was double what teachers in our area made.

"What does she need that for?" Mother replied, without looking up or losing count.

"Grace." He shook his head. His voice was firm but he sounded merely annoyed. Unlike me, my father had given up feeling angry with her for only being how she was. My mother's austere manner still caught me off guard and could sting as if experiencing it for the first time, even though I should have been resigned to it by then.

"I'll have to think about it." I said. There would be no discussing it that night.

"Yes, this is a decision to sleep on Lucy," my father said with too much enthusiasm. He always got so nervous when Mother and I were at odds. I stuffed the telegram into my dress pocket and crisscrossed the room to kiss each of them on the cheek—a childhood ritual that followed me into adulthood. Father first, then her.

"Don't worry," I said, lingering over the chair, trying to catch Mother's gaze. "At least it's in Michigan." She stared only at the large skein of wooly yarn unraveling on her lap, refusing to let anything that felt like reassurance soften her contrary demeanor.

"Barely," she finally mumbled in a voice hardly audible over the clicking needles. As a girl I'd often adopted Mother's angst as my own, without question. While I cannot claim that this was the root of all my nervous tendencies it certainly made it more difficult to combat the extreme shyness that had plagued me for years.

"Well goodnight then," I said, kissing her on the forehead, although a bit roughly I suppose. What I really wanted to do was stomp out of the room in an angry snit—a secret fantasy long-held but never acted on. I'd spent years trying to please Grace Ball and was growing tired of the endless quest. The desperation I'd always felt to get her attention and approval eased considerably once I started college and I was gradually discovering that I didn't actually need it.

Upstairs in my room I immediately grabbed the atlas that lived on the back of my desk—a gift from my beloved Aunt Rose for eighth grade graduation. I'd spent years looking at it alone at night, imagining what it would be like to live somewhere else, someplace more interesting and exotic than a farm on the banks of the Kalamazoo River. It took me several minutes to find the tiny dot that was Munising on the Michigan map, on an inset close-up of the Upper Peninsula set off to one side. It wasn't any bigger than the mark made by the sharpest of pencils pushed straight down on a fresh piece of crisp, linen paper. There it was, clinging to the shore of Lake Superior, about as far away as I could get from home without actually leaving the state.

"Barely indeed," I whispered.

I reread the telegram several times before going to sleep. My heart beat faster and my hand shook as I held it near the kerosene lamp mounted on the wall next to the bed. To me it was more than just a job offer. Somewhere in between the Superintendent's urgent words calling me to service was the message I'd been waiting for. The one urging me to leave instead of stay; explore instead of wait; dream instead of merely accept the life presented to me at birth. This was finally my chance to escape the white picket confines of the farm that had fenced me in for twenty-two years already. I couldn't possibly ignore it.

I extinguished the lamp the second I heard Mother climbing the stairs. She paused at my door for a good while before passing down the hall and I froze in place, making sure not to give her any reason to knock and start a conversation. It took forever to drift off and I slept fitfully, creating a daunting list of last minute tasks in my head as I tossed and turned. Even though I said I would think about my decision, there is simply no use in pretending that I hadn't already decided to go to Munising long before my head ever hit the pillow.

"Everyone exit the train," called the conductor as he moved through the railcar. "Door is on the left ladies," he said, pointing back behind us as he passed. "The ferry's ready for boarding."

I stood and crossed the aisle, shaking the shoulder of my friend Vera who was somehow still asleep. "Vera, wake up. We have to get off the train," I said, returning to gather my bags.

"Ferry?" Vera mumbled, rising up on her elbows, yawning. The tightly pinned bun of hair she'd left home with had returned to its natural state, framing her face in a shock of cascading, auburn curls. Vera Smith was my best friend from high school who had also received her teaching degree from Albion College that spring, in English. I was thrilled to discover that

Mr. Abell offered her a job too and we were both relieved to be embarking on this grand adventure together.

"Hurry up now!" It was the same way I scolded my younger brothers. I hadn't figured out yet that my mother's voice lingered somewhere beneath the slightly softer timbre of my own.

"Coming," she said. My admonishment did nothing to quicken her pace.

Stepping off the train, we joined a small contingent of passengers walking down a gravel berm running parallel to the tracks. The train was perched on a wide pier jutting out into the water and I could hear the sound of waves crashing ashore on either side. Assertive gusts of wind blew in off the Straits and pulled at my hair and clothes. In the distance, a row of bright lights hung high in the sky like some wayward strand of moons. The dark, hulking outline of the ferry gradually filled in the space below as we approached.

"Chief Wawatam," I whispered, its name emblazoned in red on the hull.

The ship was massive, standing at least fifty feet tall. The lights overhead were from the Captain's deck at the very top of the boat. Directly beneath that was a pristine, white, two-level passenger cabin, which ran the full length of the ship. The bottom deck was peppered with windows and doors opening onto a narrow, wood-railed promenade. Viewed from that level up, the boat looked like a stately paddle wheeler that gently glided up and down the Mississippi. It was what lay beneath the passenger deck that literally left me shaking.

The Chief Wawatam had a thick, black steel hull and a hinged, V-shaped mouth for a bow that stood wide open. It looked like the gaping jaw of a whale—as fierce and hungry as Moby Dick himself—prepared to gulp down its next meal.

Only this metal giant did not settle for plankton or fish. This ferry swallowed trains! The sight of it drew my legs to a halt and I fell back from Vera and the other passengers. It had been easy to daydream about leaving home from the safety of my cozy, peak-roofed bedroom but there I was, not even a day's train ride away, already wondering if this was all a mistake.

Our family farm sat on 240 acres just outside of Albion, Michigan and was passed down to my father through the Farleys, on his mother's side. David Farley, my great-grandfather, was a pioneer in the area and I knew from the earliest of ages that this place was as much a part of who I am as my blue eyes and brown hair. Nestled in and around a swiftly flowing fork in the Kalamazoo River at the confluence of the north and south branches, Albion always seemed bigger to me than it ever should have. Even though we lived five miles away I never tired of making the trip into "the city"—first by horse and buggy and later by motorcar. Church. Shopping. High school. Visiting my grandparents or Aunt Rose. There was always a reason to make the trek into town. Albion was also home to a fine four-year university founded in 1835, which populated an otherwise small farming community with professors and scholars who deeply valued education and learning. Albion College was one of the first institutions to graduate women and Aunt Rose, my father's sister, worked there as the head librarian. She and Mother had been roommates as students and Rose was actually the one who introduced my parents to each other, granting the college a nearly mythic standing in our family.

It was also Aunt Rose who often took me for long walks around campus, stopping to tell stories here and there about her college experiences. It was always exciting to run into people she knew. They seemed so smart to me, so polite. As a young girl, I could hardly say anything more than my name without running out of breath, but Aunt Rose never embarrassed me or made me feel bad about my nerves. She usually rested a protective hand on my shoulder when we stopped to speak to anyone and swooped in with just the right comment or question to divert any lingering attention away from me. We often walked downtown along Cass Avenue from campus and Rose would treat me to a soda or some penny candy at Parks' Drugstore. On our way back, I always begged to stop on the Cass Street Bridge to watch the rushing river pass below our feet. What a thrill it was to drop a leaf or the occasional treasured bird's feather into the frothy, dark water and see it be swept away.

"Do you think that one will make it?" she'd ask. It was Aunt Rose who taught me how the Kalamazoo meandered across the state to Saugatuck and emptied into Lake Michigan, passing on from there through Huron, Erie, and Ontario, and finally the St. Lawrence River, all the way to the Atlantic Ocean.

"Yes." My answer never changed, but sometimes I only nodded as I strained to keep an eye on whatever I'd just set free.

"I'll bet you're right," she always whispered in my ear.

Rose was the first person I told about accepting the teaching position in Munising. I stopped at the college library on the way to the post office the morning after receiving the telegram. She ran around the front desk and gave me a giant hug.

"How exciting!" she said. "But I'll miss you terribly." Aunt Rose always got things right and I was lucky for it.

"Lucile," Vera called. She stood at the bottom of a wooden gangplank, angled precariously between the dock and the ferry's passenger deck. "He needs our tickets." She gestured towards the crewman stationed there, but remained completely oblivious to the spectacle unfolding beside us.

Two sets of railroad tracks ran right up to the end of the dock where the ferry was moored, each connected to two more pairs of tracks that continued on into the belly of the ship. A trio of workmen labored to hook a line of freight cars onto the ship's own miniature steam engine, which then hauled them into the cargo hold. The ferry barely wobbled as I watched every last bit of that train disappear into its cavernous belly. It was terrifying to think of heading out onto open water after it had only just ingested a several ton meal. The moment that final rail car stopped inside the ship, a deep, rumbling horn sounded—one long blast followed by two shorter ones. The dockworkers scrambled to close the huge metal mouth-of-a-door and thick plumes of black smoke poured out of the twin smokestacks amidships. The horn continued to blare its repetitious warning, one plaintive triptych after another.

"Lucile!" Vera yelled. She glared at me, standing helpless as the crew prepared to retract the gangplank. What started as a nervous walk turned into a full run after just a few steps. I had two small suitcases and a handbag hanging off my arms, my skirt hiked up in one hand, trying not to lose balance on the shifting gravel.

"Wait!" I yelled, wildly waving our tickets in the air. The crewmen were all smiling and chuckling with one and other as we climbed the ramp. Vera did her best to stay annoyed with me but we broke into fits of laughter once safely onboard. It took several minutes for the Chief to back away from the dock and turn 180 degrees toward the U.P. The engines bellowed in protest against the weight of her hull and the strain that was shaking the deck beneath us finally grabbed Vera's attention.

"That doesn't sound good," she said, turning somber in an instant.

"I'm sure it's fine," I replied, even though my heart was racing uncontrollably. Vera was easily reassured and recovered quickly.

"Let's stay outside," she pleaded. "In back. We'll have it to ourselves." She rushed towards the stern where we stood pressed up against the railing for the entire half hour trip.

The nighttime traverse did not allow for much sightseeing but it was a beautiful night. Clear. The wind off the water gusting, but still warm from the August sun, even that far north. Looking back toward the Lower Peninsula there were few lights on the horizon and the horizontal stripes of sky, land, and water blurred together in a shadowy mix of blues, gray, and black. How odd it was to see the lake swell up beneath us and not feel the slightest impact of the waves as the ferry cut through every crest and trough like a knife through butter on a hot summer day. Even the engines settled into a soft hum that merged effortlessly with the rush of the water and the wind.

Standing there, looking out over that endless dark vista, my thoughts finally settled on Howard for the first time that day. I was caught somewhere between guilt and relief by their late arrival. The weight of Howard's departure was unrelenting and the threats he faced overshadowed everything I did back home. There was nowhere in Albion that the two of us had not been during our three years of knowing each other, nowhere I could escape reminders of him and all that was at stake. From the moment he was inducted, I'd fielded dozens of questions about where he was and how he was doing. It was exhausting telling others that he was all right when, on so many days, I could barely be sure of it myself. As the first boys from Albion began to return home injured—or worse—I could feel everyone looking at me with the same pity they offered them or their bereaved families. It had to be easier, I reasoned, to be somewhere completely unfamiliar where I could try to contain the tide of anguish threatening to engulf me. In Munising, I would simply be one of several new teachers in town and not that poor, shy, unmarried Ball girl whose fiancé left and may never return. The truth is, I might have gone mad if the telegram from Munising hadn't arrived when it did, to provide my much-needed escape.

My only link to Howard was his letters and I brought every one of them with me, packed in a tin thread box at the bottom of my bag. I read each several times when they arrived and again later if I needed to fill in the gap before the next letter showed up. We had tracked the timing of several of our exchanges and it took a minimum of two weeks, but usually more like three, for a letter to cross the Atlantic. I didn't know if Howard was able to save the ones I'd sent or if he was forced to abandon them as he disappeared further into Flanders Fields. I liked that there might be a trail of words leading to wherever he was, a path I could follow if I became desperate to see him. It was the same path I sometimes tracked in my dreams and used again to return home, bringing Howard with me by the hand, back to safety.

As the ferry pulled up to the dock at St. Ignace, she blared her horn again despite the late hour. It only sounded once this time and the crew waiting to unload the freight cars was in no hurry since this was the Chief's last crossing of the night. Our northbound Duluth, SouthShore & Atlantic train was waiting onshore. It was just two cars long in addition to the engine and Vera and I were the only passengers to make the connection.

We settled into the first car and Vera collapsed across two of the seats, falling asleep instantly. I was exhausted but kept seeing visions of Howard every time I tried to close my eyes. Bedtime was the most difficult and it wasn't uncommon for me to lay awake half the night, equally distracted by fear or lost in wonderful memories of so many happy times together.

I retrieved the tin of letters and sank into one of the seats at the back of the car where I could be alone with them. Just seeing Howard's handwriting on the outside of each envelope made me feel better. It was all the proof I needed that he was all right and rereading his tender words was enough to sustain my hopes for the future. Our future, together. I knew if we were fortunate enough to be reunited, we would never be apart again.

Chapter 2

April 5, 1918
Camp Custer
Battle Creek, MI

Dear Lucile,

I only hope that I continue to like as well and learn as much in the army as I have during the last two days. Yesterday we marched and drilled for about four hours, traveling almost 10 miles. In the afternoon I participated in a lively game of baseball and after all that exercise, how I did sleep! We have "Retreat" here every night, when all the companies in the entire camp gather in front of the barracks and stand at attention. With the sun dropping behind the hills to the west, a lone bugle is sounded before the band joins in with a national air. I shall never forget the first night I did this as a United States soldier.

No doubt you saw in the "*Free Press*" this morning that the U.S. is going to rush troops to France as fast as possible. The same talk prevails in camp and they are certainly rushing us.

I had a good talk with a man in the barracks this morning. He has been to college and our philosophies of life corresponded somewhat. We were discussing what a captain said to us men the other day. The captain was talking to us about our actions while out on pass. He told us if we "got in bad", to take a treatment as soon as we get back. That was fine and if he had stopped there, we would have respected him. But he spoiled it by saying, "Don't deny yourselves anything while you're out, just take the treatment after." Imagine that coming from an officer! It made me wonder for just a moment if my philosophy of life is wrong, but I know I must keep right for my sake and especially yours. I tell you this just as a little sample of what men must deal with in the army. Think of a young fellow hearing such talk, who had no stable foundation and did not think for himself. I expected it and was therefore prepared. I'm not complaining either, but I am going to fight to come thru with the complaining either, but I am going to fight to come thru with the "clean-been look."

Well Lucile, there is a question I both long and dread to ask – how are you getting along? I hope you are not too lonesome. You certainly were a brave girl. I never saw you shed a tear, but you saw me. I need such training.

Love to you and just one touch of lips.

Howard

Enclosures:

LINES

By a Soldier, Camp Custer.

If Death should choose me in this com-
    ing year,
To join the elements and be a part
Of earth or sky or sea; let no sad tear
Be shed for memory of a gladdened
    heart,
Whose gracious privilege it may some
    day be,
To give America my humble share—
For life and love and friends She gave to
    me.

April 29, 1918
Barracks 1366
Camp Custer

Dear Lucile,

I have never wanted to see you so badly since I have been in camp as I do tonight, but that is impossible and so we make the best of it. I'm glad you are not "blue & worrying". You and I must spend many long and anxious hours before that happy day when we can be together again, for all time.

I guess I'm just getting moody. But Lucile, I have never doubted for one minute that you love me with all your heart. And I did not separate with the least fear that another man could win your affections, even though you will have to wait a long, long time. The human heart wants love and sometimes breaks down under the strain of such waiting, but Lucile, if I am in France two years, I know who will be waiting when I get back. I have known too that you will meet bigger and more attractive men than I, but attraction is no good unless there is the "meeting of souls". And I believe that nothing can really sever two souls that have met as ours have. After all I have said Lucile, it amounts to this, and my soul says it - *I love you.*

I wish you could see the rookies coming in now. I can walk around and "kid" them and feel quite like a soldier, although I have not seen any real soldiering yet. Tell any boys under 21 for me that the army is no place for them, but a place for men. An eighteen or nineteen-year-old boy should not, as a rule, bump up against such things.

I will tell you something now, which is only conjecture on my part and must not be shared. One of the officers was saying that 6000 of the 7000 new men will be sent to a camp in New Jersey soon; in a week or so. When my time comes, I will go gladly, but we will not know until it is time to go. I regret anything that takes me further from you, but the sooner I leave, the sooner I can return.

Well Lucile I feel good, really, and must close and write to my mother for whom I feel so sorry. Enclosed is a verse that made me think of you.

XXXXXXXX
Your lover,
Howard

Enclosure:

Very touching is this exquisite little love-poem:

VALUES

By Jessie B. Rittenhouse

O Love, could I but take the hours
That once I spent with thee,
And coin them all in minted gold,
What should I purchase that would hold
Their worth in joy to me?
Ah, Love—another hour with thee!

Chapter 3

I FIRST LAID eyes on Howard Bridgman in sophomore English at Albion College in August of 1915.

The windows of Robinson Hall were propped wide open to catch any hint of a breeze, random hoots and hollers from a football game echoed around the quadrangle just outside, and the classroom was filled with students chatting in measured tones awaiting the professor's arrival. I knew everyone there except for a handsome young man sitting by himself several rows over and was quite surprised to find him already staring at me as I scanned the room. He smiled and I smiled back but then quickly turned to appear part of my girlfriends' conversation. I knew little of boys and dating but wanted terribly to glance over and see if he was still inclined to catch my eye.

"Let's get started," Professor Hembdt said, barreling in from the hall.

A hush came over the room and we all watched as he arranged things to his liking—centering the lectern, lowering the window shades behind him half-way, precisely arranging his suit coat on the back of a chair.

"Poetry is our first unit," he announced. A few of the boys

grumbled. "I'm going to pair you up to do readings," he continued, studying the class roster. He looked out over the top of his reading glasses.

"Miss Ball," he said. We had met many times through one encounter or another at the library or Aunt Rose's house. "You will be working with Mr. Blake today." Silence. "Mr. Blake?" He stared at the list, waiting.

"He dropped out," someone said. It was not uncommon to lose one or two classmates over the summer. Not everyone could afford the $625 annual tuition.

"Mr. Bridgman then?"

"Yes, sir. Right here." The new boy I'd noticed promptly stood up and made his way to where I was sitting.

"Howard Bridgman," he said, hand outstretched. He had the most beautiful pale blue-gray eyes and the kind of bright, easy smile that left me blushing.

"Lucile Ball," I replied, shaking his hand. I remained seated.

"Nice to meet you," he said.

"Likewise." I could hear my girlfriends whispering and giggling all around me, but I didn't dare look at any of them.

"May I?" he asked, motioning towards the bookshelves lining the wall. I nodded.

I took a good long look at Howard as he picked out a book for us. Trim but not slight, broad shouldered, wire glasses that flattered his face, dressed nicer than most of the other boys, though his shoes looked like they'd seen a few too many Sundays. The bag he dropped on the floor beside me had flopped open and I could see that the paper and pencils inside were new, unused; a carefully folded necktie rested on top. He was thumbing through a book and had it open by the time he returned.

"Evangeline?" he asked.

"Longfellow," I said.

"You know it?"

"Oh yes." My father was not your typical rural farmer. A college man himself, I had grown up hearing him recite excerpts of *Evangeline*, among others, as he trailed the walking plow each spring. It was my job to follow just behind, picking rocks from the freshly turned soil and I hung on his every word.

"*THIS* is the forest primeval," Howard read, taking the seat across from me.

Evangeline tells the story of a woman separated from her betrothed who spends the rest of her life tirelessly searching for him. After decades apart, they are reunited by chance but he is old and sick by then and dies in her arms. It is epic, tragic, and terribly romantic and I was impressed with Howard's interpretation—his tone, inflection, and phrasing, all perfect. I continued to study him as he read and marveled at how different he was from any of the other fellows my age. More intellectual. More serious and mature. More like a man and less like the boys I knew from high school. I worked up the courage to chat with him after class, but he was in a rush.

"I gotta get to work," he said, standing up. He returned the book, packed his bag, then paused, looking straight at me with those eyes—that smile. "It was swell to meet you Lucile." I so hoped he wasn't just being polite.

"I study at the library. My aunt's the librarian," I blurted out as he walked away. He turned. Surprised by my outburst, but then a grin took over his face.

"Well, I'm sure I'll see you around then."

"I expect that you will." I tried flashing one of the flirty smiles I'd seen Mary Pickford or Theda Bara wield at men in the movies. Mother certainly wouldn't have approved.

While Albion College remained a conservative Methodist institution well past the turn of the century and serious dating was not common among the students, I couldn't stop thinking about Howard from the moment we met. I had only gained my freedom from the farm the year before and, after a very long and tedious summer back home, was excited to be living with Aunt Rose again, throwing myself into campus life with little restraint. And Howard, as I later learned, had just taken a year off to work in one of the new automobile factories out-side of Flint, returning with enough money for several years' tuition—wanting the full college experience more than ever. Whether it was passing each other on the way to class, chat-ting at one of our sorority or fraternity gatherings, working together on the college newspaper and yearbook, or wander-ing the stacks at the library secretly hoping to bump into each other, we had little trouble spending as much time together as we desired.

My father was also in the habit of hiring college boys to help out on the farm and I immediately recruited Howard to work that fall. Born and raised on a farm himself in Manitoba, Canada, he quickly became Father's favorite.

"That Bridgman boy's the only one worth the extra money," he'd say.

The one drawback about this arrangement was having to find excuse after excuse to show up back home on the week-ends, after making quite a fuss over spending any time there during my freshman year. There was always extra work to do and no one seemed to suspect my motives even when I took to catching a ride with Howard and whichever one of my brothers was sent to town to collect him early Saturday morning, or Sunday after church. Carleton tried to rib me once as we walked up to the house, but I quieted him quickly.

"Mother didn't find that deck of cards you keep in your room yet, did she?" I asked, slipping my arm through his and giving it a good pinch. He never teased me about Howard again.

After the chores were done, Howard and I often spent time together taking long walks through the fields and talking at the picnic table or up in the hayloft. There were canoe rides on the river, endless rounds of croquet on the large patch of grass between the house and barn, and Howard almost always stayed for a meal on the days he worked. My brothers loved having him around and Father enjoyed jawing about politics or some newly acquired piece of farm equipment as Howard patiently listened, asking questions. He raved about Mother's cooking and was always the first to stand and help clear plates before dessert. His polite nature and skillful flattery somehow never failed to coax a girlish smile out of her. I had never really felt serious about a young man before, and it only felt reassuring that my family liked Howard so much.

One night, with the boys in the barn feeding the animals and my parents rushing over to the neighbors for their weekly drama group, we were left alone to wash dishes.

"I enjoy your family Lucile," Howard said, handing me one sudsy plate after another to rinse and dry. "Especially your brothers."

"Ugh!" I groaned. "They're a little tiresome I'm afraid."

"To you maybe. Not to me. But then, I'm only used to having sisters," he said.

"What are their names?" I asked. "How old?" Howard knew so much about my family, but had barely mentioned his.

"Lillian and Florence, both younger."

"Are they still in Clio with your folks?" Even though he was born in Canada, Howard referred to the small town north of Flint as home.

"Yes. With my father." He paused. "And step-mother."

"Step-mother?" I swore he'd mentioned his mother in conversation.

"My mother died when I was nine," he said, before I could ask.

I looked at his reflection in the window over the sink. He kept his head down, focusing on one last dish in the nearly suds-less water.

"I'm so sorry Howard. That must have been very hard for you and your family."

"Yes." He paused. "It was cancer that took her."

"Howard..." I didn't know what to say, but thankfully he continued.

"My sisters went to Clio to live with relatives after she passed. I had to stay on the farm with Father. It took three years before we joined them." There was little emotion in his voice. Another pause, even longer this time.

"Are you close to her? Your step-mother?" I asked.

"Very. Actually, she's also my mother's sister."

"Oh. I see," I said. He finally handed me the bowl he'd been washing and rewashing and looked up at me in the reflection.

"It's not as strange as it sounds," he said. As much as I relied on Rose for plenty of mothering, the circumstances he described were hard to imagine. "Aunt Laura never married and took such good care of the girls. She's a wonderful woman." The words rushed out of his mouth, nearly faster than he could say them.

"Well," I said. "If she helped raise you, then I'm sure that's true."

Howard smiled, but it didn't linger. He pulled the drain on the sink and began to wipe down the counter with the dishrag. It seemed this was a story he wasn't in the habit of sharing.

"What was your mother's name?"

"Louise. Father says I look like her, but I don't really see it." He draped the dishrag over the faucet, turning to dry his hands on the towel I was still holding.

"I'm sure she was beautiful," I said, lost in those eyes. The brush of his hand against mine sent a shiver through me and made my heart beat even faster.

"I should go. We've got that biology test tomorrow," he said. "You're very kind to listen to me blather on."

"It's not blathering at all. I always love to talk with you."

I retrieved the extra piece of apple pie Mother had wrapped and left for him in the icebox. Instead of taking it, Howard held me by the shoulders. His grip was firm. His gaze insistent.

"I like you so much Lucile. I hope you don't mind me saying it."

"I don't mind." I whispered, as if the words were a secret. He leaned in and I closed my eyes. I wanted him to kiss me, but not some peck on the cheek or a tentative, teenaged brush of lips—a real one, shared by two adults. Instead, he hugged me quickly and took the plate.

"Goodnight then," he said, his body still lingering in front of mine.

I could have kissed him, but I didn't have it in me. Even the most modern young man would have thought twice about any girl being so bold. I would have to wait for Howard to make such a moment between us happen, but that was the first time I knew what it felt like to really want a man. And, it was thrilling to feel him wanting me too.

From then on, Howard and I were inseparable and saw each other nearly every day. We shared a passion for learning but were equally intent to enjoy all that the college had to offer, attending every concert and theater production on campus and taking in each new movie the first night it played. Howard and Aunt Rose got along famously and he was a regular at the house, be it for a formal dinner with several professors or just the three of us drinking tea and playing Flinch or Lotto. I spent many nights studying at the hardware store where Howard worked just to keep him company. After closing he'd walk me home and we'd pause on the bridge to talk and talk, until all hours.

"Did he kiss you yet?" my girlfriends always asked, if they ever found me alone.

"He's not like that," I'd say and some of them would roll their eyes and scoff but I knew they were jealous, longing to find a nice young man for themselves.

It was no surprise that other girls took an interest in Howard and I often caught one or another looking at him, when they didn't know I was watching. Smart, handsome, honest, reliable—they were only noticing the same things I did and the fact that he wasn't from Albion only made him more interesting. But Howard never gave me reason to worry, never once. He only showed the other girls the same polite attention he offered his fraternity brothers, Aunt Rose, or a customer stopping in for a pound of nails. His eyes always brightened, his smile got wider, his voice more excited when he spotted me across the quadrangle, waved me over to the seat saved next to him in class, or whispered from the stern of the canoe to point out a great blue heron paused at the river's edge.

"Lucile," he'd say. And from his lips my name sounded like the woman I knew myself to be on the inside and not the shy thing I'd been looking at in the mirror all those years.

It was in the spring of our junior year when the country—after avoiding it for as long as possible—was finally pulled into the war that was already destroying most of Europe. Mother was worrying herself into a frenzy by then, certain my brothers would be drafted. Rose confided that the college president and all the deans were meeting privately, preparing for what most considered an inevitable outcome of the growing German threat. Howard and I avoided discussing what was happening, though it became harder and harder to study or enjoy our usual round of diversions. By the time President Wilson declared war, it came almost as a relief. For just a moment anyway.

Within a month's time the campus was unrecognizable. All sporting events were cancelled to support military training and volunteer drills were held daily on the abandoned athletic fields. The college's traditional May Day celebration was replaced by a war rally and a new, taller flagpole was dedicated in the center of the quadrangle. The graduation ceremony that year was moved up to accommodate all the senior boys who planned to enlist. Howard was lucky enough to have secured a summer job at an automobile factory in Clio before the draft began and was included in one of the initial deferred groups of eligible men. With the government rushing to convert many of the factories for military purposes, they needed the labor forces there intact. As much as I'd been lamenting our separation that summer Howard was safer working in Clio, though he was deeply torn by the exemption. We spent several long afternoons on a bench by the millpond downtown, weighing his options.

"It makes sense to wait," I told him.

"My family really needs the money I'll make this summer."

"And, you'll be back in the fall."

"There's no way to know that Lucile." He was right of course, but I didn't want to hear it. "So many men are signing up. I must look like a real coward."

"Not to anyone who knows you. You have people who count on you Howard." I took his hand and held it tightly. "I count on you."

He looked at me, his eyes full of worry. Fear. As close to tearing up as a person could be without actually relenting. He put his arm around my shoulders and I snuggled up against him. With our future so uncertain, there really wasn't more to say, but I knew I was falling in love with Howard Bridgman by the time he left me for the first time that June.

The summer passed quickly. The war effort seemed to make everything speed up when there was so much to be done to support the troops. Days became wheatless or meatless and every scrap of metal or extra splash of kerosene was something to save or reuse. We collected the pits from apricots, peaches, and plums to be burned and used as charcoal in the soldiers' gas masks. Our vegetable patch grew into a "Liberty garden", tripling in size, as did the number of canning jars Mother and I put up that fall. There were very few extra young men around to hire for threshing and all the local farm families came together to bring in each other's crops on time. Even Rose joined us whenever she could and we all worked the longest of days without even a sigh of complaint. Several Albion boys left town each week for nearby Camp Custer in Battle

Creek. Some by their own volition, some not, all with their chins up and a pair of knit socks in hand, made by the women in town in purple and gold—the college colors. Howard and I only managed to exchange a few letters and he described being even busier at the factory, with any free time spent helping his family prepare for his eventual departure. By the time we saw one and other again, we'd each had a chance to adjust to the new world around us and it was immediately clear that we wanted the same thing for our future.

"Lucile," he whispered, lingering in the doorway of Aunt Rose's office at the library, where I was working.

"Howard!" I ran into his arms. His embrace was firm, his body stronger from the heavy factory work. "I missed you," I told him without even thinking of letting go.

"Not as much as I missed you," he said.

I knew that anyone passing by the circulation desk just outside would see us holding each other, but it didn't matter. Not then. We finally did separate, only barely. I sat perched on the edge of Rose's desk with Howard leaning over me, hands resting on my hips, his torso in between my slightly parted legs. And then, it finally happened. A kiss so soft, gentle, and full of the kind of passion that only couples who take their time can ever truly know. I'm not ashamed to say that I didn't have anything to compare it to, but I couldn't imagine a first kiss to be any better.

"You're a vision, Lucile," he said and I could tell his sentiment had nothing to do with the new skirt or lace top I'd carefully chosen, knowing he was returning to campus that day.

"Oh Howard," I said and we kissed again. And again. Each one growing more urgent than the last.

I often dreamed about that moment in the early weeks

following his departure. It was always hard to wake up and realize that he was gone, that I would have to wait a long time for more of his kisses. But Howard Bridgman was the kind of man that a girl would wait for forever. At least, that was my plan.

Chapter 4

June 4, 1918
June Automatic Replacement Draft
Medical Department, Camp Merritt, N.J.

My Dear Lucile,

I can no longer tell you anything about the movement of troops or how many men came with us. From here, our next stop is France. After leaving Custer we spent a week at Fort Riley in Kansas but I was sick for most of our stay—just a cold that I'm having trouble shaking. The doctor kept me in the hospital overnight to make sure I didn't have the flu. One of the nurses told me they had quite an outbreak here back in March so they are being very careful now. They are taking good care of us Lucile, especially given the sheer numbers of men being funneled towards the Western front. I'm happy to report that I feel much better today!

Every day we get more of our gear. I am assigned to work with the quartermaster's detail, helping to equip all the men, and have been able to claim mostly new items for myself. This may seem like a small accomplishment, but I am determined to increase my odds for returning in any way possible. I also received my gas mask and we had our first drill this morning. There are classes this afternoon to learn more about the different chemicals we might encounter during battle and I heard that we will practice with real chlorine and tear gas later in the week. They have actual trenches and bomb shelters built here to give us a taste of what it might be like on the front lines.

The camp is full of shade trees and is cooler than Custer or Riley. There are spring cots and mattresses, which will be very acceptable. We are 14 miles from N.Y. City and I have an ambition to go there if I can get a pass. Upon arrival we went over to the YMCA tent where a group of ladies treated us to homemade cake and ice-cold tea. We had a sing and I feel fine and not a bit lonesome, although I could stand to see you, for a few minutes at least. I received your last Sunday's letter tonight, forwarded from Riley, and enjoyed it very much. I guess we feel the same about marriage and I am fully satisfied. And oh, when I get back! It cannot happen soon enough.

> Good luck and happy time,
> Howard

―――――――――――

June 9, 1918

Mon Ami Lucile,

Enclosed you will find a few lines. You can hardly call them poetry; perhaps "thoughts" would be a good title. I just sat down and wrote what came to mind.

Last night I was at the "Y" and heard a splendid

entertainment by 50 men and women. It brought me back to things of civilization for a little while. This was followed by a picture show, "Tom Brown of Harvard". It was good! He was honest and noble and came out ahead and of course won the girl.

Today I have also been reading the book "Lucile" by Owen Meredith (for the third time). It seems to touch a sympathetic chord in me. The strength of Lucile was wonderful and since I have known you I have liked the book even more. You are the strongest woman I know.

Earlier today, I went over to Merritt Hall, which was dedicated by a rich lady. There is a 15,000-volume library, a clubroom with lounges and rocking chairs, a cafeteria and free pool tables! It's the best I have seen in the army. I read a book of poetry and it seemed pretty good to me to revel in the words. How I look forward to the time when we can sit down, sort o'lazy like, and read some of the best things written and talk and love each other. The last sentence looks unemotional in print, but as I wrote it I was thrilled and thought of the night I read Keats' "Endymion" to you. *"A thing of beauty is a joy for ever..."* Remember?

I received your gift of candy and am still enjoying it, a little every day. I must finish it up by tomorrow when I am scheduled to see the dentist for a final check-up and cleaning before shipping out.

You will excuse the stationary, but I used the packet you gave me a while ago and it will not pay me to get any more now. I can carry nothing extra "over there".

Your Soldier Boy,
Howard

Enclosed Poem:

THOTS IN A "Y" HUT

1.

A soldier boy sat in the "Y",
THINKING
Of the happy days flown by;
WONDERING
Of the fateful days to come.

2.

It was the eve of his departure
For France.
He was thinking so much of her,
Who promised
To be waiting when Sammy returned.

3.

Tho the soldier lad may be away
Along time,
He knows that some glorious day,
If he returns,
They can be together alway.

4.

And if Sammy should not return,
Which God forbid,
He will be in that peaceful bourne
To wait
For her, whom in youth, he loved.

5.

So as the soldier-lover nears
War-scarred France
He comes not with sickening fears,
But gladly
Joins to battle the hateful Hun.

Camp Merritt N.J. June 6, 1918.

June 10, 1918

Well Lucile, I could be disappointed but there is no use. The captain just issued orders that no more men can leave the camp, so I must stay put. I'm afraid my final night in the States is upon us.

Tonight at 10 o'clock I expect to take my last communion in America. I am anticipating a great service from the camp chaplain, because the boys are anxious for it and are thinking now of where we are going, as they have not before. We will sign the "War Roll" as well, our final act as soldiers on this side of the ocean.

Lucile, I enjoy your letters! I have received one almost every other day. I just lie on my bunk and enjoy them all I can; you cannot write too often to hurt my feelings. When you get this, I will probably be in France already, but you can still write. If you do not hear from me for some time, you will know it is because I cannot write. It takes a war and a vast ocean to keep me from you, but neither can stop me from holding you in my heart.

And so, I reluctantly close. And I will say to you as others say to us soldiers, plus my love. Good luck and God bless you. I leave for Europe with one cent in my pocket, my courage on my sleeve, and the deepest vision of you in my heart.

With greatest love,
Howard

Chapter 5

"LUCILE!" IT WAS Vera. I had fallen asleep on the train, my lap covered with Howard's letters, several of them still open.

"Are we there?" I asked, scrambling to stuff the letters back into their tin box. The train was stopped at a small station in the middle of the woods. It was just barely light out. "Are we in Munising?"

"Nope. Munising Junction!" Vera's words were clipped and terse. "We have to change trains again." She stomped up the aisle, snatching her luggage from the netted rack above. "It's a good thing Mr. Abell didn't mention what a rigorous trip this would be," she snipped. She stormed out of the railcar and dropped the tangle of bags in a pile at her feet. "You better hurry," she yelled.

I joined her on the platform as quickly as I could and the train pulled away as soon as I exited. There was a tall man, perhaps a little older than us, standing with a pair of suitcases at the other end. Vera yelled in his direction.

"Do you know when the train to Munising arrives?" He checked his watch.

"In about ten minutes, Ma'am."

"Ten minutes," she repeated to me, throwing her arms up in the air, dropping down on one of her suitcases, straddling it like a stool.

"Thank you," I said, waving at the man. He smiled and waved back. Given Vera's tirade, it was no surprise that he didn't join us.

The thick forest canopy overhead blocked the streams of light from the rising sun, leaving the platform in deep shade. The air was still damp with morning dew that hadn't burned off yet—the sky, crystal clear. Somehow it looked bluer than the one I was used to back home.

"It's freezing," Vera said.

"Well put your coat on for goodness sake." I picked it up off the ground and dropped it on her. "And stop complaining. We're almost there."

"Humph," she huffed, but did as I asked. Vera was a girl who needed her sleep. When we were younger, she was always grumpy the morning after one of our frequent pajama parties.

Within just a few minutes a whistle sounded in the distance and a train pulled into the station. The three of us boarded the lone passenger car, Vera and I at the rear and the man up front.

"I'll be out here," I told Vera, retreating to the covered platform hanging off the back of the train. I was relieved when she didn't follow me out. We weren't accustomed to spending so much time together.

As the train pulled away from the Junction, the tiny depot disappeared immediately. Only the narrowest of paths had been cleared to allow the railway to proceed and the short embankments leading up to the tracks were littered with blackened stumps. The blinding periphery of pine, birch, and maple made me dizzy as it rushed by—I had never seen so many trees.

In between the steam engine's gasps and belches I could hear the distinct, piercing wail of buzz saws. Munising was born a mill town and thousands of trees had certainly been felled and removed from the forest already. Yet, as we barreled toward the shore of Lake Superior I couldn't see one single scar amid the surrounding stand of conifers and hardwood, except for the train track itself.

A wave of anxiety washed over me just as the first buildings in Munising appeared. The courage I'd mustered to accept this job so far from anything familiar was a faint shadow and I stood there on that bucking platform wondering just what this speck of a town—sandwiched between woods and water—had in store for me. The image of Howard leaving home on a train just months prior, facing much more unpredictable circumstances, stifled my fears almost instantly.

"You can do this Lucile," I told myself. Howard went knowingly into certain danger without breaking. What did I possibly have to be afraid of?

The trip into town took less than ten minutes. Two finely dressed gentlemen were waiting at the station to greet us, freshly pressed and polished from their Homburg hats to their shiny shoes—"church clothes" as we called them back home. I fussed with my hair and tried to smooth the wrinkles on my dress, but twenty-four hours of travel had taken its toll. The passenger from the front of the train got off too.

"Welcome to Munising!" the first gentleman said, arms outstretched as if the rail platform was his stage. "Harold Abell, Superintendent of Schools. So good to finally meet you all." Everyone shook hands and made introductions.

"Yes indeed, welcome!" echoed the other man. He handed

Vera and I each overflowing bunches of wildflowers. "T.G. Sullivan, Mayor of Munising. But you must call me T.G."

"Oh, Mr. Sullivan, I couldn't," I said. Mother would have a genuine fit if she ever heard me addressing such a prominent man by his nickname and for once I wouldn't blame her.

"I insist," he said, nudging Mr. Abell. "Lord knows, I'm called much worse behind my back!" The Superintendent laughed, but looked terribly uncomfortable. "You're all here to help this town in our time of need and I'm here to make sure you get anything you require during your stay." Still holding my hand, he patted it gently before letting go. The mayor certainly wasn't old enough to be my grandfather, but that was the warm feeling I got by first impression.

"This way everyone," Mr. Abell said. He and the mayor took our bags and led us around to the back of the red brick depot where a magnificent Model-T bus was idling.

"This is Shorty Leslie," Mr. Abell said. A rather squat man in a white shirt with suspenders and a tweed flat cap ran over and took the luggage.

"Thomas, you'll be staying with me as we discussed," Mr. Abell said to the man from the train, another substitute teacher. "Ladies, I have to say goodbye but I'm leaving you in T.G.'s capable hands. I'll see you both tomorrow at the school."

"Thank you," I said.

"Goodbye," Vera said. The two of them left on foot and the rest of us piled into Shorty's bus.

"We thought you would be more comfortable together at the inn," T.G. said. "Best pie in town." He turned and winked at us. The mayor pointed out several landmarks as we passed, none of which I would recall later since I was literally nodding off. Shorty took us all the way to the lake before stopping the bus under a sign for "The Beach Inn".

Munising's finest hotel was a three story, beige brick building with a wide, open porch at the front offering panoramic views of Lake Superior. A wooden boardwalk extended out from the inn's main entrance to the shore, no more than fifty feet away. It cut across a grassy expanse that was cleared of all trees to highlight the view. A teenaged boy ran out to retrieve our luggage and T.G. escorted us to the front desk. He introduced us to the inn's manager, Mr. Charlie Samms.

"Welcome to The Beach Inn ladies," Mr. Samms said. "We'll get you right up to your rooms. I know you've had a long trip." He handed two keys to the boy with our bags. "301 and 303," he directed.

"Charlie here can get you anything you need while you get settled," T. G. told us.

A large, elaborately cross-stitched sign hung behind the desk. *The Best Is Not Too Good!*

"Anything at all," Mr. Samms said, crossing to the stairs, waiting to show us our rooms.

T.G. leaned in close to Vera and me. "The rooms are a bit small, but very well appointed. Restaurant's the best in town and the Sunday dinner spread is legendary. You must take advantage of it tonight," he whispered.

"Thank you T.G., I'm sure we'll be quite comfortable." I had to think carefully to even speak. At that point, a canvas cot in the corner would have felt glorious.

We followed Mr. Samms up to the third floor. He pointed out the one shared bathroom just off the second-floor landing as we passed and led us all the way down to the end of the hall.

"These are our quietest rooms," he said. "We get a lot of

salesmen and they come and go at all hours. They won't bother you down here." I decided right then not to mention the salesmen to my mother. "Good day," he said, turning to leave.

Vera and I retreated to our rooms without speaking. It was barely eight in the morning, but all I managed to do was get my hat and coat off before falling into bed. When I opened my eyes again ten hours later I saw them crumpled on the floor next to me. I just looked at them for several minutes, my limbs too heavy to lift.

The room was filled with sunlight and pleasantly warm. A gentle breeze moved the sheer curtains in and out of the open windows. I listened for any sign of Vera next door but only heard waves lapping at the shore outside. I slowly ran my eyes around the room—a padded wicker lounger in one corner, a small desk and chair in the other, a nice sized dresser with a lovely porcelain pitcher and bowl set on top was in between; the coordinating chamber pot rested on the floor next to the bed. I could hardly make myself realize that this would be my home for the next nine months, but it seemed comfortable enough and was much larger than my bedroom at home.

I finally got up and unpacked my clothes and the few personal items that made the trip with me. The most important was a framed picture of Howard taken on one of our canoe rides. He is crouched on a rock, smirking at the camera, quite pleased with himself for jumping from the boat onto a perch completely surrounded by the river. I put it on the dresser where I could see it from anywhere in the room, my precious tin of letters beside it. The hallway was deserted when I went to the bathroom and after cleaning up and changing into a fresh dress I knocked on Vera's door several times without any reply. I peeked in her room and was surprised to find that she'd taken the time to unpack and even change into her nightclothes and was sound asleep under the covers. I was on my own for dinner. The idea of eating alone was daunting and I almost settled for some water and the leftover cookies sent by Rose for the long trip.

"Greetings Miss Ball." It was Mr. Samms passing through the lobby, his jacket off, sleeves rolled up to the elbow, wearing a starched white apron tied snugly across his hips. He was balancing an impressive armful of bed linens and towels. "You look rested. Were you able to get some sleep?"

"Oh did I. Thank you for asking. The room is just lovely and very quiet, as you said."

"Glad to hear it. Will you and Miss Smith be dining with us tonight?"

"Just me."

"Come right this way," he said. He piled the linens on the front desk and escorted me into the dining room. It was nicely sized, but not spacious, crowded with ten or twelve tables, about half of them filled with diners. The room went silent as Mr. Samms led me to a table at the front of the room with a "RESERVED" sign on it and the best view of the lake.

"I'll send my girl right over," he said.

I fidgeted with the napkin and silverware, waiting for everyone around me to resume their conversations. The menu sat folded like a tent in the middle of the table. It was typed on heavy paper and astonishing for all its choices. There were several first courses and salads, a roast chicken or prime rib entree, three kinds of potatoes, and four desserts. The idea of choosing from so many equally enticing options was completely foreign to me and seemed entirely extravagant. As a child, it was understood that there were no sweets if I didn't eat everything on my plate and I was more than satisfied with that compromise when I encountered something I truly couldn't choke down like headcheese or sweetbreads. I was very excited to place my order when the waitress arrived.

"I'll have celery hearts to start, please. Roast beef and the new potatoes. And cantaloupe a la mode for dessert," I told her. Ice cream on a melon—I couldn't even imagine what that would taste like!

While the waitress was very friendly, the view from my table just lovely, and the room lively with the other diners, as well as punctuations of laughter coming from the bar next door, it was lonely eating by myself. Even when I arrived home late from campus, Aunt Rose or my mother always dropped what they were doing to sit with me at the kitchen table. It was a loving gesture that I hadn't even taken notice of until that evening. I did eat faster than usual and was sure to leave a small tip, just as Aunt Rose had instructed me to do.

Stomach full, head still fuzzy, Vera sound asleep—I went right back to bed after dinner, even though the sun clearly had no intention of setting for several hours. It was all a little disorienting, lying there in bed in this strange new place I hadn't even heard of just over a week ago. My eyes locked on the picture of Howard. Even though he'd been gone for four months it seemed impossible that he was in a foreign country, fighting as a soldier, at war. It bothered me quite a bit that he wouldn't know about this job or where I was for at least another week or two. If he stared at a picture of me that night he would think of me in Albion—on the farm, at Rose's, or perhaps one of our favorite haunts on campus. Even though I knew he'd understand my decision to come to Munising, I prayed that he wouldn't worry about me or my situation. I knew what worry could do to a heart that was filled with love. I felt it take hold of mine the day Howard's draft notice arrived. Its grip was brutal and it hadn't let up one bit ever since.

Howard received an Order of Induction in late February and was called to Marshall, Michigan to appear before the draft board on March 6, 1918 as an alternate. The board would send fourteen men into service that day and with volunteers still enlisting in great numbers it was highly unlikely that he would be needed to fill their quota. Howard used this fact to downplay the risk and convinced his family to forego coming all the way from Clio to accompany him to the Calhoun County Courthouse, but the same argument had no effect on me.

The scene at the courthouse was unexpected. Calm. Organized. Free of the nervous bustle I'd anticipated as befitting a nation going to war. The draft board was seated in a vacant courtroom and interviewed each man individually before sending him on for a physical, vision and hearing screenings, and a brief aptitude test. The men were escorted around by a draft official and not allowed to interact with any friends or family once they were taken away. All fourteen men in Howard's group were present for the nine o'clock check-in, but he and the two other alternates were also being interviewed, in case someone in the main group was disqualified.

"You won't have to go through the screening process again next time, Mr. Bridgman," the lady checking his papers at the door told him. Her voice was entirely too cheerful for the job.

Next time, I thought. The only thing worse than Howard having to leave that day was the idea of going through another long, drawn-out goodbye. His escort appeared shortly after he checked in.

"Howard H. Bridgman, Albion, Michigan," the man

announced into the crowd. Despite having a clipboard and wearing a badge declaring him an "OFFICIAL", he looked like anyone's friendly, older neighbor—clearly just a volunteer.

"Yes sir. Right here," Howard replied. He bent down to kiss me.

"Hurry up," the man said. "There's time allowed to say goodbye later."

"Thank you for coming with me." Howard said, his face right next to mine.

"Mr. Bridgman. It's time," the escort said, suddenly sounding more official. I glared at the man, but Howard ignored him completely, his eyes locked only on mine.

"I love you." He lingered on each word.

"Me too." I made sure not to be the one to look away first. And when Howard stood up, I watched him walk away. Just down the hall and into some room, but I knew that no matter the day's outcome, this was the beginning of him leaving me.

The tears I'd only shed in private started pouring down my face. I couldn't have stopped them if I wanted, but I didn't try. My whole body began to shake, more out of anger than fear. I wanted to fight what was happening to Howard. To me. To us. I felt trapped and filled with panic, the kind a fish displays just below the surface of some placid lake when it finds itself hooked and dragged somewhere it does not want to go— toward a net with holes too small to slip through, back beneath the still waters. Howard would soon be gone and there was no way to prevent it.

Such public displays of emotion would have normally embarrassed me greatly, but I was not the only woman in tears. All the people accompanying the would-be soldiers were held in one of the courthouse's drafty vestibules, which was closed off as a makeshift waiting room. Seated on stiff, wooden folding chairs we had to keep our coats and hats on to battle the cold air pouring in under and around the doors. My breakdown was hardly noticeable compared to the wailing from several of the other women. No one bothered to make introductions and we all avoided any eye contact as we sat there. Once I regained my composure, I took to watching the recruits parade back and forth through the hallway in front of me.

I studied each man for any noticeable defects that might create a need for an alternate. None of them limped, only two wore glasses, and from what I overheard as they checked in, all had enlisted voluntarily, except one. The young man who'd been drafted was easy to spot—hunched over, always on the verge of tears, his lip quivering every time his mother waved. I wanted to feel sorry for him but I couldn't help believe that his anxiety might warrant a dismissal, putting Howard at risk. I stared at those men as if they were the enemy. As if some future alternate's loved ones wouldn't stare at Howard in the same self-ish way when his final call came. It's easy to fool yourself into thinking that there might be a way to control what's uncontrollable. Make sense of something that doesn't. The waiting was torture, and I finally had to get up and leave. I walked to Schuler's Restaurant across the street and got a cup of coffee, settling in on a park bench near the empty reflecting pool in the center of the main traffic circle. From there, I had a clear view of the courthouse door and the clock tower overhead. The board was supposed to conclude its review of the men by 2 PM. I would have my answer then.

"Just fifteen more minutes," I told myself. It made no sense that the alternates hadn't been dismissed yet if they weren't needed. I'd been waiting for over an hour and just finished a third cup of coffee.

By the time the clock struck two, I was already barreling toward the courthouse. Dodging traffic across the circle. Pushing past anyone in my way. The doors swung open just as I reached the bottom of the stairs. It was the check-in lady and one of the volunteer escorts. They were chatting. Smiling. Glad to be going home.

"What's going on in there?" I demanded. "They're supposed to be finished."

"Should be any time now," the man said. They stepped around me, picking up their lively conversation just a few steps away.

I sat down on the stairs. I had a terrible headache and realized I hadn't eaten all day. The black coffee was gnawing at my stomach. The door behind me opened and the click of a pocket watch snapping closed gave Howard away. He came and sat next to me on the cold, dirty marble treads. I held my breath and looked at him. He was pale and expressionless.

"We can go home." He sounded completely drained, not relieved.

"Thank God," I said.

"I'll be called for sure next time, Lucile. Within a month."

"A month," I repeated. I leaned against him, hard. He took my head in his hand and nuzzled my neck.

"I don't know how I'll ever do it," he said.

"Go to war?" I asked.

"Leave you," he whispered.

The next few weeks went by quickly, and slowly, at the same time. On March 20th, an article in the newspaper served notice that Howard was among the next group of local men called to serve. His name was at the top of the list. Twelve days to say goodbye.

Trying to make every last moment with Howard special was exhausting. I felt numb and deeply sad most of the time. I did my best to hide it but I'm sure I was fooling no one, least of all Howard. We both relied on the routines and events of our regular lives to pull us forward into the future, even though it was void of all promise or pleasure.

Everything on campus was moving quickly to graduate as many men as possible before they were all called away. Classes met six days a week. Academic finals were in March instead of May. And military drills filled in any extra time that remained. Despite the fast pace, Howard would still be gone before graduation, but we were able to attend the Senior Convocation together. Held in the chapel, it was a ceremony sponsored by the professors to honor the senior class, and that year it was dressed up more than usual with caps and gowns, carnations for the women, and a larger reception afterwards attended by both of our families. Before the ceremony, Howard and I posed reluctantly for pictures at Aunt Rose's, in front of her prized stand of lilacs. We stood there, arms at our sides, a space between us. Although we were never apart during those final weeks, we were already practicing being separate and alone. The bushes behind us were peppered with tight, lavender buds but their promise was lost to us. The only thing having that extra time to say good-bye accomplished was to clarify that what we really wanted, more than anything, was to be together.

Howard wouldn't allow anyone to accompany him to Marshall for his final induction on the 2nd of April. Instead, we said goodbye at the train station in Albion, surrounded by his family and several other groups of people bidding farewell to their own soldiers. Seeing his parents and sisters again under these circumstances was more like a competition, than a reunion. We all wanted Howard's attention and any time given to someone else couldn't help but feel like a loss to the others. Fortunately, the train schedule required the Bridgmans to leave for their return trip to Clio before Howard's train departed for Marshall. It was heartbreaking to watch them say goodbye, which I did from a distance.

Howard's sisters took the lead, hugging him ferociously then rushing onto the train, crying. Mr. Bridgman was next, stepping forward to shake Howard's hand with the same two-handed grip his son favored. He patted him roughly on the back, pulling him forward just far enough to plant a kiss on his forehead before stepping aside to allow his wife a turn. She reached out for both of Howard's hands, staring at him for a long time without saying anything. Of all the responsibilities this woman accepted in raising her sister's children, sending her nephew off to war must have certainly been the most unexpected and painful. Howard removed his hat and kissed her on the cheek and she pulled him into a big, gentle embrace. The current Mrs. Bridgman loved Howard enough for two women. I couldn't imagine the strength it took to say goodbye for two, as well.

"Are you alright?" I asked, as soon as Howard returned to my side. In the time it took him to go into the depot and purchase his ticket after his family left, the train to Marshall had pulled into the station. Its stopover would only last a few minutes. He nodded and handed me a lemonade he'd purchased inside.

"Are you?"

"I'm fine," I lied, but didn't look at him as I said it. We

stood facing each other, passing the lemonade between us until it was gone. I rocked back and forth on my toes and shook my hands at my side. I couldn't get warm even though it had to be at least fifty degrees, standing there in the sun. Howard rubbed my arms briskly, keeping an eye on the train. He checked his pocket watch.

"Three minutes," he said.

I dropped my head on Howard's chest and wrapped my arms around him, clasping my hands together behind his back. I could feel his heart racing through his coat and I pulled back far enough to reach up and cup his face in my hands. I stared at him fiercely even though his eyes were shut, and tried to memorize what it felt like to have all of his love, so close. He found my mouth with his and kissed me. His warm tears dropped onto my cheeks and the saltiness gradually worked its way in between our lips.

"ALL ABOARD," the conductor called. "First call for Marshall and all points west." A rush of passengers headed for the train. No one wanted to be stuck in the compartment directly behind the engine because of the noise and soot.

"Let's go," Howard said, grabbing my elbow and leading me down the platform. It's ridiculous, of course, but I actually thought we were leaving. Escaping. But we were only headed toward the rear of the train. Away from all the people.

"ALL ABOARD!" This train bound for all points west. Final stop Chicago, Illinois. Have your tickets ready," the conductor barked repeatedly, pacing back and forth beside the railcars.

"I have something for you," I blurted, remembering the small gift in my pocket. I handed him a bundle of plain stationary and stamped envelopes tied together with a scrap of grosgrain ribbon. Tucked under the bow was a small, sturdy fountain pen and a picture of me taken out in a canoe on the river. "This will get you started."

"Thank you." he said. "Who knows, maybe I won't even need all these?"

"Who knows?" I replied. I could tell he was so nervous. We both knew it would take more than thirty letters to mark his journey back home.

"Last call folks," the conductor shouted in our direction. Howard was the only passenger left on the platform.

"I guess this is it," he said, picking up his duffel bag.

"Be safe Howard."

"I will."

"Keep warm," I added, not knowing what else to say. I smiled at him deliberately, determined that his final vision of me would be a pleasant one.

Howard dropped his bag and lunged at me, draping his body across mine with such force that it took all my strength to brace myself and hold him up. His lips moved roughly across my face and forehead and he pawed at my coat, trying to find something to hang onto. I patted his back and tried to pull away, but he fought my efforts to contain him.

"Howard," I said, as firmly as I could without being scolding. "I hate it, but it's time."

The train started moving forward. The screech of metal on metal seemed to get his attention and he let go. He stood mere inches away from me and quickly composed himself. The small gap between us already felt like the Grand Canyon.

"I'm coming back Lucile."

I nodded. Still smiling.

"You know that. Don't you?"

I wasn't sure if I could speak without sobbing. The train was picking up speed and Howard grabbed his bag and started following it, walking backwards, faster and faster.

"Say it," he said. "Say you know I'm coming back." He was jogging to keep up with the train.

"I know you will," I called. He ran to the stairwell of the nearest car and jumped on board. "Goodbye Howard. I love you."

"I love you too."

And then, he was gone.

The tears did not overwhelm me until I saw Aunt Rose. She sat with me in her parlor while I cried and did not try to comfort me with the usual platitudes people rely on when they really don't know what to say. There was no way to know how or when Howard's time away would end and I had to start making peace with that the moment he left. I could have accepted his absence with a guarantee of safety or the date of his return, but that isn't the nature of war. Or life either, I suppose.

But somehow, the latter is easier to ignore.

Chapter 6

At Sea

My Lucile,

I do not know where to start. I have dropped short letters to many people who are interested in my whereabouts but I am writing to you last because I always eat my cake last. And Lucile, we can write as freely as ever. The censor pays no attention to personal matters. It does not cost me anything to write you, but I'd still do it even if it did.

Well my love, I am on the bounding blue sea with water everywhere. I saw the Statue of Liberty the morning we left New York. And as she stood there lifting her mighty arms toward the clouds I felt proud that I am a soldier of democracy. I got seasick on the second day but only missed one meal. I feel good now and actually enjoy the roll of the ocean! Last night I had a salt water bath in a real tub and a change of clothes plus a hair cut today makes me feel new again. So many men in the army get into carelessness along these lines, but it pays to be at my best for many reasons. I am trying to keep awake mentally in spite of the long hours of boredom, when I am not free to do as I please, but merely idle. I spend many evenings at the railing looking out over the great sea, dreaming and absorbing its dark beauty.

Today I read Russell H. Conwell's famous lecture, "Acres of Diamonds". Perhaps you recall how he states that we all have riches in our own backyards but we have to look for them and not always seek something better, elsewhere. All I want is to live a quiet, useful and prosperous life with you. I'll never forget our dreams of the future Lucile, which I hope some day will come true.

When I made it up on deck this morning, I was thrilled to see land on the port side. I suspect what it is but cannot say. We will probably debark tomorrow and how happy I'll be to get on land after almost 2 weeks on board this ship. I can hardly realize yet that I am actually going to war to kill men. When I looked out this morning at the beautiful hills and rising sun I almost couldn't make myself believe that men, millions of them, are doing all they can to KILL each other instead of enjoying the great free gifts of God. No doubt the events of the next few weeks will impress upon my mind that I am, indeed, at war.

Dinner will soon be ready and so I will close. Send me some strawberries Lucile. How I wish you could.

Au revoir mon Ami,
Howard

July 9, 1918
Somewhere in France

Ma Amoureux,

We just finished a long, dirty trip across country and are now situated in a beautiful valley with wooded hillsides and a silver stream meandering down the center. I counted 8 villages nestled in among the trees during a stroll earlier today. I tramped over scenes of past fighting—not much remains except old trenches and shell holes. I am told the battles here were fierce during the early part of the war.

I am sitting on a litter in the door of my tent. I was just down by a pond near here to do some washing. I built a fire, boiled my clothes with soap and rinsed them out. I am getting to be quite a tramp Lucile—living and sleeping outdoors.

We had a gas drill this morning that consisted of running thru the woods, picking up sticks, etc. with the mask on. It is rather an uncomfortable contraption, but much preferable to the chlorine gas used by the diabolical Huns. If we had as good of protection from bullets we would be quite safe. This morning several of the fellows picked up pieces of shrapnel around the buildings from a battle overnight. Most of the men ran down to the cellar during the bombardment, but I never heard a thing as I slept and could hardly believe it when told about it this morning.

Many things have impressed me in France so far. The beauty of the country is undeniable, even as it's being ravaged by war. I have seen an old castle with a moat and an avenue of trees leading up to it. I toured a chateau built in 1724, that has certainly known the footsteps of more than one French nobleman. Yesterday I walked thru a large cathedral over 400 years old. The architectural work both inside and out must have required infinite time and patience. There were 365 steps leading up to the tower alone! Last week, I went swimming in the (CENSORED) river and could hardly believe I was in France. I associate with the local people as much as I can and am learning to speak the language rapidly. Although the French are at war they seem to be cheery. Why not?

There are several college men and a Baptist minister in my unit. Also, some bums—but we are all equally classed in the army. By now, I am used to meeting strangers and all men in khaki are brothers. As we travel nearer and nearer the front lines Lucile, I realize how far away I am from you. I do hear stories from other fellows of their girls getting married after they left, but I have no fear. I only pray that I may return.

With all my love,
Howard

July 21, 1918
Somewhere in France

Dear Lucile,

This is rather hideous paper to use, but it is all I could find. I don't know where the poor fellow is who had it before me and I'm quite sure I do not wish to know either.

I have not written to you because I have been where I could not; where we were too busy; where there was too much hell.

It would be useless to try to describe to you what I have seen. Rather, I will have to tell you in person. I do like my Red Cross work very much. Often one just gives a cup of cold water, but it helps assuage the suffering of some poor fellow and many of them suffer more than I have had to yet. I slept 2 hours in the last four nights and that on a stone floor, but I survived my first trip into active service. You no doubt read in the papers about our great victory. I saw one of the German generals who was captured and "beaucoup" prisoners. When I first came over I entertained a rather humane attitude toward the Germans as human beings. After seeing a little of the results of "Boche Kultur", I loathe them and believe that most good Germans are dead ones.

We are staying in a charming little town near the front lines, now vacant of all civilians. I can tell it was abandoned quickly and think about how frightened the villagers must have been, especially the children. I wonder how long this awful carnage must continue? I suppose it is a lovely Sunday morning in Michigan and it seems that I must see you.

I will be glad when I begin to receive mail again. A letter came for me the other day but I was away from the company. We are moving so much and there are so many other things more important than mail but now I must wait even longer to hear from you. After what I've seen in the past few days, I realize that none of us should complain so long as we can hasten the end of this terrible war.

To answer your question—no, I am not worrying about your "disposition" all the time. I guess when I get out of this rough army life I will have some improving to do! I am well and praying for the coming of a better day.

As ever – your soldier man,
Howard

XXXXX – I dreamed the other night they were real.

Chapter 7

VERA AND I were reunited at breakfast the day after arriving in Munising. Her room was empty by the time I got up and dressed and I found her in the dining room, surrounded by several meals worth of plates.

"You just help yourself," she told me, waving her fork at the large buffet set out at the back of the room—eggs, bacon, biscuits, hotcakes, oatmeal, juice, even cold cereal. What a treat it was to eat a large bowl of corn flakes without anyone huffing about it. Mother and Aunt Rose thought cereal was a poor substitute for a hearty breakfast and refused to keep it in their cupboards. To me, it was a delicious taste of freedom. Vera and I chatted and lingered at the table for over an hour, as if we were on vacation.

"Mr. Samms gave me directions to the high school," Vera said between her last two gulps of coffee. "It's just three or four blocks up the street."

We emerged from the inn and Lake Superior looked like a sparkling jewel in the soft morning light. A large, heavily forested island hovered in the water directly in front of us.

The city dock was at the end of the street to our left. I hadn't noticed either one in the exhausted haze of our arrival.

"Gitche Gumee, indeed!" Vera marveled, recalling the lake's Ojibwe Indian name from *The Song of Hiawatha*, a poem we'd studied in high school. I wondered if anyone who lived there ever tired of that view looming on the periphery from everywhere in town. It seemed impossible, but I suppose it grew invisible like most anything familiar can.

Founded just before the turn of the century, the city of Munising was the exact same age as me. It sprung up overnight to accommodate hundreds of immigrants who came for work at one of the area's many lumber mills. At first glance, it reminded me of one of the frontier towns I pictured while reading the western pulp magazines Aunt Rose indulged in after a long day studying more academic tomes at the library. Dusty dirt roads lined with uneven, wooden sidewalks. Simple one and two-story frame buildings crowded together, interrupted by newer and taller brick ones in between. There was a bank on every corner and a boarding house on every block. Even with cars becoming popular, horses and bicycles remained the favored means of transportation. Munising was the kind of place with more saloons than churches, fewer women than men, and a movie theater that opened on Sunday after church, playing to a packed house. It wasn't anything like Albion and that was the most exciting discovery of all.

Vera and I passed through the business district just two blocks up from the inn. It extended down Superior Street for several blocks on either side of Elm Avenue. From that one spot I could see three or four drug stores, a half dozen grocers, and at least as many theaters, restaurants, and newsstands. One store called The Marks Block filled an entire corner and was *the* place to go for almost anything—fresh food, dry goods, clothing—all sold together in one place. There was the post office, a mortuary, a beauty shop and tonsorial parlor, and several hardware stores, the largest of which housed the city clock on its roof. Electric lights and iron fire hydrants marked each corner and telephone wires hung draped across the streets like streamers. The sidewalks were busy and a near constant tinkling of bells filled the air as shop doors opened and closed, up and down the street.

"Good morning ladies," a policeman said, approaching from a small, enclosed shelter built right on the sidewalk. "Can I help you find something?"

"No sir, we're just headed to the high school," Vera told him.

"You must be two of the new teachers," he exclaimed. "Welcome!"

"Thank you," I said.

"Joseph Pelissier, Chief of Police." He shook hands with each of us. "My two oldest are at the high school this year. Annie and Joe Jr."

"How wonderful," Vera said.

"We'll look forward to meeting them," I added.

"If you ladies need anything, just stop by. I'm here all day. My night watchman's Tom Poff. I wouldn't recommend it, but if you're out past ten and need help, he's your guy."

"Thank you," we said, walking away.

"Do me a favor," the officer shouted. "Cross over to the other side of the street. There's a group of men hanging out in front of the boarding house on the next block. They're harmless, but I don't want 'em giving you any trouble."

Vera grabbed my hand and we crossed over right away,

spotting the sizeable crowd of third shift mill workers loitering on the sidewalk. They were standing there in clumps of two or three, talking and laughing loudly, smoking cigarettes. Their conversations stopped abruptly and there was some mumbling and a whistle or two as we passed. I held on to Vera tightly and kept my head down, like we were doing something wrong. Such behavior was unheard of in Albion, where everyone knew each other and the occasional teenaged boy who stepped out of line risked a public scolding and an immediate call home. By the end of the week we learned how to zigzag our way through the streets to avoid the daily round of hoots and whistles.

Rows and rows of small houses filled the neighborhoods just off the business area. Most of them were quite neglected, in need of something more than what a simple coat of paint might provide. There was evidence of children everywhere from jump ropes, balls, and bicycles scattered across tiny, fenced-in yards to colorful pictures proudly displayed in some of the homes' windows. Many children were out enjoying the last week of summer vacation—the younger ones running around playing, the older ones sitting and talking, pretending not to notice two of their new teachers clomping uphill. Their stares were almost as intense as the ones from the men we'd just passed.

"Good morning," Vera said to each group in an entirely cheery but overly familiar way.

"Hello," I said simply, much more intent on maintaining the distance and formality that I thought proper for a teacher. I was very much aware that only four years separated us from many of the older students.

We finally found the school at the top of the hill, sitting there all by itself, looking as much like a sentinel or a crown jewel as it did a place of learning. Central High was a large, red brick and sandstone building with oversized windows and a white wooden cupola straddling its peaked roof—the whole thing topped by a single round finial. Mill money had paid for the school and it took up the entire block. Although it served fewer students, it was easily twice the size of the high school in Albion.

"What a beautiful building," Vera said.

"Yes," I replied. I'd never expected to find such an impressive school in such a remote locale. "I can't believe I'm here," I said to myself.

"Me too!" Vera groaned. She might have been talking about the long walk uphill or the hectic week preceding our arrival but I was referring to something else altogether. I had dreamed of being a teacher since I was a little girl and standing there in front of that school—about to take over my own classroom—was a remarkable moment. So far from anything I could have imagined the day I stepped into a tiny one-room rural school for the first time back home.

I was so shy as a child that I didn't even start my formal education until just before my eighth birthday, though I'd been studying letters and numbers with Grandma Ball at our dining table for years. Even though it was the middle of the harvest—his busiest time of year—Father took me there in the horse and buggy, just to ease my nerves. It was understood that I would be walking the two miles on my own from then on, starting that same afternoon with the trip back home.

"Lucy, this is one of your teachers, Miss Brunner." Everyone at the schools knew Elmer Ball. He served as the clerk of the school board for many years and it was his name signed on the bottom of every paycheck.

"Hello Lucy," she said, bending down to meet me face to

face. I buried my head in Father's dirty overalls. They smelled like gasoline and manure, but I liked it.

"She prefers Lucile. I'm the only one that still gets away with Lucy," my father explained. He stroked my hair. "I gotta get back now," he said, his hand dropping to my back, nudging me forward. It just made me lean into him harder.

"Lucile, are you feeling nervous?" Miss Brunner asked. I nodded. She gently, but firmly tugged at my hand until I transferred my tight grip onto her. "I think you just need someone to show you around." She immediately escorted me further into the building as my father stood in the doorway for several moments, despite claiming to be in such a hurry. "She'll be fine," Miss Brunner told him. I didn't really believe her and I'm not sure he did either.

Dawn Brunner was the assistant to the head of Holmes School and had just graduated from high school herself. She took charge of the younger students who were learning the basics of reading, penmanship, arithmetic, and geography—all subjects she could handle easily with only a secondary diploma. I'm not sure if it was her soft, patient voice, the endless supply of encouraging words or her sparkling hazel eyes and shiny auburn hair, but I latched onto Miss Brunner like a newly hatched chick following its mama hen around after just one glance.

A one-room school was a wonderful place to learn and grow, especially for a shy and tentative girl like me. My instruction was as likely to come from an older student as it was from one of the teachers and later I took my turn tutoring the younger ones too. I can still hear Miss Wartman, the head teacher, calling out over the disgruntled groans of the eighth-grade boys being pressed into service.

"There's as much to learn from teaching someone else as there is from being the student. If you can't explain what you know, then you don't really know it." Her words were adamant but never harsh and even then, I knew she was right.

The lessons there were often quite practical with the notion that learning by doing was really the best way. Collecting individual chalkboards and erasers from everyone's desk helped the little ones practice counting and sorting. Making pies and jam from the enormous stand of rhubarb behind the school required careful measuring and work with fractions. Reading to the youngest students was a favorite job and each time I did it a small bit of shyness slipped away without my even noticing. For fun, we played Hide and Seek or Run Sheep Run on the grassy area out front and in the winter, there was sledding and snowball fights or ice-skating on nearby Farley's Pond. Come spring, after the summer ice was cut and stored, the boys caught bullfrogs at the pond using broomsticks with nails on the end as spears and we girls would fry up a big batch of frog's legs for lunch the next day. After those initial weeks of uncertainty, I fell in love with school and always knew that teaching was my calling for a career.

Entering Munising's Central High School, Vera and I were greeted by the school secretary who immediately disappeared into the office behind her desk to fetch the principal, Calvin Smith.

"Hallelujah" we heard a booming voice say, before we even saw him. Mr. Smith was a tall man, crossing to the counter to greet us in two quick strides. "Such a pleasure ladies," he said, reaching for my hand.

"Nice to meet you," I said. "Lucile Ball."

"Lucile," he said. "And you must be Miss Smith."

"Glad to be here," Vera gushed.

"Not as glad as I am," Mr. Smith said. "The draft took almost all my teachers just last month. It's a miracle I got the two of you to venture all the way up here."

"Happy to be of service sir," Vera said, sounding like a soldier herself.

Mr. Smith gave us a thorough tour of the school before dropping us each off in our classrooms. I had a large corner room on the second floor, facing the street. It was outfitted with all the expected necessities—tables, chairs, bookcases or chalkboards lining many of the walls, and a large oak desk and matching lectern centered at the front of the room. I quickly set about arranging it to my liking, parting the furniture down the middle so I could move the desk to the back. I preferred having as many students as possible working at the chalkboards and needed space up front for that. Sitting behind the students also allowed for easier monitoring of the weekly quizzes I favored and allowed me a break from commanding everyone's attention—a part of the job I was still getting used to. I started to seesaw the heavy desk across the room as best I could. "Need some help?" It was the gentleman from the train. "I heard all this commotion and came to investigate." He motioned to the jumbled mess surrounding me.

"Would you mind?" I grabbed one end of the desk and waited for him to join me.

"Let me get Mr. Smith and we'll set it all up just how you want it," he said, smiling at me as he tried to leave the room.

"That won't be necessary," I said. "I've got this end if you can manage the other." His smile grew bigger.

"If you say so." As soon as he was in position, I counted to three. Even though he held his side higher and I had to shuffle my feet twice as fast to keep up, we quickly had the desk in its new spot.

"Thank you," I said, proceeding to move all the tables and chairs back into neat rows.

"You're welcome," he said. "I don't think we were properly introduced yesterday. Thomas Fremont. I'm the science teacher."

"Lucile Ball. Mathematics."

"I guess we're neighbors. My classroom is on the other side of the lab next door."

"I guess so." I finally stopped to take a break and faced him, hands on my hips. "Do you need help moving anything?" I asked. He chuckled loudly.

"No. No I do not Miss Ball. But if I do, you will be the first to know." He turned to leave.

"Do you know who I see about textbooks and supplies?" I asked.

"Mrs. Watkins, in the office. They seem very well stocked."

"That's good to hear."

"I'll see you tomorrow," he said before disappearing into the hall.

A few deep breaths helped my racing heart settle down. I told myself it was just the heavy lifting that left me winded but the truth is, Mr. Fremont was quite handsome and I think I missed the attention of a man more than I realized. I felt so fortunate to like each and every one of the teachers and staff at the school. They were a good lot and everyone made us feel most welcome.

By the end of the week I was exhausted and more than ready for the students' arrival on Monday. Vera and I left work early and were relaxing on the Beach Inn porch, eating bag lunches the cook there provided for us, when a couple charged up the front walk. Linked arm in arm, nattily dressed with matching straw hats—we presumed they were guests of the inn. Instead, they marched up the stairs and stopped right in front of us.

"Miss Ball and Miss Smith?" the man asked.

"I'm Clara Doty and this is my husband Marcus," the woman explained, without even waiting for us to confirm our identities. "We've come to take you sightseeing."

"Mr. Smith just rang us up and said you were done for the day so we came right over," Mr. Doty said.

"Forgive us for just surprising you like this, but please say you're free to join us," Mrs. Doty added.

"That would be lovely," I said. It seemed these two were accustomed to getting what they wanted.

"What's the harm," Vera added. She'd already stood up and was slipping on her sweater.

"Wonderful then. You two take your time getting ready and meet us by the car," Mr. Doty instructed. A shiny Model T was sitting out on the street directly beneath the Beach Inn sign. Vera and I were already familiar with the Doty name even after just a few days in town. Marcus Doty was one of the wealthiest men in Munising—a real entrepreneur—with stakes in several local mills, the electric company, and owner of the city's first automobile garage.

"Follow me ladies," Mr. Doty said when we joined them minutes later. "The boat's this way." We followed him out onto the city dock to a small but beautiful wood paneled lake cruiser.

"You haven't seen Munising until you've seen The Pictured Rocks," Mrs. Doty said as we settled onto the padded benches lining the open-air stern. I glanced at Vera carefully and widened my eyes dramatically, making the slightest grimace. We had all but written off this scenic area east of town as a waste of time. Hawkers gathering tourists for sightseeing trips often crowded the entrance to the inn, badgering us for money. If the natural beauty wasn't wildly over-exaggerated by those filchers, it would certainly be spoiled anyway by the crowds they carted out there.

As we floated away from the dock the vast, steely plane of water that is Superior immediately enveloped the boat and I suddenly understood how large the lake is in a way that's not possible from land. Munising vanished behind us, its denuded city center quickly receding into the forest that crowded the outskirts of town. Mr. Doty pointed out a few of the nearly two-dozen sawmills that ringed the bay. What a thrill it was to see several flat rail cars stopped on the shore, tipping out loads of freshly cut timber right into the lake. The once towering trees sounded like thunder from a receding storm as they rolled over each other and smacked into the water to be cleaned, then pulled up to the mills on conveyer belts for processing into lumber, shingles, and barrel staves.

"I'll take you to one of my mills some time," Mr. Doty said and we quickly accepted his offer.

"It's not much further," Mrs. Doty said after we'd been motoring for some time. It was nearly impossible to converse over the roar of the engine. "Just around that bend," she continued, daring to release the death grip she had on her floppy hat long enough to point out over the bow.

Mr. Doty stood up and stretched past us to pound on the door to the tiny pilothouse and the boat instantly slowed. The silence was remarkable. Not only had the engine been reduced to a muted purr but we were actually far enough from town to escape the constant din of screeching planers and the clock-work call of steam whistles at the mills. The water was glassy and barely rippled as the Pictured Rocks slid into view.

"They're over 200 feet tall," Mr. Doty announced, like he had sculpted them himself.

Stretched out before us were towering cliffs of glacial sand-stone rising up out of the lake as far as I could see. The jagged edges of rock looked like an enormous chisel cleaved them, shards of broken stone laying in irregular piles at the base. The soft rock was layered with thick stripes of mineral ores—iron, copper, and manganese. The metal laden water running over the cliffs left vertical stains of brown, black, tan, and ochre on the surface. The colors were shockingly vibrant and as richly hued as any paint on an artist's palette, applied by the heavy hand of Nature herself. The shoals at the base of the cliffs shimmered in the sun in the most beautiful shades of emer-ald, aqua, and turquoise, providing a stunning contrast to the earthy murals above.

A procession of fanciful shapes revealed themselves as our leisurely promenade continued. Miner's Castle. Lover's Leap. Indian Head. Battleship Row. Once solid outcroppings had each been gradually carved by the elements into turrets, arches, pillars, and bridges. It was like staring at the clouds to find pictures in the sky, only not as fleeting. The Pictured Rocks were more impressive than any words used to describe them and the Dotys couldn't have been more kind or hospitable to give us a private tour. It was a perfect afternoon even though I longed to share it most with the one person who couldn't be there with me.

We were back onshore by dinnertime and the Dotys insisted we accompany them to their home for a meal. Vera was too tired and declined but I joined them, even though it was most unlike me not to succumb to second thoughts or nervous anticipation. The ride up the hill to their house was lovely in Mr. Doty's immaculate touring car, one of only a few vehicles in town to brave the terrible, pockmarked roads. Nearly everyone we passed stopped to wave and I worried if anyone would balk at seeing one of the new teachers being carted around like royalty.

The Dotys lived in what was easily the nicest and largest home in Munising. The three-story, white clapboard house was generously proportioned and solidly built with large leaded glass windows facing the bay featuring completely unobstructed views.

Mrs. Doty deposited me on the wraparound porch facing the lake and I happily sunk into the most comfortable wicker chaise I'd ever sat in. While I didn't make it a habit to concern myself with how other people spent their money, the Doty's outdoor furniture was certainly more expensive than anything in my living room or even Aunt Rose's parlor. Within moments, a young girl arrived carrying a tray with a pitcher of lemonade, several tall glasses, and a large bowl of chipped ice. The latter was a special treat in late August, a full five months or more after huge blocks of ice were cut from the lake or nearby ponds and packed in sawdust. It had to be the last of their supply. We were always running low on the farm by then and drank our lemonade warm, saving what was left for the icebox.

"You must be Lyle." I reached out to shake her hand. The Doty's only daughter was quite pretty.

"Yes ma'am. And Mother tells me you're my new mathematics teacher."

"Yes. So nice to meet you, I…"

"Sweetheart!" Mrs. Doty called from the house. "You forgot the chips dear."

"Excuse me," Lyle said and skittered back inside. She reemerged holding a basket lined with a white napkin and filled with one of my favorite treats—fried potato chips.

"Are those from Peters' Grocery?" I asked. Vera and I had noticed the large bin at Mr. Peters' store where the thin salted chips were scooped into wax bags for customers, who often stood in line out the door whenever a fresh batch appeared.

"They are. Mother has two tins delivered every week. Please, help yourself." She placed them right in front of me and I did just that, but with as much restraint as I could muster.

Lyle and I chatted about the coming school year and all the changes brought on by the war. She was only a freshman but already quite confident and well-spoken, so unlike me at that age. Mr. Doty joined us and smoked a cigar as he quizzed me about my family, Albion, and how I came to be in Munising. I wasn't wearing my engagement ring, so there was no need to mention having a fiancé overseas. Munising seemed farther away from the war than Albion did and I hadn't felt so relaxed in some time.

"Dinner's ready," Mrs. Doty said, emerging from the house with a stack of pasties and a fresh tomato salad. A gourmet cook, she was not content to serve such simple fare to a guest without some sort of flourish. Instead of being filled with just a traditional savory blend of meat and potatoes, Mrs. Doty's pasties were also half sweet—stuffed on one side with apples, apricots, and brown sugar. The mill workers often carried the crescent-shaped, short crust pies in their pockets for lunch but these pasties would never have fit. I must admit that despite their size I finished every morsel—famished after spending the afternoon on the lake, in the wind and the sun.

To top the day off, Mr. Doty treated us to an impromptu violin recital right there on the front porch. As a trained orchestra musician, he was quite adept at classical music and warmed up by playing a few short etudes. Mr. Doty's real talent however, was his ability to imitate current and popular tunes by ear after listening to them just a few times on the Victrola. His repertoire included ragtime standards and new jazz songs, as well as a lively Sousa March made popular by the war. Mrs. Doty, Lyle and I were clapping and laughing so loudly that I wondered if Vera might possibly be enjoying the show through an open window, down the hill in her room.

The performance ended with a heartfelt rendition of "Till We Meet Again", a sentimental love song about a soldier leaving his girl. My throat tightened the moment I recognized the tune and had Mrs. Doty not started to sing, I might have been able to get through it without revealing myself.

"*Wedding bells will ring so merrily*," she sang. My heart grew impossibly heavy. I looked away to try and maintain my composure but it was already too late.

"*Every tear will be a memory. So wait and pray each night for me.*" My brimful eyes finally reached their limit.

"*Till we meet, a...gain.*" Mrs. Doty's voice trailed off awkwardly when she noticed the tears. She was at my side before Mr. Doty released the final note from his bow.

"Pa," she said, "what have we done?"

"No, no" I said, concentrating on keeping my voice from shaking too much. "It's just that so many of the college boys I know are over there." They both nodded. It wasn't a complete lie. "There's so much at stake." I dabbed at my eyes and nose with a napkin. Mrs. Doty remained close.

"Well put, my dear," Mr. Doty said. "Those Germans can rot in hell for all I care." Mrs. Doty glared at him, but couldn't actually disagree. I stood up abruptly.

"Thank you all so much. I really should be going." I gathered my things without looking directly at any of them. "Vera will be so envious when I tell her about the delicious food and swell entertainment." I rushed toward the porch stairs.

"Our pleasure Lucile," said Mrs. Doty. "Pa will drive you." He stood on command. "I insist."

"You are both too kind," I said. "I would love to accept a ride some other time but a walk is just what I need." I scrambled down to the street in front of their house before either of them could argue. "Goodnight. See you on Monday, Lyle," I called, just before the sorrow completely overwhelmed me.

My busy week had helped me hide from the continued strain of Howard's absence, always wondering if he was safe and all right. I missed him desperately and as much as I'd hoped coming to Munising might distract me from the peril he faced overseas, each new experience only made my longing for him that much greater. There was so much I wanted to tell him and writing it all down just wasn't the same. Chief Wawatam and our endless trip north. My new classroom and all the wonderful people I'd met. I wanted him to know about pasties that were part dinner and part dessert, and massive cliffs of sandstone that looked like castles and Indians. I yearned to tell him that I was being brave and make sure he knew that even though I was all right, my heart ached for him ever single moment we were apart.

The inn was quiet and deserted by the time I got back. Mr.

Samms was in the dining room, readying the tables for breakfast when I entered the lobby.

"Lucile," he said, jogging to the front desk to retrieve something from the mail slots behind it. "These came for you today." He walked to the stairs and handed me two envelopes.

"Thank you, Charlie," I said without looking at them, afraid they might only be from Mother or Aunt Rose.

"I think they're the ones you've been expecting," he told me. I had taken to asking about the mail at least once or twice each day and he'd even caught me checking behind the desk myself if he stepped away for a moment. "Goodnight," he said.

"Goodnight," I replied, waiting for him to leave the room. I turned the letters over. He was right. They were from Howard.

Chapter 8

Mon Amoureaux Lucile,

Il est après midi Dimanche et j'ai peu des minutes ecire. I am sitting in a "Y" hut close to the lines where we have entertainments and where soldiers can buy cookies and cigarettes (not me on these).

Several days ago, I went down over 500 feet into a large salt mine! Holes are drilled into the walls, filled with dynamite and exploded. The salt is then conveyed to the shaft by a new <u>electric</u> train, hoisted to the surface, and refined. It is filled with many long tunnels and even a dance hall built of solid salt, with a fireplace and electric lights! It has been running for over 100 years. Very interesting.

Last night, when I returned from a walk in the country, they were holding mass in the large cathedral opposite our camp. At twilight, with the pale evening sun drifting thru the stained-glass windows, the service was impressive. The large pipe organ played and choirboys sang. The priest was clothed gorgeously, the people in attendance were all cleaned up and flowers decorated the altars. It was an anniversary service for 4 years of war with prayers for success of the Allied armies. A few other soldiers attended with me and the entire congregation wanted to shake our hands before we could leave.

As my company follows the front lines, I continue to see scenes of desperate fighting from earlier in the war. Today I saw a place where the river ran red with blood and was almost damned by human bodies. I saw the grave of one old woman killed by the Hun. And there are rows and rows of wooden crosses over graves of French and American heroes. But the Boche only came this far, but no farther thanks to the Allies! I am sorry to say it, but why shouldn't we hate the Hun?

I must close and go to supper. How I long to see you this beautiful Sunday evening. As each day closes, I think one day less of war and one day nearer the time I can come home to you. There is a French girl here who has been waiting four years for her lover's return. Hopefully you will not be required to be as patient as her!

With love,
Howard

———————————

August 7, 1918

Dear Lucile,

Today I am out in the woods expecting to go up to the front at any minute. If you don't hear from me, you will know it is only because I do not have the opportunity to write.

Yesterday we had a severe hailstorm and it rains almost every day, but I am clothed in wool and have not suffered much yet. Last night two German planes flew over our camp and seven more again this morning. Our planes went after them and soon the air was free. A part of a bomb did fall close to the camp kitchen. Well, that is war!

Also, the other night there was a shortage of ambulances to transport the medics to the front, so they called for 30 volunteers to walk. We hiked three or four hours and still did not get to our destination. Finally, about 2:30 AM we stopped and "flopped" by the roadside. The nights here are cold and I only had a thin raincoat—five or six of us laid there together, like pigs. I slept for about an hour and then woke up, oh so cold and stiff. I stayed up and walked around until morning, never wanting to crawl into a real bed so badly in all of my life. Now I smile at it as one more of my "experiences".

Lucile, I often lie on my bunk or on the ground and dream of the past and plan for the future. I wonder if I can make myself worthy of you, but I am learning invaluable lessons here and pray that someday I may have a chance to "try my hand". As I think of what a happy life is possible to properly paired couples, it seems that I cannot wait. When we can sit down of an evening in front of the fireplace, or go for a canoe ride and talk over those happy Albion days, or I will come home from work and tumble around the floor with our children. My eyes are dimmed with tears as I think of the happiness you bring me. Your pleasures in playing with children, told about in your letters, are extremely worthy—so much better than frivolous things. We must pray for the future Lucile. I do every night and I feel quite sure you do the same.

Have you been getting my letters quite regularly? Please

let me know if I have been overstepping the line and they are severely censored. Success to you in teaching, though I haven't yet heard where that will be. I must close not knowing when I can write again, but I will be brave and hope and expect to come back to you.

Your soldier lover,
Howard

Chapter 9

TO SAY THAT I was relieved to be in touch with my beloved again would be like reporting that the Pictured Rocks are somewhat beautiful or that my mother was a little particular—wholly inaccurate and unduly restrained.

Overjoyed. Ecstatic. Full of hope.

Reading words from him that were only two or three weeks old was a real luxury and I couldn't stop smiling the rest of the weekend. I'm not sure why, but I didn't tell Vera about the letters right away. Good news was something to be cherished and savored—there was never any way to be sure if or when the next bit might come.

"I finally heard from him," I said plainly, in the middle of breakfast on the first day of school.

"What? When?" Vera asked, dropping her toast mid-bite. She had stopped asking me about his letters when it became obvious that telling her there weren't any was wearing on me.

"The other night. When I returned from the Dotys'." I regretted being so specific the instant I said it.

"Lucile, that's wonderful! I'm so glad," she said. Her face crinkled and fell a little. "I wish you'd told me sooner."

"Oh Vera, you know me," I said. I was much more reserved than she was. "You're still the first person I've told." That seemed to please her.

"How is he doing?" she asked.

"Well, I think."

"What do you mean, you think?"

"As far as I can tell, he's doing fine. But he's certainly not sharing everything with me," I said.

"Like what?"

"The conditions in the trenches or at the front. How dangerous it is. How scared he feels." I had a much longer list of concerns stored in my head.

"He'll make it home Lucile, you've got to believe that," Vera said.

"You know I do. But I just can't help worry what the war is doing to him. What toll it's taking on the inside? On his mood? His spirit?"

"His joie de vivre," Vera concluded, with a slow nod. We had taken French together for all four years of college.

"Yes, exactly!" I said. "Howard was so alive when he left." I'd been torturing myself with these thoughts for weeks. Suddenly my throat closed. Vera reached over and rested a hand on top one of mine until I could speak again. "He has to work so hard to hold on to who he is over there. To what's important." All I could do was shake my head. I didn't want to show up at the school with red eyes.

"He's a good man Lucile." Vera squeezed my hand tight and stared at me until I looked back. "A good, good man. And he loves you."

"Yes. I know that. I really do." But, there was no way to be sure if that would be enough to protect him. Good men certainly died in battle and others who managed to make it home, often slowly suffered in silence long after the final shot was fired.

"We need to get going," Vera said, looking at her watch. She jumped up and I stayed seated, my mind somewhere in France.

"There's no excuse for tardiness," she said, in a reverse falsetto. It was her best impersonation of one of Mr. Smith's favorite sentiments. I couldn't help but share a laugh with her. I had long treasured Vera's friendship, but never more than during Howard's absence.

My first days of teaching went very well and, as expected, the desks were filled mostly with mill worker's children. Many of the families originally hailed from places much farther away than Albion—Scandinavia, Eastern Europe, the United Kingdom—their pedigrees read like the index of the atlas at home on my desk. The majority of my students were hard workers and eager to learn, demonstrating a real motivation to please both me and their parents. The immigrant experience was familiar to me from my own grandparents who settled in the Midwest from Germany and that connection inspired me even more to be the best teacher possible.

Once school began, my life became a whirlwind of activity. I spent many late nights memorizing elaborate seating charts to learn every student's name and going over each of my lessons two or three times, actually reciting them out loud in my room. Several of my students' families were poor and I was always stopping off at Tredway's Pharmacy to restock my classroom supply of pencils, erasers, and paper for their use, offering it to everyone so that the children who really needed it didn't suffer any embarrassment. I was also touched when two large boxes showed up from home filled with dozens of cookies that Mother and Aunt Rose had made for me to distribute—devoured by the students and staff alike. I opened my first bank account, hiked to several nearby waterfalls buried deep in the woods, and swam up to my neck in Superior's bone chilling fifty-seven-degree water. Everything about those early days in Munising was adventurous and new, but that all began to change by the end of the second week of school.

"What's going on?" Vera asked, stopping abruptly to take a good long look around. We were walking through downtown on our way back to the inn.

"I can't imagine," I replied.

The streets and sidewalks were completely deserted. Only a few shoppers milled around, not a sound was coming from the large saloons nearby and the Delft Theater looked like it wasn't even open yet for the early show. You would have never known it was a Friday afternoon—payday at the mills.

"Maybe they're offering overtime today," Vera said, resuming our trek with a shrug. The mills operated around the clock and sometimes added extra men to the overnight shifts.

"Maybe," I said, but the flags flying half-mast over the New York Store and post office left me certain that the explanation wasn't that simple. Without needing to dodge the usual throng of bicycles on the sidewalk we made it down the hill in quick time. Charlie was at the front desk sorting mail when we arrived.

"I don't suppose there's anything there for me?" I asked. Charlie was continuing to keep an eye out for Howard's letters.

"No. Not yet," he said. He flipped through the stack of envelopes without looking up. It was very unlike him to be so abrupt.

"Charlie, why is it so quiet in town this afternoon?" Vera asked. If anyone would know, he would.

"You two haven't heard?" He stared right at us, not even blinking.

"Heard what?" Vera said, managing to sound both annoyed and intrigued by his subtle scolding tone.

Charlie slid a copy of the Munising News off the top of a stack of newspapers on the counter. He tapped the headline. "That's my ma's second cousin. Nice guy too."

Munising's First War Casualty: Army Private Prato's Funeral on Sunday. My heart sank further with every word.

"Well, that explains it," Vera said, clearly more relieved to have an answer than concerned about the news. It was terribly obvious that she didn't have any loved ones overseas.

"We're so very sorry for your family's loss Charlie," I said.

"Yes, very sorry," Vera added, taking my lead, but turning to head up to her room.

"How is Helen holding up?" The inn's waitress had only mentioned once that her brother was overseas and I was so wrapped up in Howard's plight that I didn't give it much thought.

"She's as good as she can be. They found out a couple weeks ago but didn't tell anybody until his body was returned."

"Please give her my condolences." I headed for the stairs.

"No supper on Sunday," Charlie announced. "We can bring you up a plate if you like. The inn's hosting a reception after the funeral. I got 'em a real good deal."

"We'll make other arrangements," I said. I walked back to the counter and reached for the paper he'd laid out, the smiling soldier staring up at me. He looked younger than Howard. "May I?"

Charlie nodded. I could see he was looking at the picture too.

"He looks very kind. Such a handsome face," I said.

"Thank you, Lucile." There was just the slightest crack in his voice. His eyes looked bloodshot up close. "There's nothing here from your beau. Sorry," he said, placing the final envelope in someone else's mailbox.

"That's alright." At least I could expect more letters some other day.

I took the next hour before dinner to read and re-read the news article about Roderick "Buck" Prato. I had to know everything about his military service and death so that I could try to determine the amount of risk Howard faced in comparison. It was not surprising to learn that Mr. Prato was killed in active duty on the front line and even though Howard served as a medic there too, he usually went in after the worst of the fighting was over. The Prato boy had enlisted early and was sent to France months before Howard was even drafted. Perhaps his time had come I reasoned, the odds working against him given his length of service. There was no mention of a Mrs. Prato and even though his family was certainly grieving it felt more tolerable to me that a heartbroken young woman wasn't suffering nearby—no Prato children asking when their daddy was coming home. It saddened me terribly to realize that poor Helen knew about her brother's death for some time, serving me dinner every night all the while keeping the heartbreaking news to herself.

The following day was the annual teacher's picnic on Grand Island. Already postponed once due to rain, it went ahead despite the funeral scheduled for the next day. The island, just a half-mile ferry ride from Munising, is covered by virgin forests, dissected by old fur trapper's trails, and outlined with coarse, sandy beaches. We spent the day hiking, beach-combing, and for a brave few, swimming. The extraordinary setting, plus the mild weather and enormous amounts of food provided by the Women's Auxiliary, made it easier to relax and nearly forget any troubles back on shore. With sunburned cheeks, windswept hair, and my skirt rolled up several times at the waist to keep the hem dry, it wasn't until the boat ride back that I finally thought better of having such a gay time in the wake of the city's grim news. It was quite sobering to return to the echoes of the local Finish Band practicing for the funeral somewhere up the hill. All of us rushed to put ourselves back together as best we could before the boat sidled up to the dock. As Vera and I scurried back to the inn I could tell there was sand in my shoes, rubbing my feet raw in several spots. With Mother's voice ringing in my head, I didn't dare risk sitting down and having anyone see me shaking them clean while strains of Amazing Grace drifted in the air.

It seemed everyone in Munising attended Roderick Prato's funeral except Vera and I and a small group of church ladies setting up the reception at the inn. We heard it was standing room only at Bowerman & Son with latecomers literally spilling out onto the streets, straining to hear the speeches and tributes through the open doors. A funeral procession out to Maple Grove Cemetery stepped off at 3pm, led by the band with Shorty Leslie and his bus close behind carrying the flag draped casket and the Prato family. It was a moving sight to see the crowd of townspeople fall in behind the bus, filling the street from curb to curb as they wound their way out of town. Vera and I walked up the hill to pay our respects and joined the procession for a few blocks before heading back to the inn to relieve the women who wanted to attend the graveside service and burial.

After the reception began, we joined two other teachers for dinner and a movie. The streets were teeming again with people partaking in their usual Sunday evening outings. The only sign of the day's events was an occasional program from the service lying crumpled on the sidewalk or in the street, the same picture of Private Prato from the paper being stepped on and tattered by pedestrians and horses. At the last minute, I declined to go to the movie and after the girls disappeared into the theater I set about collecting as many of the programs as I could. I carried them with me to the lake and threw them away in the trash barrel at the City Dock. I found a lone bench nearby and sat facing the water, waiting for the reception to conclude. I reached into my purse to retrieve the small box I'd been carrying with me all day. It was my engagement ring, purchased by Howard's mother from one of the finest jewelry stores in Flint with a portion of his soldier's benefits that he'd saved and sent to her after he was drafted. I received it right before leaving for Munising and hadn't worn it more than a time or two to try it on. I somehow thought that I could keep my two worlds separate—the one with Howard and the one without. Just looking at the box still made my heart race and my cheeks flush. I had never been angrier with my mother than the day it arrived.

"Lucile!" Mother yelled from outside.

I had dozed off in the parlor, waiting for her to come in from hanging laundry so we could cook dinner. Father and the boys were in town running errands. I opened my eyes and saw the sheer curtains whipping about wildly in the open windows next to me. I glanced outside to see that a violent summer storm had advanced toward the house with little warning. The western sky was pitch black and filled with huge, anvil-shaped thunderheads, illuminated from the inside by jagged bolts of lightening. Simultaneous cracks of thunder accompanied each flash.

"Lucile! Come help," she yelled again.

Heavy raindrops began randomly falling from the sky even though the sun was still shining. Storms like this were commonplace in central Michigan, where cool winds off the Great Lakes converged, encountering thick walls of hot air that often sat stagnant over the gently rolling farmland.

"Coming," I yelled. The raindrops started to organize themselves, falling together, faster. As I made my way to the door I paused at every window on the storm side of the house long enough to lower each one to within an inch of being shut. It would keep the rain out but allow us to take full advantage of any cooling effects the storm might provide. I ran outside and straight down the porch steps, veering toward the clothesline where Mother was standing.

"Get that," she called, just as one of my father's work shirts was ripped from her hand. I grabbed it as it flew past, stopping to overturn the wicker chairs in the yard. The rain was pouring down and I was already soaked to the skin. Mother had managed to stuff most of the clothes into the baskets at her feet but the bed sheets were impossible to retrieve in the wind. Without breaking stride, I hit the first one head on, taking fistfuls of fabric and running straight down the row. Each clothespin popped off easily and I handed it to her, running back and forth five more times until all of the sheets were collected. We each grabbed a basket and ran for the porch.

"What a mess," Mother said. She was standing barefoot in

a pile of laundry, frantically searching for anything clean. "I'll have to redo everything." Friday was washday and it pained her to change the weekly schedule. I knew she'd be up half the night to still get it done on time.

"I'll take care of dinner." I said. She didn't respond.

I stood there and just watched while she continued to sort through the clothes and linens. Her thin grey hair, normally drawn back into a neat bun, was hanging in clumps across her neck and forehead. Her light summer dress was dirty and clung to her thin body. The wet fabric was almost transparent. Her feminine curves were subtle, whittled down by hard work and little attention. She looked frail, even though she wasn't, and I could see glimpses of the old woman I was destined to become.

"Look at you," she said. I blushed. Unsure if she caught me staring.

"I can only imagine," I replied. I was covered in mud from the knees down.

"You go check the windows upstairs." She was already pulling her hair back and pinning it up, panic gone, back to work. "Get out of that wet dress. I'll take care of this."

I retreated to the bathroom my father had put in the attic and did my best to sponge off at the sink. My bags for Munising were packed with all my best clothes but I found an old skirt and blouse in the closet that would do for one last night at home. By the time I returned to the kitchen the baskets of dirty laundry were gone, the mud we tracked in mopped up, and every window wide open. The patter of steady rain surrounded us and a hint of something cooler was finally starting to blow through the house. Mother met me at the table where she'd set out two glasses of lemonade and a plate of cookies.

"This came for you," she said, placing a small parcel on the table, much closer to her, where I couldn't reach it easily.

"Is that my ring?" Mrs. Bridgman had called several days prior to say she was sending it.

"Yes. It is." I stood up and grabbed the box, almost knocking over both of our drinks. "I want to talk to you before you disappear with it," she said.

"When did it get here?" I asked. I already knew the answer. It was my routine to make the half-mile trek to and from the mailbox by the road just before supper. Father liked to go through the mail at the table after we ate. I hadn't collected it yet that day and I'd been in town shopping and saying goodbye to Aunt Rose the evening before.

"Yesterday." At least she was honest.

"How dare you keep this from me for even one minute," I said, waving the box at her. "Really Mother. How could you?" I stood up to leave. She could make dinner by herself and explain to father why I spent my last night at home alone in my room.

"I'm sorry," she said. I reeled back around.

"I don't care," I snapped. "You can't just do what you please and think that an apology afterwards will be enough. I'm tired of it."

"Please sit," she said. "I just want to say one thing and then I'll let you be." This conversation had been brewing for days. There was no avoiding it, but I remained standing.

"I'm listening."

"You have a fiancé now. Your place is here. Waiting for him." She couldn't stop herself from saying her peace but she couldn't look at me either. "He needs to know you'll be here for him whenever he returns."

"He knows that whether I'm in Albion, Munising, or Timbuktu!" If the box weren't so important I would have thrown it across the room.

"Well I don't agree, Howard won't..."

"Won't what?" I screamed. "Won't have me? Want me? This isn't about Howard." I lunged toward her and smacked my hand square on the table directly in front of her. "It's about you and what you think is right and proper!"

She finally looked at me. "Well I AM right about this one Lucile," she yelled, through clenched teeth. Her vehemence hung there between us and I stared back until she dropped her eyes. She wouldn't dare talk to me like that if Father were home.

"Mother," I said in strictly measured words. "Howard would never ask me to just sit at home and wait for him. He asked me to be his wife. Not his housekeeper and not his cook. He *wants* me to teach. For goodness sake, he wants you and I to both be able to vote." I had never spoken to her like this. "I'm leaving for Munising tomorrow and there won't be any more discussion about it."

She didn't move, but tears collected at the edges of her eyes. It was as close to crying as I'd seen her since Aunt Kit was committed to the state hospital in Kalamazoo. I stood up and walked out of the room and went all the way to the bottom of the stairs before going back. She was still at the table. Crying, but in control—unhappy, but resigned.

"I hope we can all have a nice evening together when Father and the boys get back," I told her.

"I'd like that too," she said. And I believed her.

Once I left for Munising, Mother accepted my decision without any more trouble. She wrote often and I'd received two calls from home since my arrival. I'm almost certain that some small part of her actually admired that I'd stood up for myself. Demanding that things be a certain way was something she understood. She just wasn't too familiar with anyone else making the demands.

I stared at the ring box for quite a while before opening it. Even though his mother took great care to pick a beautiful stone and setting, it was disappointing to become engaged by proxy. Our decision to get married was made during those final weeks before Howard was inducted, when there wasn't time to plan a wedding and the mood was anything but romantic. Howard never officially proposed to me—no bended knee, no asking for my hand. We knew we wanted to be together but there simply was no possible way to stand before God and our families, faithfully vowing to love one and other "'til death do us part". Not with his name getting higher and higher on that draft list with every passing day.

I finally opened the package and slipped the ring on my finger. There was no hiding from the war in Munising, no managing my fear better by keeping Howard and our love a secret, no protecting myself from losing him once I'd already given my heart away. That ring became a symbol of hope for the future and whenever I looked at it I was reminded of all that was still to come. I knew that if Howard came back to me, he would be mine forever and I would most happily be his.

Chapter 10

Dear Lucile,

It is such a beautiful, sunny morning in France and I am off duty after being on guard last night. While walking my post, a friend brought out 5 letters from you. I carried my rifle in one hand and read them in the other. I cannot tell you the pleasure and inspiration that comes to me from reading them! I can only feel it Lucile, and it fills my heart. Being away from you and associating with the coarsest fellows is mentally and spiritually depressing. I read my Testament and pray each day but I need more than that. I need you. I reread your letters this morning and life seems infinitely more worthwhile than it did this same time yesterday.

The tone of your letters was entirely cheering and I like the touches of everyday life you mentioned. It seems strange to be reading about your summer on the farm and your struggles with your mother when I know that you will be teaching by the time you receive this. Uncle Sam promises mail to the trenches in 17 days. Some receive it sooner, but they are way back from the line. I have been within the sound of shooting since July 3rd.

Yes my dear, I am well fed, though not like at home. There is plenty of meat and potatoes and white bread with almost every meal. I buy milk and eggs from the French farmers whenever possible. About the only thing I miss is fruit. I just received new "socks with names", my first pair in France. I still have the Red Cross socks and sweater I got in Albion and will receive more clothing when winter sets in. Sometimes I grow impatient at the apparent slowness of our progress here, but our goal is to defeat the Hun and whatever that takes is the right course.

I am glad to hear that there are now three Ellerbys, because they both longed for the touch of little fingers. I dream of that some day too for us. As I walked post last night I lived over some of our happy days, which will always be with me while memory lasts. The moon was big and round and silver and I imagined that you might have been looking at it too. What a night it would have been for canoeing.

With love,
Howard

———

August 24, 1918

Lucile,

I intended to write you yesterday, but was too busy with drills in preparation for inspection today. Everything went well.

Tomorrow there is a big parade before General Pershing. I hope to see it if it passes thru this cantonment.

Lucile, I sometimes feel badly that I did not go to officer's school. But, we cannot all be leaders. All work in the army is honorable and I've told you that I believe I am learning some vital lessons. The greatest one of course is that I am willing to make the supreme sacrifice, if necessary, for my country. I have been at the front and seen other men making it. There was a truck driver who was hit by a shell and it cut a jagged hole right thru his head. He had a ring on his left hand and I thought of the pain to that woman who was to receive a little card with the words "killed in action". The same shell shot the right leg off of a French Lieutenant and it removed the calf of his left one too. I helped dress his wounds. New and different men will come back when the soldiers of the U.S. return. Some will be sick in soul as well as body, never to be the same physically, mentally, or spiritually. I am so thankful for previous training and for the thought of you to get me through.

Last night I had the privilege of hearing an entertainment group from N.Y. City. Two artists made several rapid crayon drawings that were both frivolous and sensible. One of them has done many covers for the Saturday Evening Post. They also gave a little playlet and sang a couple songs. The soldiers yelled and cheered for them until it was deafening. It was a mighty good show, so near the front.

Yesterday, I also saw a simple, French military funeral. The soldier had drowned in the river the day before. I saw him as he struggled in the water and some American soldiers rushed across, pulled him out and tried to resuscitate him, but failed. I was saddened to later learn that he has a wife and two children at home.

In the Literary Digest I see that the U.S. has done wonderful things during our first year in the war. The Germans are certainly out of luck. Does the Kaiser think he can beat the men of the A.E.F.? It's impossible.

I must close and write a few more letters. How I savor any word I receive from the good old U.S.A., but none as much as yours. Good-bye for now.

Your soldier boy,
Howard

Chapter 11

IT WAS DIFFICULT to remember how isolated Munising was when my day-to-day life there was so busy and full. Keeping up on news about the war was especially challenging since the local paper only came out on Fridays. Besides immediately funneling Howard's letters to me upon their arrival, Charlie became my main source of information about the war. He had several city papers brought in from Marquette, Detroit and Chicago for guests at the inn and even though they were a day or two old by the time they made it to the U.P., he was the first one to read them.

"The boys are really pushing 'em back, Lucile", he'd tell me if the news was good. "It won't be long now."

When the inevitable setbacks occurred he would simply say, "They can't win 'em all, now can they?" His reports were very discreet and came to me as a wink or a shrug if I passed through the lobby with anyone other than Vera.

When I was alone, and if he wasn't busy, we might stand at the front desk and chat for a half hour or more, mostly about the war but sometimes our conversations turned more personal. Like me, Charlie grew up on a farm and we shared a few stories about our experiences from childhood. An accident with a horse caused him to lose a toe and even though you wouldn't know it by watching him walk, it was enough to keep him out of the draft. He was a year or two older than me but didn't mention having a girl and though he never said it directly, I don't think he finished high school. His job at the inn was a good one and the owner, Mr. Redfern, let Charlie run it without much oversight. Charlie was polite, a real sharp dresser, and he knew all the businessmen in town who favored the inn's bar over the saloons off of Superior Street—as did their wives. It was just a matter of time before he fell into an even more lucrative position with one of them.

Like every city or town across America, Munising put on quite a show for the 4th Liberty Loan Drive at the end of September. With the troops having more success against the Germans early in the month, there was a real sense that all they needed was one last push from home to get the job done. Mrs. Doty headed the organizing committee planning the parade. She engaged the volunteer firemen to decorate the entire town in red, white, and blue for the event, had the Finnish Band brush up on all the patriotic songs usually reserved for the Fourth of July, and even convinced the mill owners to shut down their lines for two hours that Saturday so that everyone could attend to show their support. The First National Bank opened its doors well before the parade stepped off and a line formed out the door and around the corner within the first few minutes. Every teller window was in use all day long until the last few people in line purchased their bonds.

"How much for you today, Ma'am?" the clerk asked me as I took my turn. My parents had bought bonds in each of the previous drives but this was my first purchase.

"Fifty please." It was the lowest amount allowed and required a $4 deposit right then and twenty-three weekly $2 payments, made well into the next year.

"And what name would you like to appear on the bond?"

"Doesn't it have to be mine?" I asked.

"You can purchase a bond in anyone's name."

"Howard Bridgman," I said, without pause. "No "e"." I had heard him provide the same explanation dozens of times.

"Your fiancé?" The young woman glanced at my ring while filling out the paperwork.

"Yes."

"Overseas?" she asked. I nodded and we shared a reticent smile.

"Mine too." She held up her hand and flashed a ring at me. "Let me get the certificate for you," she said, walking away.

A small flyer posted on each window showed the terms of the twenty-year bond and what different amounts would be worth in 1938. I pictured Howard and I spending our modest windfall on something frivolous when it came due. What a relief it would be to have two decades between us and the war, our time apart barely even a memory.

The streets were packed for the parade. Several Four Minute Men, who normally spoke while movie reels were getting changed at the Delft Theater, stood outside on the sidewalk giving their quick, inspirational speeches about the war effort. Many of the larger businesses had constructed simple floats, draping horses and automobiles in flags or patriotic bunting and displaying a variety of placards encouraging people to buy bonds.

Lend as they fight.

Every bond you buy is a bayonet thrust at the Kaiser.

That Liberty shall not perish from the Earth.

Participation in the loan drive was voluntary, but it was organized to help everyone feel obligated to give something. The "honor roll" of subscribers—people who bought bonds—was posted outside the bank and a crowd gathered each time the list was updated. Everyone received a 4th Liberty Loan pin once their transaction was completed and people proudly displayed them on their collars and lapels for weeks afterwards. I felt especially uplifted by the patriotic air that day. It was a relief to have other people sharing responsibility for supporting the troops and many of my new friends and acquaintances did notice my engagement ring.

"Why didn't you tell us, my dear?" Mrs. Doty said, grabbing my hand and lifting it to examine the stone. "No wonder Pa and I left you in tears."

"It wasn't the right time," I said.

"What's his name?"

"Howard. Howard Bridgman."

"Has he been gone long?"

"Since July. He's a medic at the front."

"Well, you've already given more than most of us," she said, adjusting the pin on my coat and patting my shoulders. Clara was older than me but not old enough to be my mother. Everything she did was proper, beautiful, and just right. She reminded me so much of Aunt Rose; the highest compliment I could pay any woman.

Following the loan drive, everyone in town turned their attention to the Alger County Fair, held in nearby Chatham. Usually a mid-summer event, it had been postponed and nearly cancelled due to the war but the local mayors banded together to reconvene it and give people something to look forward to.

I was spoiled as far as fairs go. Albion's Calhoun County is home to Michigan's oldest county fair and it was the highlight of every summer I could recall. That week in August was one of the few times my entire family stopped working to relax and have fun together—one last hurrah before the harvest. We spent hours roaming the midway trading in the strips of 5¢ tickets Father bought for rides, games, and treats. We gorged ourselves on smoked meats, fried dough, giant marshmallows, and fresh churned ice cream. As a youngster, I always entered at least a dozen contests from embroidery, tatting, or art projects to baking, canning, and raising chickens. I brought home a number of blue ribbons and even when I didn't, the experience always boosted my confidence. A highlight each year was watching my parents' dramatic group perform a short play or read an excerpt from Shakespeare or some other classic work. It was thrilling when their act drew a big crowd and wild applause, but I didn't ever know what to make of the practiced and daring woman my mother became onstage. As a tradition, I ended every fair season with a ride down the giant slides and one final turn on the Ferris wheel with Father. I skipped it for the first time that August, unwilling to go without Howard who had attended with us the previous two years. The fair in Alger County had no such associations and only felt fun to me from the day it was announced.

At my urging, the teachers sponsored a booth to display artwork made by our students. Children in all grades were encouraged to participate and we used any free time we could muster in our schedules to allow them to complete their pieces. Thomas volunteered his carpentry skills to construct a display booth with wood donated by one of the mills. The night before the fair began he and I were both working late at the school.

He was down in the basement painting the charming, shingled structure he'd built and I was in my classroom labeling and organizing all of the entries. Despite our early introduction, Thomas had kept mostly to himself although he was very friendly whenever we passed in the halls or out on the street. It seemed awkward for him to find his place among an all female teaching staff and it wouldn't have looked right to socialize with a group of young, single women—more for us than for him. Teachers were important and well-known figures in the community and what they did was noticed and mattered.

Returning from the washroom, I found Thomas standing in my room, back towards me, examining the artwork. He was holding a large paper bag.

"Well hello there," I said. No response. "Thomas?" I said again, a bit louder. He finally turned around.

"Oh. Lucile. You're still here." His sleeves were rolled up, his arms splattered with blue and white paint.

"I'll be here for a while I'm afraid," I said. It seemed every student had provided at least one entry for the display. "How's the booth coming along?"

"Almost done. It needs one more coat." He held up the sack. "I just ran out for some dinner. Got you something too, just in case."

"You didn't have to do that," I said, reaching for my purse.

"Keep your money," he said. "It's just a sandwich."

"Thank you. I'll see if there's any water left." I grabbed the cup I kept on my desk and the mug I used for hot tea in the morning and walked to the end of the hallway. The older boys in school took turns filling large buckets with water from a stream around the corner. They were kept in the stairwells on every floor—a single ladle in each, shared by all. It took some tipping but I was able to get enough for the two of us.

"I hope you like egg salad," Thomas said when I returned. He had cleared off one of the desks and laid out the sandwiches, chips, two apples, and two cookies.

"What a feast," I told him. I was starving by then and quite happy for the company.

"Where's Vera?" he asked.

"She took a couple of the senior students to a show tonight. Some play they've been studying," I said.

"I thought she'd be here helping. You two are like twins."

"I guess you're right," I said. Silence. I finished unwrapping one of the sandwiches and said, "So Thomas, where are you from?"

"Detroit."

"What brought you up here?"

"You mean besides the job?" I nodded, my mouth full. "Honestly?" he asked, waiting for me to actually give him permission to answer. I nodded again. "Girl trouble," he said.

"Oh, I see." I didn't know what to make of his confession.

"Did you just get engaged?" he asked quickly. I'd noticed him following my ring up and down from the table each time I took a bite of food.

"Yes," I said. "Well, no actually." His direct manner left me a bit flustered. "I just received the ring. But I've been engaged for several months."

"Congratulations," he said, though his voice remained rather flat.

"Thank you," I replied. Again, we fell silent. "Can I ask you a question Thomas?"

"Bum ear," he said, pointing to the right side of his head.

"Pardon me?"

"I was born deaf in that ear. They wouldn't let me fight because of it."

"Lucky for you," I said. "But that's not what I was going to ask." I wasn't usually so forward, but he'd opened the door. "What was your girl trouble?"

"Bum ear," he repeated. "She left me for some soldier shipping out." I knew a couple of girls in Albion that threw themselves at boys they barely knew who were headed overseas, just to be in on all the excitement. It sickened me.

"That's terrible. I'm so sorry." No one with genuine feelings could be happy or excited about sending a lover into the trenches. "You're better off," I said.

He shrugged. "It's just not easy being the one who stays behind."

"I'm sure it isn't," I told him, recalling how Howard had even struggled with waiting to be drafted instead of enlisting.

Thomas helped me finish organizing the artwork after his painting was done and insisted on walking me down the hill when we emerged from school, into a dark moonless night. It felt nice to be in the company of a man again, especially one that reminded me of Howard—smart, quiet, thoughtful. Thomas was taller than him though, and had the dark features and thick, shiny hair of someone from a movie poster or in the pages of Harper's Bazaar.

Shorty carted several of us teachers and the booth over to the fairgrounds in his bus early the next morning. Vera and I, along with two of the elementary teachers, manned the booth into the early afternoon, showing students who stopped by where to find their artwork and helping everyone cast votes for their favorite pieces. Thomas stayed on too after assembling the booth and appeared to grow more comfortable being the only man in a sea of women. It was a real pleasure to meet so many of the parents and most couldn't have been happier to find their child's artwork hanging there for everyone to enjoy. When our shift ended I asked Thomas to join us to explore the rest of the fair and he seemed happy for the invitation.

The fair's off-season schedule allowed the county to book a very reputable traveling carnival company to provide the rides and games and an unexpectedly large assortment filled the midway. After trying my favorite games of chance—penny pitch, ring toss, and guess your weight—I got up the nerve to give the numbers wheel a try. Without Mother's stringent rules against gambling to limit me, I stood and bet on the wheel for almost half an hour, winning a dollar or more at one point. In the end, I lost all the money I'd spent on tickets, just as Mother warned would happen, but the excitement of watching my number spin around towards the arrow at the top of the wheel was so enticing, that I just couldn't help myself. Vera and I delighted our students by entering and winning a sack race and Thomas drew quite a crowd to the High Striker game in the center of the midway. It took him six or seven hits with the big rubber mallet to ring the bell at the top twice, but he was intent on winning teddy bears for both Vera and me. The food selections included a number of local favorites including pasties, potato chips, and spicy venison sticks and I was charmed to see that they still called cotton candy "Fairy Floss", a term I fondly recalled from my childhood.

Even though the line was huge, we happily waited our turn to ride on the fair's biggest attraction—the Ferris wheel. It was a new, bigger model the carnival company brought in by train to test out, and all rides were free. Screams of delight, tinged with fear, filled the air surrounding the ride. We just happened to be in line at dusk when the large wheel's lights were turned on. A series of bare bulbs lined the spokes radiating out from the center hub and the crowd gasped and applauded wildly when the switch was flipped, illuminating them.

"Are you cold, Lucile?" Thomas asked as we waited. I had dressed for working the booth in the sun, not the cool October evening that emerged after dark.

"Oh, a little bit, but I'm fine." I looked at Vera. "We're headed back to the inn after this anyway." She agreed. Thomas removed his cardigan and slipped it over my shoulders.

"Thank you," I said. It was warm, with a faint smell of aftershave.

When it came time to board the ride, Vera jumped on first and sat in the exact middle of the car.

"You know I love to rock it," she said. "You ride with Thomas." It was true. Vera and I had always brought a different best friend to the fair with us as children just so she could indulge her desire to make every ride as terrifying and stomach-churning as possible.

"Fine," I said and stepped back to wait with Thomas. We sat in the next car and the attendant clipped a chain across our laps. The car rocked each time the wheel stopped and started, loading other riders below us. I sat there, staring straight ahead, trying not to lose my nerve.

"Are you okay?" Thomas asked. The seat was so small that there wasn't a way to leave any space between us, our bodies pressed fully together from knees to shoulders. Our faces were mere inches apart if either of us should turn toward the other.

"This is really something," I said, purposefully not

answering him. I had a slight fear of heights and didn't realize how tall the ride was until it was too late.

"Here we go!" Thomas called out when the wheel lurched skyward. I heard Vera screeching and laughing as she reached the top. When our car peaked, it paused first and then tipped down sharply, gaining speed.

"Whoa!!" Thomas and I both screamed and, without thinking, I grabbed his hand—but only for a moment. I was glad to find that the ride smoothed out a bit once it got going.

"I had a wonderful time working with you the past couple days," Thomas said.

"It has been fun." I did my best to sound casual and relaxed, but all I was aware of was how close we were sitting.

"You're a swell girl, Lucile," he said, looking at me in that deep, steady way people do when they mean it. His brown eyes were endlessly dark. "Your fiancé is a lucky man."

"That's very kind of you." I said. I could tell he was looking right at me, willing me to return his gaze.

"We've hit it off so well, I just can't help wondering…"

I turned to stop him from finishing his thought, right as our car reached the top again. The ground below a blur of color and light. The garbled sound of people talking, screaming, and laughing bouncing around in my head, threatening to drown out the voice inside that told me not to do it. Thomas leaned in, even closer than we already were. I felt my own body drift toward his ever so slightly.

"No. I can't," I said, at the last possible moment.

"What? All right," he replied, quickly pulling back.

"I'm sorry. I just can't." I pressed my body up against the side of the car as best I could, desperate to put any small bit of distance between us, as impossible as it was.

"Of course. Forgive me," he said.

I couldn't respond and we rode the rest of the way down in silence. Howard was the only man I'd ever kissed and if it weren't for Howard, I may well have responded differently to Thomas' advances. Shaking and already sick with guilt, I knew almost instantly—even though the exact words eluded me—it wasn't Thomas that I would have to forgive.

Chapter 12

Dear Lucile,

It is just after dinner and I am at a French "Y" tent to spend a few hours reading and writing. Yesterday I was out all day on a maneuvering expedition. It was a sham battle and we had to establish our dressing stations to care for the wounded, the same as if it were real. But, the front line is the true place to learn. I suppose the American papers are full of the Allies' success. Just the other night we saw the light from a terrific explosion, so far away that I could not hear it. It was reported that we blew up a German munitions plant. May God speed our victories and give us uncanny power in crushing the spirit and force of the Hateful Hun!

I wish you could see some of the places I've been in France. About the first thing we American soldiers do in a French village is clean it up. The people and animals live almost together. There is a perpetual odor. Children are playing on the dirty streets, their mothers usually "jawing" them about something. One or several peasant women are often seen pushing ponderous wheelbarrows of clothes to and from the public washhouse.

There is plenty of wine in France and more than one American boy learns to drink here. I have tasted it, but that was sufficient. Just yesterday, traveling along a road in the ambulance, we passed a gang of workwomen. One of the younger girls waved at us and raised a bottle of beer to her lips to drink, and not for pretend. They smoke too, for I have seen it. Some soldiers yield for the moment and stay with these girls but I want that my body should rot on the French battlefields than return to you in such a condition! Well, I did not intend to say all this but if the censor passes it, then you will appreciate the picture it gives. It's only a small part of what I am experiencing.

Almost every night after dark, when the barracks are noisy with fellows gambling or playing cards and dingy with tobacco smoke—I go for a walk under the starlit arch of heaven. How I need such time, almost daily, to get my bearings and a new grip on life. I try to pick some worthy subject and let my thoughts linger upon it until I feel like myself again. Last night I let myself wonder if you are enjoying yourself in Munising; what you are seeing; who you are meeting. I have no doubt that you are liking your work and succeeding. Remember me to Vera and don't teach her any bad habits! I should probably worry more about the opposite happening. I expect we will be moving soon, so I may not be able to write for a few days. We may be going up to the front but I never know until it happens.

> With love on a beautiful evening in France,
> Howard

September 17, 1918

My dear Lucile,

Since writing you last, I have been at the front for four days in the great, all-American victory you have read about in the papers. I could write several pages about my experiences there and some day I hope to relate them to you in detail. Right now, I'm just glad that I lived thru them.

I am writing to you on German paper, which I found in an old French chateau used as a Red Cross hospital by the Germans. I stayed there one night and slept several hours in a real spring bed! Too soon, shelling chased us to the bomb shelters. The next night the chateau was blown to pieces. I am sending you a piece of German money given to me by a prisoner as a souvenir.

During the last two days, I received 14 letters! Two of them were the first from my mother. I learned from her (and then from you) that you received the ring and my wish is that it is entirely satisfactory. I told Mother to get a good one, but my only regret is that I was not the one to slide it on your finger. When I got the letters, the Germans were shelling the town and I sat in the door of our dug-out, reading and listening to the explosions all around. That same afternoon I was bathing in a little creek when a shell exploded nearby and two pieces struck the water just ten feet in front of me. The day before we were out patrolling for wounded and I decided to move from where I was resting and, in a few minutes, a big shell exploded right there. I do not tell you this Lucile to frighten you, but just to show you a little of the excitement.

In the villages we freed there were so many pitifully happy French civilians who had been prisoners for 4 years. How they love the American soldiers and how I hate the Germans! The night we marched in it was raining and we walked thru brown, "mud-gravy" often up to our knees. It was a narrow road and more crowded with men, horses, and guns than any city street. The German shells were fierce but no one was hit. Enough of this—all you really need to know is that I came back and feel well.

I have sometimes wished that you could come over here as a "Y" worker or a nurse and have some of these experiences but you are too young to qualify and one of us bearing these hardships is enough. I know of no better way that you can do your bit than by teaching. As I see the ignorance and consequent squalor of some other countries I realize that education is a fine profession. It touched me a little when you spoke about leaving home. I have done it and can feel your emotions. I am glad you and your mother reached an understanding.

Do not worry about me. I'm having the biggest experience of my life so far. Success in your work! Hope for the future! Love for all time!

Howard

Chapter 13

IT WAS AFTER 11 o'clock by the time the Dotys dropped Vera and I off at the inn after the fair. I was exhausted from working all day and reeling over the encounter with Thomas, still wearing his sweater, leaving so quickly that I forgot to give it back. All I wanted to do was go to bed.

"Lucile," Charlie whispered from across the lobby before I could even close the door. "I have a telephone message from your mother. She called three times," he said, handing me a note. It instructed me to phone home as soon as I received it, no matter the hour. Mother was the last person I wanted to talk to.

"I wonder what's wrong?" Vera asked.

"I can't imagine," I said. Part of me didn't care, but the rest of me worried that something bad may have happened. An accident in the fields, Rose's heart, perhaps Aunt Kit had finally passed.

"Anna Sherman's working the switchboard tonight. She's expecting your call," Charlie said, cupping my elbow and guiding me to the front desk.

"Did my mother sound upset?" I asked, even though there was no way for him to know that.

"She was very persistent." Charlie placed the candlestick phone on the counter. Vera picked up the receiver and jiggled the cradle to signal the switchboard.

"Hi Anna, it's Vera Smith. Can you place that call to Albion now? Lucile's right here." She handed me the phone. Vera pressed up against me, her ear next to mine with the receiver in between. Charlie stood right there too and I appreciated their company, not knowing what kind of news I was about to receive.

"Lucile?" Mother said. "Are you there?" Her voice was clear, but sounded small and distant.

"Is everything all right?" I was practically yelling and hated talking so loudly with people sleeping just up the stairs.

"Yes, we're fine. So far, at least. I was calling to see if you are all right."

"Of course I am Mother. What's going on?" I rolled my eyes and shook my head at Vera and Charlie, sending them away with a wave. Her call didn't need to keep us all awake. "Why are you calling?"

"The flu. Has it hit up there yet?"

"What are you talking about?" I didn't even try to be patient.

"The influenza outbreak Lucile. We've had one hundred cases here in the last two days. They say it's going to get worse."

"Mother, it's just the flu. Stop worrying. I should go. It's late."

"The college is quarantined. Robinson Hall is being turned into an emergency hospital. There's talk of closing the schools and banning public gatherings—even church!" she sputtered. "Here, talk to your father."

"Lucile," Father said. He only used my full name when he was being serious, but I felt certain he was only trying to appease her.

"Will you please calm her down?" I directed, without even greeting him. "I need to go to bed."

"Your mother and I have talked, Lucile. We want you to come home right away."

"What?" I suspected she had put him up to this, knowing I'd be more likely to comply if he asked. "No," I told him, without a hint of hesitation.

"I know it seems overcautious, but we want you here with us. Your grandparents are moving in tomorrow and Rose is next if things get any worse." There was a long pause and some hushed mumbling on Father's end. "*All right, all right. I'll tell her,*" I heard him say off to the side. "Lucy." Another pause. "There's been one death here already." The words took their time to even make sense in my head.

"Who?" I finally asked.

"Mrs. Flannery." My old piano teacher.

A lump formed in my throat. "It can't be that bad," I whispered into the mouthpiece. Father remained silent. "I can't just leave."

"What if I came and got you?" I pictured him standing in his coat and hat, ready to run out the door.

"No. Vera's here with me. We'll watch out for each other." We were hardly children, after all. *People didn't just die from the flu,* I told myself. Mrs. Flannery was already old back when I knew her.

"If it gets bad up there, promise me you'll come home," he said.

"It's just the flu," I repeated. He had had a case of it himself in the spring.

"It's different this time. You call us first thing next week. Sooner if you need to."

"I will."

"Goodnight then. I love you Lucy."

"Goodnight Daddy. I love you too." I waited for the line to go dead. "Thanks Anna," I said to the operator before hanging up. Mother was one thing, but I couldn't ignore an urgent call from my father.

"Charlie," I said into the shadows surrounding the front desk.

"I'm in the dining room." He was sitting at one of the tables, sorting through the basket of newspapers kept for guests. There were several kerosene lamps surrounding him, gathered from around the room. The single, electric chandelier overhead was on but hardly cast enough light for reading. "It's got to be here," he said. "Yep. This is the one." He pushed the basket aside and spread the newspaper open in front of us—a recent Chicago Tribune. "I didn't think much about it because the article was buried so far back." He was flipping quickly through the paper, scanning each page intently. "Found it," he said, tapping one of the shorter columns of fine print. I began to read it to myself.

Liberty Loan Drive may have spread the disease…
Surgeon General recommends closing public facilities.
Six thousand new cases last week.

"That sounds like a lot," I said.

Over 600 deaths…

I looked at Charlie, who was reading every word with me. "Should we be scared?" I asked.

"Nah," he said. "It's worse in the big cities. There's nothin' to worry about all the way up here."

"I suppose you're right," I said, but the call from home left me shaken. I excused myself and went right to bed though I didn't sleep well, plagued by a string of crazy dreams.

Mrs. Flannery giving Howard a piano lesson in a front-line trench, bombs going off all around. Thomas and I back on a Ferris wheel operated by my mother—the ride getting faster and faster. Me at the chalkboard in my classroom, turning around to find myself as a child sitting alone in a sea of empty desks. I was crying because everyone had died from the flu. Sleep completely escaped me while it was still black outside and I left for work as soon as the foggy shadows of the lakeshore and city dock first appeared out the window.

Early October in Munising was spectacular. The autumn shores of Lake Superior glowed in vivid hues of red, yellow, and orange, each as clear and bright as a box of crayons on the first day of school. The inn was packed with tourists who came just to see the colors and even the locals gushed about the show. I followed a longer route to school that morning—winding my way around the edges of town—and could see that the leaves were dropping quickly, the dark skeletons underneath just starting to make their appearance. There was hardly a pause between seasons in the Upper Peninsula and by the time the ground was freshly carpeted with the remnants of fall we would be waking to frost nearly every morning. The reprieve of an Indian summer, so often relished back home, seemed unlikely here. Once the frosty tendrils of winter found their way down out of Canada there would be no turning back.

My thoughts were not my own that morning. Instead they lingered with Mrs. Flannery, recalling her strict but fair approach for lessons countered by a genuine delight when I mastered a difficult passage. I'd studied with her weekly for almost eight years. I also kept picturing my family retreating on the farm to avoid being infected, protected by the fence that I had only ever pictured holding me back. I still couldn't believe there was any truth to the alarm they sounded. It made no sense that the flu could become a killer.

Mostly though, I thought about Howard and how I'd come so close to kissing another man. I didn't know how to fix what I'd done or what to do next. I felt guilty of course, but deep inside I had to admit that it had been just a little exciting too, and that was what caused me the most heartache. By the time I mounted the steps to Central High my head was pounding and my stomach was in knots. I could have easily taken a sick day. Instead, I went straight to Thomas's room and returned his sweater, prepared to see him but relieved he wasn't there. I retreated to my desk with a cup of tea and set about grading mid-term exams. It wasn't long until I heard someone walking down the hall, headed for my room.

"There you are," Vera said, passing through the door. "You forgot your lunch." She dropped a paper bag on my desk. "You left so early."

"I came in to get a start on these," I said. I hadn't even finished grading one of them.

"You know they're not due until the end of the week. You should have slept in." She sounded genuinely concerned. "I brought you some toast in case you didn't have breakfast either." It was wrapped carefully in a napkin and she set the bundle next to my cup. Her simple, caretaking gesture was all it took for me to break down.

"Vera, something happened," I said. She sat right beside me, still in her coat.

"What is it?" she asked, handing me a handkerchief from her pocket even though tears weren't falling yet.

"Shut the door," I sputtered. She only left my side for a few seconds but I was crying hard when she returned.

"Lucile, what's going on?" she asked. "It's Howard, isn't it?" Hearing his name made the pressure in my chest get even tighter.

"No, it's Thomas. We nearly kissed." I could barely make myself say it.

"What? When?"

"On the Ferris Wheel. I never should have let it happen."

"It's not your fault. He had no business trying to kiss a woman engaged to be married," Vera announced with the conviction best friends reserve for each other regardless of proof.

I shook my head no but remained silent. I didn't know if I could tell her.

"What kind of man takes advantage of a lonely woman like that?" She stood up and started to pace back and forth. "And he seemed so nice." She was being too loud. If Thomas had been at school I'm quite sure there would have been no stopping her from confronting him directly.

"It's not his fault," I whispered, staring at the door, willing her to quiet down.

"You don't have to defend him, Lucile. There's no excusing this kind of behavior," she continued in full voice, still pacing.

"Part of me wanted him to kiss me." Now I was practically

yelling. "I almost let him, Vera. We're both to blame!" She stared at me, confused.

"You wanted him to?" I looked her straight in the eye and nodded. She came and collapsed onto the chair next to me. "Oh Lucile."

"You must think I'm horrible."

"No," she said. The several seconds it took for her to gather her thoughts felt like minutes. "I admire how you've been holding up actually. I couldn't do it—send the man I love off to war." Even though my revelation required her to reorganize her thoughts about me, I knew she meant it. "Will you tell Howard?" she asked.

The very thought of it sobered me instantly. "Never." It hadn't even occurred to me. "Why? Do you think I should?" She shook her head no.

"But it can't happen again." I wanted to get mad at her for presuming I didn't know that, but she had every right to say it.

"I know. And Vera you have to swear not to say anything to Thomas."

"We'll see," she said. Somehow, she still seemed to blame him.

"Vera, I mean it."

"Fine," she said. "I won't."

Vera got herself a cup of tea and we shared the toast she'd brought. It would take days before I could eat anything without feeling nauseous and I had to stay very busy just to keep that moment at the fair from constantly playing over and over in my head.

As soon as the fall colors faded and the final sightseers cleared out of the inn, Charlie insisted on moving Vera and I into two of the larger rooms on the second floor. They both had small sitting areas overlooking the lake and were much closer to the bathroom—a welcome convenience as the inn's unheated hallways grew colder and colder overnight. Except for the regular contingent of traveling salesmen, we had the entire place to ourselves, acting like it was some mansion whose owners were away on vacation. With the days getting shorter we both spent more and more time inside, helping Helen wash dishes after dinner, spreading out in the dining room to mark tests and papers, or reading a book next to the hearth in the parlor where Charlie kept the embers glowing, always just one log away from a roaring fire.

One night, about a week after the call from home, I walked into the parlor to find a group of men gathered there talking. Arguing actually.

"We can't close the schools, everyone will panic!" It was Mayor Sullivan yelling and pointing a finger at Superintendent Abell. The men were sitting in a semi-circle around the fireplace. There were four of them, including Mr. Doty and another man I didn't know. Mayor Sullivan spotted me first. He was smoking a cigar, unfazed by my appearance.

"Miss Ball," he said, throwing his head back to exhale a large puff of smoke. It sounded like he was welcoming me to a party. The other three turned toward the door, unable to hide their surprise and discomfort.

"Lucile dear," Mr. Doty exclaimed, standing to greet me. The superintendent attempted to smile but could only manage a nod. The man I didn't know went to refill his drink from one of several open bottles scattered on the mantle.

"Hello, gentlemen," I said. My cheeks became instantly inflamed. "I'm sorry for interrupting. I had no idea you were in here." I tried to retreat as quickly as I could.

"Join us, won't you?" the mayor said.

"T.G.!" the man I didn't know replied. He delivered a slow, very clear shake of his head the mayor's way.

I remained in place, waiting for their showdown to end. It felt like I was going to cause trouble no matter what I did. Mr. Doty finally took charge.

"You can have my chair," he said, shifting his over to make room for another. I sat on the edge of the seat, keeping the book and pile of papers I needed to grade in my hands. I took a deep breath. The room smelled like cigars and liquor. The setting reminded me of one of many gatherings I'd attended at Aunt Rose's home with several of her professor friends. We'd adjourn to the parlor after dinner to discuss art, politics, and more recently the war, over dessert and just a bit of sherry. The debates there were always lively, but never as moody or intense as the exchange I'd walked in on.

"I believe you know everyone here," the mayor said. He gestured toward the other men with his drink. A bit of it sloshed over the sides.

"Not everyone," I said, looking at the man next to me. He started to extend his hand but then withdrew it.

"Theodore Scholtes."

"*Doctor* Scholtes," the mayor announced. "Munising's Health Officer."

"Lucile Ball. Nice to meet you."

"I'm sure you must be wondering what this is all about," the mayor said.

Although very curious, I felt obliged to say, "Gentlemen, I'm quite sure none of this is my concern. I should let you get back to your discussion."

"On the contrary, dear. Maybe a fresh perspective is just

what a group of stubborn men like us needs," Mayor Sullivan continued, staring at Superintendent Abell and releasing
another dramatic puff of smoke. "You see, we're discussing the
influenza epidemic headed our way and whether or not to close
the schools. I for one would love to hear a teacher's opinion on
the situation."

"You've had your fun T.G. Let her leave," Mr. Doty said.

"It's not appropriate to be involving this young woman in
official city business," Dr. Scholtes added.

"Now just hold on!" The mayor drained his drink and
slammed the glass on the table next to his chair. "I want to hear
what she has to say." Gone was the inviting tone used to lure
me in. This was a command performance. Despite the other
men's protests, I could feel all four sets of eyes looking at me,
waiting.

"I can't say that I know enough about it to offer an intel-
ligent opinion, sir."

Besides the call from home, details of the flu had only just
surfaced in the most recent issue of the Munising News. The
article featured an interview with the U.S. Surgeon General
and read like a high school primer detailing how influenza
spreads and ways to keep from getting sick. *Cover up coughs
and sneezes, get plenty of rest, stay away from others who are contagious.* I'd heard Mother issue sterner warnings to my brothers
over a runny nose.

"Ted?" the mayor said. "Why don't you tell Miss Ball
what we were talking about?" The doctor shook his head and I
expected him to refuse.

"Well, I was explaining to everyone that this strain of
influenza is extremely virulent. It actually started last spring in
the military camps but there's so much contagion in crowded

conditions like that that no one understood what was happening. Thousands of soldiers died before even heading overseas."

I had read Howard's letters so often I could immediately recall the one from Camp Riley, when he'd been sick and stayed overnight in the hospital to be monitored for the flu.

"Apparently," Dr. Scholtes continued, "it's in the trenches too. Word is that the Germans got it so bad they might actually lose the war because of it."

"What about the AEF?" I asked.

"They've got it too but no one's talking about it with a war to win." My head was spinning and I wished I'd never walked into that room.

"So, the question is how to prepare for the flu here in Munising?" the mayor said.

"And I've told you that the only precaution that really works is to keep people from being exposed in the first place," Dr. Scholtes said. "That means keeping people at home and off the streets. No meetings. No movies. No saloons. And certainly no school," he continued, raising his voice as he ticked through his list.

"People aren't going to listen if they think we're overreacting," Mayor Sullivan countered. "It's the God damn flu, Ted! No one closes school for the flu. They'll think we've lost our minds!"

"Good!" the doctor yelled back. "I want people to take notice. To be scared. You're not the one getting telegrams from Lansing every day. The fatalities in Chicago and Philadelphia are shocking and Detroit's not far behind. Pretty soon, you won't have a choice!"

"You can't compare us to the big cities. We're not even on

the main train line," the mayor said. "A lot of people stay inside this time of year anyway, for Christ's sake."

"Everyone except the children," Doctor Scholtes said—slowly, precisely, and smugly. If their argument was a game of chess, then his retort was checkmate. The mayor stared at him for as long as it took to take a final, full drag on his dwindling cigar. He started to carefully stamp it out in an ashtray beside him, staring as he rolled the stub back and forth.

"This is my dilemma Lucile," the mayor said. "Do I take precautions before the epidemic has even surfaced and risk scaring everyone or do I wait until it arrives and hope that it doesn't spread too quickly?" He turned to me. "What are your thoughts? As a teacher."

"Well," I said, pausing to choose my words carefully. "I'm sorry to say it, sir, but if the students are at all at risk then you have to close the schools. I think parents would understand and appreciate your caution." The mayor stared at me and chuckled.

"Well, I got my answer, didn't I?" he said, reaching into the breast pocket of his jacket for another smoke.

"The schools in Albion have been closed for two weeks," I added.

"Gentlemen," Mr. Doty said, standing up and taking me by the arm. "I'm going to see Lucile upstairs. Feel free to continue without me." The only sound from the room behind us was the pop and crackle of the fire. He kept me moving until we reached the bottom of the stairs.

"I regret you got dragged into that Lucile."

"I didn't know it was so serious," I said. "My father called the other night and told me to come home because of the flu and I told him not to worry." I tried to whisper but the panic in my voice wouldn't let me.

"Do you want to go home?" he asked.

"I can't leave my students just because I'm scared." My voice trembled and broke with the admission.

"Well then, you tell your father that you'll come stay with us if anything happens. Or we can collect your things right now if you want. Clara and Lyle would be thrilled." Mr. Doty winked at me.

"Thank you. I'm fine for now, but I will tell him."

"I should get back," he said.

"Goodnight." I turned to go up to my room.

"Lucile. You know you can't tell anybody about this?" I nodded.

"I know."

"Not even Vera," he said.

"I understand." I knew it would be hard not to say anything but by the sounds of what I'd just heard, it wouldn't be long until everyone found out for themselves.

Chapter 14

Dear Lucile,

I have not written you for several days. I have been hiking, riding in ambulances and on freight trains, and now I'm in another, more beautiful part of France. I just returned from visiting an old cathedral built in the 15th Century. It is very elaborate for such a small town—beautiful stained-glass windows and figures carved in stone. I wish to send you a picture, but that is not possible. Perhaps we can revisit some of these places together one day.

I know you are following closely the success of the Allies now. It is especially cheering to us soldiers and we think what we are seeing may be the "beginning of the end". I thoroughly believe that God is with us and that He is bringing confusion and consternation to the ranks of the enemy. I pray for this every night and then again in the morning when I wake. Think of the millions of war weary hearts who are anxiously waiting and still valiantly fighting for that end. I see that some of the big German war lords are still outwardly confident but, as we soldiers say, "They are out o' luck!"

Do you remember a year ago when I asked you to go for a walk that Sunday afternoon? That was the beginning. I also remember when I would call you on the phone and we would talk for hours; those two nights in Newberg; and our three-mile, moonlit walk down Jackson Road in February. I shall never forget the feelings that thrilled me that night. Re-living such simple times gives me enormous pleasure.

The weather here is getting more disagreeable, turning rainy and colder. I am well, however, and just as determined to come home to you. I have received no more letters for some time. In a day or so I am expecting a feast of mail. It seems I cannot wait to partake.

With love,
Howard
XXXXXX

Chapter 15

"YOU LOOK TIRED," Vera told me the next morning. "Did you stay up late reading again?"

"No. I just didn't sleep well." I wasn't hungry either and sat across from her dragging my fork around a plate of cold scrambled eggs. "Do you mind if we just get going?" I said. "I need some fresh air."

Keeping a secret from Vera wasn't the worst part about the clandestine meeting I'd walked in on the night before. It also wasn't Mayor Sullivan's gruff behavior or even learning that there was an influenza epidemic bearing down on us. Rather, it was finding out that Howard might be facing even greater odds than I realized, two enemies instead of one. Guns, flamethrowers, chemical gas—I had no choice but to accept the usual and expected threats of the war, but it was shocking to learn that something as common and benign as the flu could end up taking him from me.

When Vera and I arrived at school all of the teachers were gathered in the hall outside the main office, still wearing their coats and hats. Our friend Grace Selke, the music and drawing teacher, came over the moment she saw us.

"Cassie told us to wait down here," she whispered.

"What? I've got papers to correct," Vera grumbled. She was always behind in her grade book.

"Mr. Smith wants to talk to us about something," Grace said.

"Now what?" Vera replied. She had recently been scolded for leaving her classroom windows open overnight—a squirrel got into the school and left quite a mess. She went and stood at the bottom of the stairs by herself, pouting.

"I wonder what this is about?" Grace said. I shrugged even though I had a pretty good idea. Thomas stood several feet away chatting softly with another teacher and it was the first time we'd been in the same room since the fair. I considered going over to say hello but before I could work up the courage, the office door swung open and Mr. Smith walked out along with Cassie and Caroline Gardner, the school nurse.

"Good morning everyone," he said. "Sorry to keep you waiting, I know the students are arriving shortly but I need to share some important information with you before they get here. Please give Nurse Gardner your full attention." He ended his remarks by looking squarely at me. I felt sure Superintendent Abell had told him about our encounter.

"Thank you, Ross." Caroline Gardner was older than any of the teachers and the only one in the building who ever addressed the principal by his first name. I turned to look at Vera. She was standing several steps up the staircase, ready to bolt for her room.

"There is a very serious strain of influenza going around the country," Nurse Gardner began. "It is highly contagious and I need your help monitoring the students for illness. Send anyone displaying symptoms to my office without delay—head or body aches, flushed skin, severe fatigue, and especially sneezing or coughing. If you hear any students talking about illness at home, alert me as well. I will handle it from there." She stepped back for Mr. Smith to speak again.

"Students with any sign of influenza will be excluded from school until the contagion passes," he announced. "The same goes for all of you. Don't even come in if you have any of the symptoms Nurse Gardner listed." His warning was gruff and sent a wave of wide eyes and stolen glances across the room.

"Cassie will distribute circulars with information about influenza to your rooms by the end of the day. Please make sure every student takes one home. This is serious folks, but please remain calm. Any questions?"

"What about the water buckets?" It was Avis Rice, the science teacher. "All it would take is one sick student using those ladles...you know how they are." Mr. Smith's eyebrows arched dramatically and he turned to signal the secretary. Cassie was taking notes in the small notebook she carried whenever she followed him around the building.

"We'll figure out a solution for that right away. Anything else?" he asked without really waiting long enough for a reply. "Have a good day then." We were dismissed with his customary nod.

Between constantly monitoring the students' health and more than my usual amount of worrying about Howard, it was very hard to focus on teaching that day. I must have sent at least a dozen students down to see the nurse and all but one was sent back up. As a precaution, I kept the window nearest my desk cracked open for fresh air and had to ignore numerous complaints that it was too chilly. The water buckets at the ends of the halls disappeared and everyone was instructed to bring their own ladle or cup from home. I don't think the students fully understood what was happening yet so I required everyone in my homeroom to return the circular to me on Monday, signed by a parent.

Charlie seemed to be watching the door when I arrived at the inn after school that day. He waved for me to join him at the front desk and, as usual for a Friday, had a copy of the Munising News spread out in front of him.

"The disease is presently in Munising," he read aloud from the second paragraph of an article simply titled, *Spanish Influenza*. It contained all the information I'd heard discussed in the parlor and was signed by Dr. Scholtes. He called on citizens to keep well and avoid spreading the illness if attacked.

"If the general public cooperates as it should, Munising may pass through the epidemic without going through the experiences of eastern cities and almost surely without serious interference or loss of life," Charlie said, reading the last line of the article. "See, I told ya. There's nothing to worry about."

I considered telling him that Dr. Scholtes and the mayor were planning the city's response to the epidemic in secret. That the situation was almost certainly worse than anything they'd print in the paper and that if we waited to read about what to do, it might be too late. But, I'd promised not to tell anyone, so I kept quiet.

That weekend there were signs of the coming epidemic starting to surface all over town, but only if you knew what to look for. Stacks of extra boxes containing gauze and Vicks Vaporub crowded the aisles at several local drug stores. Bissell and Stebbins Hardware sold out of ladles and camphor balls. The line outside the Delft Theater was shorter than usual and many saloons kept their doors and windows wide open despite the frigid temperature. Sitting alone in the parlor at the inn, I overheard two salesmen talking in the lobby. One had just arrived from Newberry, sixty miles to the east.

"They got sick people in tents lined up all around the courthouse," he said. "I'd skip it if I were you."

"Aww, I can't. Not this week. How many folks you figure got it?" the other fellow asked.

"Didn't stay long enough to find out. But I'm tellin' you, it's bad."

"I'll get out as quick as I can. See you next week."

"Good luck."

There was a slight pause before the one man walked out and I could just picture the two of them shaking hands. Being polite. Spreading germs. When I turned in later that night I was careful not to touch the banister on my way upstairs, just in case.

I was not surprised to get a call from home that Sunday evening. My father's plan to keep the family isolated on the farm was working—not one sign of illness among the seven of them—though reports from Albion weren't as favorable. The schools there were still closed, including the college and 400 cases of the flu had surfaced in total. There were also two more deaths.

"Haven't been to town since the last time we talked," Father said. "But we're doing fine. With the cows and the hens and all that canning you and your mother did, we're eating like kings." He sounded nearly giddy with pride. "I had Rose churning butter just this morning," he added. "Here, she wants to say hello."

"Lucile?"

"Aunt Rose. It's so good to hear your voice," I said. It was the first time we'd talked since I'd left and I could feel myself tearing up.

"How are you, sweetheart?"

"Fine, I guess. I'm so glad that you're all healthy and not driving each other mad yet."

"Healthy yes, but no one said the latter, dear." We both laughed. "What about Munising? Any sign of influenza yet?" I didn't know what to say. "Lucile? Hello?" She must have thought our connection had dropped.

"I'm here," I said. I couldn't bring myself to lie to her. "Don't say anything to Mother or Father, but yes, it's here now too. I'm sure it won't get as bad as it is down there," I added.

"Oh, I see," she said. Then whispered, "Have they closed the schools?"

"No. There's a plan to keep everyone out who might be sick. To stop it from spreading." There was a long pause before Rose responded.

"They tried that here too, Lucile. I have to tell you, it only worked for a day or two." Her voice grew even softer. "Be careful," she said. "This isn't the kind of flu you're used to."

"Oh, tell Father that Mr. Doty invited me to stay with his family if it gets bad up here. I'll be fine."

"I know you will," Rose said, even though I knew she worried about me. "I should go, dear. Someone else just picked up the line."

"Goodbye," I said. "I love you. Tell everyone I said hello."

"I love you too."

Saying goodbye to Rose was difficult. Hearing her voice, knowing my family was together at the farm—cooking, laughing, playing games—taking care of each other. It was really the first time I'd longed for home since leaving Albion. Waiting for the epidemic to wind its way to us, across the Straits and along the train lines, was maddening. It reminded me of those weeks after Howard was turned down as an alternate in the draft and we knew that his next order of induction would be the one that took him away. Knowing that something bad is going to happen without having any way to prepare yourself. Not really.

As expected, a number of students stayed home from school on Monday and we all did our best to cope with the mounting pressure, especially in front of the children. Mr. Smith visited the home of every student who was absent and confirmed that all were out as a precaution and not due to illness. Miss Gardner was busy, but not overwhelmed, checking students showing any symptoms, the ladle-less buckets were back in the halls, and my classroom was no longer the only one with open windows. Miss Rice used her science class to teach all of the students the singsong reminder printed in the paper—"*Cover up each cough and sneeze, if you don't you'll spread disease*"—and the art teacher had students create flyers and banners with the saying for display all over the school. The mood in the building was alert, but calm, and dare I say even a little excited. There was a sense of preparing for the arrival of something important or a relative you hadn't seen in a while. But, "The Spanish Lady"—as this particular strain of influenza was often called—was hardly the kind of visitor anyone really wanted to make welcome.

Upon returning to the inn that afternoon Vera and I walked into quite a scene. There were people everywhere and a wall of nervous chatter greeted us at the door. Dr. Scholtes was at the center of it all, set up behind a large dining table someone dragged into the parlor. People crowded around, waiting for their chance to talk to him—like he was royalty—his throne one of the wingback chairs from next to the fireplace. An oversized street map of Munising sat on an easel next to him with three red X's drawn on it, all on the same block. The mayor, Superintendent Abell, and Principal Smith were there too, each surrounded by their own smaller contingent of people. Mrs. Doty sat in a corner of the dining room talking and making lists with another woman. Helen Prato was racing in and out of the kitchen with pots of coffee and pitchers of water and Charlie carried out stack after stack of towels and sheets from the inn's linen closet, filling the buffet with dozens of each. No one even noticed when we stepped into the middle of the lobby and we went undetected for several minutes.

"Hello girls." It was Miss Gardner walking in behind us. "I got here as quickly as I could."

"Caroline," Superintendent Abell said, barging in to collect her. "I would shake your hand, but..." He turned and greeted us too. "Listen, if it's all right with you Caroline we might as well have these young ladies join us," he said.

"That's fine," she said. We all followed him into the parlor and found Mr. Smith and Cassie who were already seated. There weren't enough chairs, so I sat perched on the arm of Vera's.

"Well, as some of you have heard the mayor received a proclamation from the governor this morning that calls for banning all gatherings and meetings across the entire state, effective immediately," the superintendent explained. I looked around and wondered what the governor might have to say about the crowd filling these two rooms.

"The order includes churches, theaters, saloons, and any other places of public amusement," he continued. "After consulting with Dr. Scholtes and me, Mayor Sullivan decided to close the schools too, even though they weren't included in the order.

"Not yet anyway," Principal Smith said. I let a hand drop onto Vera's arm and squeezed it firmly, without looking at her.

"Are the X's on the map cases of influenza?" I asked.

"Yes. The ones we know about at least. Which brings me to all of you," Superintendent Abell said, scanning the seats where the Nurse Gardner, Vera, and I were sitting. "At Dr. Scholtes suggestion, I'm going to ask the teachers to conduct daily health surveys all over the city to check for illness." Vera looked up at me, shocked and scared. A flash of regret came over me and I wished then that I had given her some warning.

"Caroline," he said. "You will be in charge of the survey. I'll need you to arrange the teachers into pairs and assign them to one of the districts drawn on the map. We need this up and running tomorrow morning." If Nurse Gardener was surprised by her assignment, it didn't show.

"What if someone isn't comfortable with this kind of work," she asked him.

"I'm not expecting them to put themselves at risk here," he said. "They don't have to go into every house. Talk to people through a door or a window. Hold up a sign. I don't give a damn how they do it." He turned to Vera and me. "Do you ladies have a problem helping out?"

Shaking my head, I said, "I certainly can't imagine *any* of the teachers having a problem with it Mr. Abell." Vera nodded in agreement.

He turned back to look at the nurse. "That's what I was counting on," he said. He sighed and then his voice softened. "But I'm certainly not going to require anyone to participate if they don't want to."

"Thank you, Harold," Nurse Gardner said. "I'm sure we'll have plenty who are ready to help."

"Excuse me." It was Dr. Scholtes. "I need to talk to Miss Gardner, if I may."

"Go ahead, we're done," Superintendent Abell said, abandoning his chair. The doctor leaned in close to Caroline but made no attempt to keep his instructions private.

"I need you to talk to Mrs. Doty and Mrs. O'Brian," he said. "They're in charge of the Red Cross effort and will be outfitting the old Froebel School building as an emergency hospital. You'll need to keep them apprised of the number of cases your teachers discover every day so they can determine when to open the extra beds. I want to keep the flu out of the main hospital if we can. Also, contact Mrs. Bissell. She's making a list of all the nurses in the area who could be called on, if they're needed. It's been difficult getting volunteers over in Luce County," he said.

"What? Why?" Nurse Gardner asked. She was shocked by the news. He paused and turned to look at all of us, then back to her.

"Everyone's terrified of getting sick," he said.

"Who can blame them," Cassie whispered. She looked pale and her voice quivered. No one else was bold enough to agree with her, but we were all thinking it.

"They waited too long to get ready over there," Dr. Scholtes informed us. "I'll be damned if I'm going to let that happen in Munising." He marched back to his table where people were standing three deep to speak to him.

Vera and I stayed late into the evening helping with the preparations. Miss Gardner put us in charge of contacting the other teachers to inform them of the school closing and our own call to service. As anticipated, everyone agreed to help with the survey, without any hesitation. With that done, Mrs. Doty sent us to the grocery for more food and we returned to help Helen prepare a light, cold supper for all the volunteers. She also instructed us to buy as much gauze as we could find, along with plenty of elastic ribbon, thread, and needles. After everyone ate and all of the men went home, the women sat in the dining room together, cutting and folding the gauze into wide, multi-layered strips and sewing elastic to the ends to fashion masks that would be distributed as the epidemic took hold. Teachers would be the first to receive them the next morning and Vera and I each took ours upstairs when Nurse Gardner sent us to bed sometime after midnight. I slipped the mask on and looked at myself in the mirror before going to sleep. It was hot and uncomfortable and covered the entire bottom half of my face. I could tell that once I put on a hat, only my eyes would still be visible. Standing there, I noticed the picture of Howard I kept tucked in the corner of the mirror, posed somewhere in France wearing a gas mask. I inhaled sharply but couldn't exhale until I pulled my own mask back off. I stared at his image and wondered how I'd ever stand wearing it for hours, let alone days at a time, and wondered if he felt the same.

The teachers reported to work the next morning to greet any students who hadn't heard about the closures. The children had different reactions to finding us standing outside in front of the high school, wearing the masks and passing out flyers with a simple message printed in large, dark capital letters: SCHOOL CLOSED. PREPARE FOR AN EPIDEMIC.

Several of the boys thought it was funny—some sort of joke. Two of them kept playfully trying to snatch Thomas's mask off his face and he finally had to raise his voice to get them to stop. A few of the girls started to cry, especially the younger ones. We did our best to comfort them but the masks were unsettling and made that nearly impossible. We were told to instruct the children to stay close to home, avoid playing in large groups, and remind them that there'd be no loitering in the parks or on the streets with school out.

"Are we going to be all right?" many of the students asked.

"Of course. We'll be back in school soon," I told them. What else could I say?

After the last students went home the teachers were immediately paired off and given an area of the city to check for illness. Miss Gardner was kind enough to put me with Vera and I was relieved to find that the homes we were assigned included many of our students as well as the Dotys. While knocking on doors checking for influenza was never going to be mistaken for a social call, knowing many of the families made it much less awkward. I felt badly for Thomas who was paired with Mr. Smith and had to call on several of the town's less reputable boarding houses and a half dozen mills, closest to town. Our eyes met as he turned to leave and we shared something close to a smile, as much as was possible given the gravity of our new jobs and the masks covering our faces. The first survey took us well into the afternoon to complete, though we stayed at the Doty house longer than most when Clara and Lyle treated us to a quick lunch. Everyone we spoke to was full of questions, some were scared and others angry, especially anyone whose livelihood was threatened by the mandatory closings. But despite the stress, all the people we met were respectful and gracious, aware that we were only doing our job and trying to help. It was a masterful plan to send teachers into the community at a time of great peril. Who else could ask such prying questions and be expected to get a cooperative response?

I returned to the inn by myself late that afternoon, completely exhausted and looking forward to a short nap up in my room. I could tell something was wrong with Charlie from across the lobby as soon as I entered. He didn't look up at me and there wasn't even a newspaper spread out in front of him to hold his attention. When I approached the front desk, he stood and retrieved a letter from the mail slots behind him.

"Charlie?" I said. It was both a greeting and a question. He slid the letter across the counter. His hand was trembling.

"This came for you in today's mail." His voice was dull and flat. There wasn't one drop of color in his cheeks and he still avoided looking at me.

"Are you all right?" I said. I felt for the gauze mask in my coat pocket. I wondered if I was about to discover my first case of the flu.

"You need to look at that." He stared at the envelope.

I picked it up, assuming it was from Howard but I immediately noticed that the stationary was different, much nicer than the thin tissue paper issued to the soldiers. I turned it over and saw my own handwriting on the front. It was one of the letters I'd sent to him a while ago. Returned. Unopened. A splash of red ink cut across his name.

My heart flipped violently in my chest, my pulse walloping in my ears as I absorbed the crimson message. The letter fell from my hand when my arms went limp at my sides.

"I'm sorry Lucile," Charlie said, finally making eye contact. He ran around the desk to keep me from dropping.

The air rushed from my lungs and I couldn't refill them no

matter how hard I tried. I turned to go to my room but knew with the first step that I would never make it. A metal taste filled my mouth and a terrible moan escaped my lips, crying out in unison with the roar in my head. I sank to the floor on my knees. White-hot tears pouring down my face.

WOUNDED it said on the envelope.

Address, not known.

Chapter 16

Chapter 17

THE FIRST THING I recall after finding out Howard was wounded, is Vera kneeling on the floor next to my bed.

"What can I get you?" she asked.

"Nothing." The letter was laying on the nightstand.

"Get that away from me," I said. She snatched it off the table.

"What should I do with it?"

"Put it in your room. I can't look at it." Vera immediately ran out into the hall, but left the door wide open. I didn't want anyone to see me in such a state but I couldn't pull myself out of bed. My eyes were burning and nearly swollen shut. My sides ached, my throat was scratchy and dry and the pillow under my face was damp from tears.

"What time is it?" I asked, when she returned.

"Just after seven. You fell asleep for about a half hour. Helen's keeping a plate warm for you, I'll go get it." The room was littered with things Vera had already fetched for me—used handkerchiefs all over the bed, two glasses of water and a steaming cup of tea on the nightstand, a hot water bottle at my feet. I let her go even though I knew I couldn't eat.

Howard was wounded but I didn't know how badly. If it took my letter two weeks to return to the States then there was no way to even know when he was injured. He could have been dead already by the time it got back to me. In between bouts of sobbing, all I could do was replay the last fourteen days in my mind, scouring each second for some clue, a sign that he was in trouble. But there was nothing, no sense that anything was wrong. I had lived my life normally while Howard was lying somewhere bleeding and in pain, vulnerable, alone, almost certainly thinking of home. No doubt, more aware than ever, just how far away he was.

I don't know how long I cried but there was an endless supply of tears for as long as I did. I managed to sleep a few hours but only because Vera laid down with me and was there for comfort every time I woke with a start, seeing Howard get injured countless different ways in my dreams. I didn't ever stay asleep long enough to see if he survived.

In the morning, Vera tried to convince me that she should do the survey on her own but I knew she'd hardly slept either and I really couldn't face being left alone. We completed our rounds faster than the day before, now that everyone knew about the schools closing and the ban on public gatherings. We spoke to most people on their front porches and tried to at least put our eyes on each of the children. The original three cases of influenza were recovering rapidly and no other sign of illness turned up anywhere, leaving many citizens frustrated and angry with the mayor, just as he'd feared. Vera took the lead talking to people and I did my best not to appear too somber.

The only exception was at the Oas home when I asked Albert Oas if I could speak to him privately. He was the city records keeper and head of the local draft board. I showed him the letter.

"I don't know if you can help, but I sent this letter to my fiancé overseas and it was returned to me yesterday." I thrust it into his hand.

The red ink explained it all in one glance. "Oh, I see," he said.

"Do you know if wounded might really be code for something else?" I asked. "Something more serious. Perhaps as a way to warn people. To give them a chance to prepare?" I heard what I was saying and couldn't believe that I was talking about Howard.

"Miss, I get men ready to leave for the war because I have to, it's my job." He handed the envelope back to me. "I'm afraid I don't know anything about how they return. I wish I could help. I really do." He touched my arm when I started to cry. "If he was dead the army would just tell you. It's no secret that we're losing a lot of men over there. You should keep your hopes up."

"Thank you," I said. I found Vera and left as quickly as I could—confused, scared and embarrassed. I considered asking Helen Prato if this was how it went with her brother, but I did not want to upset her and wasn't sure I really wanted to know the answer.

After completing our survey, we reported to the Froebel School to help get the abandoned building ready for its new life as a makeshift hospital. It was a sturdy, two-story frame structure with a tall stone foundation, plenty of large windows on all four sides, and gingerbread trim at the eaves that reminded me of the farmhouse back in Albion. The building had sat empty since the high school was completed in 1907 and even though it looked to be in fine shape there was eleven years worth of cleaning to do before it could accept any patients. A small group of women were methodically working their way from room to room—washing walls and windows, scrubbing floors and woodwork, disinfecting the bathrooms and a small kitchen. Miss Gardner had several reliable high school boys stacking old desks and bookshelves into one of the classrooms for storage, carting in all of the donated supplies piled out front, and setting up cots as soon as each room was cleaned.

"We're here to help," Vera said to Miss Gardner upon our arrival. The school nurse was passing through the foyer, clipboard in hand.

"Know any nurses?" she snipped. Usually calm and patient, I had never seen her look or sound so strained. But she immediately grabbed Vera's arm and apologized. "I'm sorry. You're both dears for coming by."

"Is there a problem?" Vera asked.

"Oh, they can't find a single nurse willing to assist me. There's plenty registered but no one wants to work during this epidemic."

"People are getting scared," Vera said.

"What kind of nurse is scared to be around sick people?" Nurse Gardner huffed. "Being exposed is part of the job." She looked at me and put her hand on my forehead. I had yet to say a word. "Are you feeling okay Lucile?"

"Just tired," I said.

"Get some rest then. Don't let yourself get run down. It's an invitation for getting sick."

"Yes, you go rest. I'll stay here and help," Vera said.

"I guess I will." I didn't have the energy to protest and left immediately.

I fell straight into bed when I got back to my room and slept well past mealtime. There was a tray of food outside my door with a note from Vera telling me she was downstairs if I needed anything. I ate alone in my room. Then, I did something that surprised me but it had been my routine for so many nights that it would have felt wrong to stop. I wrote Howard a letter.

It didn't take long to fill three pages with news of everything that was happening. I wrote about my debate with the mayor and the school closing that soon followed. I described my new assignment patrolling the streets of Munising looking for influenza and the gauze mask I had to wear all day, then boil in strong antiseptic each night. I wanted him to know that the thinnest crust of ice was starting to form on the lake and that once it froze solid you could skate out a mile from shore. I also did reveal that I had learned of his injury. I reminded him that he was strong, that he would be home soon, and that I would be waiting and ready to take care of him and help in any way necessary. Then I sealed the envelope and walked downstairs to say goodnight to Vera. I gave her the three cents for a stamp and asked her to post it for me in the morning. It felt good writing to him but I couldn't drop the letter in a mailbox myself, knowing that it might be back in my own hands just a few weeks later. Since April I had spent all my time wanting the waiting to end and now I would gladly wait for many months more to receive the only news I longed to hear—that Howard was alive and safe and on his way home to me.

In the coming days I fell into a welcome routine of busyness, which kept me occupied from breakfast until bedtime despite being relieved of my duties in the classroom. The emergency hospital was fully outfitted and waiting, the residents were still grumbling but had adjusted to the bans and closures, and our routine health surveys became the highlight of the day even though all of us teachers were on edge, waiting for the epidemic to surface. We really came to know each of the families we visited more intimately and they all quickly grew to see us more as friendly guests than nosy intruders. That's how Vera and I instantly knew something was wrong at the Schultz house when Anna's husband answered the door. He worked at one of the mills and should have been gone for hours by the time we knocked. Mr. Schultz was still dressed in his coat and boots, ready to walk out.

"She's in bed," he said. "Just collapsed. I had to carry her up." The smell of tobacco and beer poured off him as he paced in front us. I could see their toddler in the kitchen at the end of the hall, sitting in a high chair, wailing. Vera rushed to check on him. He'd clearly been crying for some time. "I can't wake her up," Mr. Schultz said, still pacing. "Do you think she's got it?" This poor man wasn't much older than me, I realized.

"I don't know but I'm going to get the doctor over here," I said. "Do you have a phone?" We'd been instructed to call the Dr. Scholtes' office if we found signs of illness.

"No," he said. It was a convenience not everyone could afford. "Please, you have to check on her," he pleaded, pulling me toward the steep stairway crowding the front door. "She was fine when the baby got up earlier."

"I'm sorry, but we have to call the doctor first. I'll get my friend to do it and be right back," I said, motioning down the hall. I walked to the kitchen, took the child, and sent Vera out the back door to call from a neighbor's house.

"Don't go inside. Have them place the call for you," I reminded her.

I returned to the front hall and handed the baby to Mr. Schultz. "The doctor will be here shortly. I'll just wait on the porch so he knows which house to come to." If this was influenza, I had to make sure no one came or went before a quarantine sign could be posted.

"No," he said, grabbing my arm. I didn't struggle with him, but he was holding it tightly and it hurt. "You're a nurse, you've got to check on her." He was yelling and it made the baby start to cry again. All this man knew was that his wife was sick, he was late for his shift, and I was someone sent to help. I didn't dare try to explain that I was just a teacher.

"All right," I said. "But you'll have to stand outside. The baby should get some fresh air anyway." I waited for him to let go, but it took several seconds. I fetched an afghan from the living room to tuck around the child. "Don't talk to anyone and don't let anybody inside." He nodded but wasn't really looking at me. It might have been the mask. A lot of people weren't used to them yet.

"She's in the room at the top of the stairs," he told me. He took his time stepping onto the porch and closing the door, watching to see if I was really going up. I wasn't able to catch my breath until I heard the latch click into place. I knew I shouldn't check on her by myself but was more afraid of his reaction if I didn't.

I first heard the rattling noise as soon as I reached the second-floor landing. It came from the bedroom. A sound similar to the crackle of cellophane being pulled off a Whitman's Sampler at Christmas. Only it was slow, drawn-out, repetitive.

"Hello?" I said. "Anna, it's Lucile. I'm here to check on you." No response, but the crackling sound continued uninterrupted. I approached the door, which was open just a bit. I went to place my hand on the worn brass knob and thought better of it at the last second.

Cover up each cough or sneeze, if you don't you'll spread disease.

"Anna? I hear you're not feeling well. Can I come in?" I opened the door with a push of my elbow and that was when the dreadful smell hit me, even through three layers of gauze. An unidentifiable mix of bodily fluids. "Anna?" I said again, a little louder. "I'm coming in now."

Buried under a pile of blankets in the middle of the bed, the poor woman was curled up in a fetal position. Her labored breathing and the putrid air made me suddenly feel short of breath myself. I walked to the side of the bed and gasped out loud, shocked by the look of Anna's face. Her skin was severely mottled, covered in a rash of deep purple blotches. Her lips were dry and cracked and had a blue cast to them, her eyelids too. There was a light pink stain on the sheet near her face. A foamy, reddish liquid oozed in and out of her nose with each labored breath. Her body shook with fever and I went to feel her forehead but realized I couldn't risk touching her. If this was really just influenza, it wasn't like anything I had ever seen.

"Lucile!" It was Dr. Scholtes. He was half way up the stairs by the time I made it back out to the landing. He pushed past me, pulling up the mask hanging around his neck without pausing. "Wait outside with Miss Smith," he ordered.

There was a small crowd gathered in the yard when I emerged and we waited in silence on the stoop as they stared at us and whispered. Dr. Scholtes returned after just a few minutes and took Anna's husband off to the side, speaking to him in a hushed but firm tone before sending the man and his child back inside the house.

"He accepted the quarantine for now, but I'll have to come back and take her to the hospital," he said to Vera and I before rushing out to his car. He returned with a long piece of fabric that appeared to be a ripped-up sheet. It was painted black and he tied it like a bow around the porch railing. There hadn't been time to print the official signs yet and this makeshift solution had been ordered by the mayor.

"Lucile," Dr. Scholtes said. "Come with me." I wanted to stay with Vera but knew I had to go. I ran to keep up with him and was barely able to get in the car before he pulled away.

"You shouldn't have been up there! That woman is extremely sick," he yelled.

"I'm sorry. Mr. Schultz insisted I check on her. He wouldn't take no for an answer," I yelled back, though not as sternly.

"What do you mean?" he asked. I had been rubbing my arm through my coat. The car swerved when he noticed and looked at me. "Did he hurt you?"

"Not really. He grabbed my arm when I tried to step outside."

"Get that mask off. Stay close to the window," he told me with an urgent, but noticeably softer tone. "Don't touch your face until you can wash your hands. I won't have you getting sick." His voice cracked and as he reached down to shift gears I saw that his hand was shaking. Dr. Scholtes wasn't angry with me at all. He was scared.

"I'll be okay," I said softly. "I was very careful not to touch her and no one sneezed or coughed while we were there."

"I'm glad to hear that at least." He stopped abruptly in front of the emergency hospital and sat in the idling car with me. His voice had settled completely. "Your job is to check on people," he said. "That's it." He finally looked at me.

"I understand," I said.

"And don't you worry, I'll have Officer Pellesier deal with that bum Schultz."

"He's scared. I feel quite sure he didn't mean to hurt me."

"That's no excuse. Now you go inside and wash your hands thoroughly, all the way up to the elbow. And throw that mask out right away. I'll bring you a new one."

"Thank you," I said.

"Of course." He sounded exhausted. It wasn't even noon.

By the end of the day there were twelve patients in the emergency hospital, including three people from a single family. Nurse Gardner was able to piece together how the epidemic finally made it to Munising. The Harvey family entertained a visitor from St. Ignace the night before and the train their guest arrived on stopped in nearby Newberry, which had suffered thirty deaths by then. Not only were the Harveys infected but so was their cook and server for the night, Anna Schultz.

CITY WILL OBEY INFLUENZA BAN.
PREPARE FOR AN EPIDEMIC.

Word of the flu's arrival finally made headlines in the Munising News. The official order from the Governor of Michigan that closed all public establishments and banned all unnecessary meetings was reprinted on the front page. Mayor Sullivan and Dr. Scholtes provided statements as well, warning all citizens to take necessary precautions, but not to get excited. I had to shake my head when I read that. As more and more people saw what I had seen, when it was their loved one lying in bed, blue in the face and fighting for every breath, there would be no staying calm.

A dark mood fell over Munising in the days to follow. The

teachers issued gauze masks to everyone in the city during our rounds. The streets became nearly deserted, day or night, and those who ventured out had to wait their turn entering stores one or maybe two at a time to purchase basic goods and necessities. The Beach Inn continued to serve as headquarters for the epidemic effort and was visited that week by a speaker from the State Board of Health, sent to check on conditions. I stood with Charlie at the front desk listening as Dr. G.R. Hill addressed city officials and several local physicians. His ideas for averting a high death toll were extreme and I could see the mayor and others in attendance cringe as he listed the precautions that might become necessary.

"Incoming trains should be watched and any suspects picked up and examined," he told them. "A man who expectorates on the streets should be arrested forthwith, for that man is worse than a murderer!" Dr. Hill did commend Dr. Scholtes for the low infection rate in Munising, but encouraged him to take action sooner than later. "Don't wait until your funeral car is in daily use to send out the emergency call for relief." He concluded his remarks by stirring the group with a simple but powerful piece of advice. "Safety first at any cost."

The mayor and Dr. Scholtes took this seriously and maintained tight restrictions even though incidents of illness remained low for another week. While they saw this as proof that their strategy was working, many citizens were growing tired of the warnings and took to openly disparaging the mayor. People gradually returned to the streets, larger groups of children were seen gathering in backyards and parks, and the masks started to come off too. The community's disregard for the bans only caused Dr. Scholtes to become more adamant and inflammatory with his own warnings.

"Disabuse your mind if you have concluded that the danger period has passed," he said in the next of his weekly newspaper interviews. He squarely blamed the people of Munising for what he called an inevitable and violent epidemic. "It would be an act of divine providence if Munising is spared the siege," he concluded. It became increasingly difficult to defend the decisions made by city officials when I was in people's homes every day, seeing the hardship caused by the restrictions, though I did remain silent when anyone aired their complaints in front of me. With Howard still missing somewhere in France, I had bigger concerns than when the pool halls and churches could open or how many people were allowed to shop in The New York Store at one time.

Every day I rushed back to the inn as soon as my patrol duties ended. I took to coming in through the bar, which was closed to the public, just so I could rub the twin, bronze pig statues mounted by the door. It was rumored to bring good luck.

"Anything?" I would call out to Charlie as I passed through the dining room and into the lobby.

"Just the usual," he'd say from behind the front desk, indicating that more of my letters to Howard had arrived. They were trickling back, often one at a time but sometimes two or three. There was no getting used to the red mark next to his name, and seeing it again each time cut through me as if it were the first. Charlie gave me a box to store the letters in and I organized them by date to present to Howard when he came home. I was determined for him to know that I never gave up trying to reach him. It wasn't lost on me however, that his safe return was actually less and less likely as that box slowly filled, but to sit with that for more than the slightest of moments would have driven me mad.

I was so glad to receive a call from Howard's sister Lillian after their letters started coming back to Clio too. Try as he might, his father was having no luck getting information from the army about Howard's status. The same day that they learned he was wounded, Mr. Bridgman borrowed a neighbor's car and drove all the way to Battle Creek. He stood at the front gates of Camp Custer clutching his son's birth certificate and picture until someone would talk to him. He was told there was no way to handle specific inquiries about individual soldiers, especially since Howard was probably separated from his unit after the injury. It was heartbreaking to think of Mr. Bridgman being turned away still not knowing if his son were dead or alive. I asked if I could speak to him, but he declined.

"He's still feeling too emotional," Lillian whispered. "He doesn't want to cry in front of you."

For much the same reason, it took over a week for me to feel up to calling home with news of Howard's situation. Even then, I could barely get the words out before breaking down with Aunt Rose. She and Howard had become very close during our senior year and the news hit her hard, though as always, she did her best to focus on what I needed.

"I'll come stay with you if you want me to," she said. Her offer made me cry even harder, though I couldn't dream of accepting. I did impose on her to tell the rest of the family about Howard's injury, though I knew it would hurt my parents not to get the news directly from me. I longed to hear father's calm voice and tender words but also knew that Mother's response would likely be upsetting. She spent every day of her life so tightly wound that a broken curio or some sour milk was often cause for alarm, depending on her mood. She certainly couldn't handle news of this caliber without overreacting. Rose agreed to the favor immediately.

I was so on edge to receive news of Howard's whereabouts and condition that it was hard not to panic when Dr. Scholtes turned up at the inn late one evening to speak to me. I felt sure he was there to deliver the news I feared most.

"Hello Samms," he said. "I'm looking for Lucile." I was in the parlor and heard him come in.

Of course, I thought. It made perfect sense that the doctor, or the mayor, or even my boss, Superintendent Abell, would be the one to deliver a telegram bearing news of Howard's death. I sat frozen in my chair.

"She's in the parlor sir," Charlie told him. And, with a few quick strides the doctor was standing in front of me.

"Good evening, Lucile." I didn't look at him and remained silent. "Lucile? I need to talk to you about something. It's important."

"It's Howard, isn't it?" I said. I gripped the arms of the chair tightly waiting for his reply to hit me. "You have news about my fiancé."

"Oh, dear Lord, no!" he exclaimed. He dropped his black medical bag to the floor and fell into the chair across from me. "No, no, no, that is not what this is about."

"What?" I said. I was flooded with relief. As much as I wanted some news, I really only wanted it if it was good.

"I'm so sorry Lucile. Of course that's what you thought." He grabbed my hand and patted it. "Samms," he yelled. "Bring in a glass of water." It took a few minutes before I was ready to hear the real reason for his visit.

"So why are you here?" I asked.

"You know, now's not a good time for this. It can wait 'til tomorrow," he said.

"No, tell me," I said.

"I need your help. But before I ask I have to say that it's completely all right if you decline. Agreed?" I nodded. "I need someone to work at the emergency hospital. Caroline is exhausted and I have to get her some relief."

"What about the list of nurses Mrs. Bissell compiled?"

"Mrs. Doty spoke to every woman on that list personally and I'm ashamed to say that not one of them is willing to step in." He rubbed his face with open palms and pushed his hands back through his thick, prematurely white hair. "Same damn thing that happened over in Newberry. I have half a mind to publish that list and let their friends and neighbors learn about their decision." A look of complete disgust took over his face, like he'd just bit into a rotten apple.

"I'll do it," I said. He looked surprised.

"You should think about it. Talk it over with Vera, your folks perhaps."

"There's no need. I want to help."

"There are risks, Lucile."

"I know." I could still picture Anna's blue face.

"Well, I'll give you all the details tomorrow then." He stood up. "Do you know if Miss Smith is around here somewhere?"

"Should be up in her room. I'll get her for you."

"Stay put. I'll find her myself," he said. He made it all the way to the doorway before stopping. I was trying to find the page I'd been reading when he first came in, when our eyes met across the room.

"Thank you, Lucile. You're a brave young woman," he said.

Truth be told, I felt anything but brave and courage had nothing to do with my decision.

I knew if Howard was alive somewhere in France there was a trail of people who'd risked their lives to care for him: a medic dodging bullets to carry him to safety and dress his wounds, a doctor patching him up in some crude hospital near the trenches, nurses taking care of him right then, right as Dr. Scholtes asked me to help others in need. I would never meet any of the people who assisted Howard but I owed them all a deep debt of gratitude. And it was a debt I wanted paid in full, whether Howard returned home to me or not.

But especially, if he did.

Chapter 18

I WAS RELIEVED to learn the next morning that Vera and I would be working together at the emergency hospital. There must have been a terrible need for help, we joked, if we were the best candidates Dr. Scholtes could come up with. Between the two of us, we didn't have one single bit of nursing experience and I had never even stepped into a hospital. Beyond the stories of rampant illness and high death tolls in the large cities of the Lower Peninsula, it felt like influenza couldn't really hurt us, like it was something happening to other people, in other places. Even Anna Schultz, as sick as she was, was slowly recovering.

Our stint at the Froebel School began right away. Dr. Scholtes met us there early to issue our uniforms—white starched full-length aprons, white linen hats, and new gauze masks that we could dispose of and replace anytime we liked. He showed us each of the hospital's four wards, including the empty quarantine area on the first floor, reserved for cases of pneumonia, should they develop. Two cots were set up in the corner of the kitchen where we would be sleeping. We were charged with running the hospital during the day so Nurse

Gardner could rest. She would take the overnight shift when we, in turn, would sleep. There were only five cases of influenza in the hospital that day and all of them were stable and close to discharge.

At first our duties really felt more like babysitting or caring for a sick family member than anything close to risking our lives. Vera and I took turns checking on patients—fluffing pillows, tucking in loose blankets, and taking temperatures and pulses every hour. They were all younger than expected and we spent a lot of our time sitting with the ones who were awake—chatting, reading magazine articles out loud, or playing hangman on one of the chalkboards lining the walls of the old classrooms; anything to relieve the boredom. I took charge of what little cooking there was, making simple foods like soup, custard, and toast. Squeezing oranges for juice. Vera and I were both looking forward to greeting our fellow teachers as they checked in that afternoon. I was having so much fun pretending to be a nurse that I didn't even notice when several of them hadn't returned on time.

"There they are," Vera announced, spotting our friends Grace and Nellie out the window. They were two blocks away and running towards the school. We were all feeling a bit cooped up by the circumstances and it looked like they were having a friendly foot race to relieve some stress. I stepped outside to greet them.

"Hi you two," I chirped. I was anxious for them to notice me in my full nursing regalia. As they drew closer I could see they weren't smiling or laughing and their pace did not slow at all until they reached the top of the stairs.

"Dr. Scholtes wants you to get ready," Grace said in between heaving gasps for air. Her gauze mask flapped wildly in and out across her mouth, her normally soft and wispy voice unexpectedly assertive and demanding.

"We found nine cases in one family," Nellie exclaimed. She sounded both proud and terrified of their discovery.

"Influenza?" Vera asked. The revelation was hard to believe, even after all the time spent preparing.

"Come in, come in," I said, shuffling them into the kitchen at the back of the building. I didn't want to alarm the other patients. The four of us stood in a tight circle, whispering intently.

"We saw Mildred and Lola flagging down the doctor on our way over here," Nellie said. "They must have found some cases too."

"How many beds are made up?" I asked Vera.

"Eight or ten. I'm not sure." We had spent more time visiting than working.

"Can you girls stay?" I said to Grace and Nellie. They both agreed and I sent them upstairs with armloads of linens to make up all the beds as quickly as possible. Vera and I rushed to hang a sheet across the doorway of the room where the healthier patients rested. None of them asked what we were doing, having each lived through their own delirious arrival. All five would be sent home that evening to protect them from the possibility of re-infection.

"Should I call Caroline?" Vera asked. Her eyes were wide and frantic, filling in the gap between the top of her mask and the bottom of her nurse's cap.

"No, she'll find out soon enough." Although I did wonder if a real nurse would be better equipped to manage the onslaught.

Another local physician, Dr. Tearnan, arrived first with two sawmill workers from one of the boarding houses laid out head to foot in the back of his car. The doctor was supposed to have retired that fall but agreed to keep working until the epidemic passed. He half walked, half dragged each of the men upstairs. They looked more like they'd been found passed out in front of some saloon instead of their tiny, single-bed rooms, lying limp in puddles of sweat.

"There's so many," Vera whispered as the doctor pulled away.

"It's starting," I told her. Before we could even check on our two newest patients, Dr. Scholtes arrived with a whole bus full of victims.

"Lucile! Vera!" he called from the doorway. The sight of him stopped me cold. He was standing there in the hall holding two children, one each foisted lifelessly over his shoulders. One of them was Lyle Doty.

"Help me," he said. Vera grabbed the smaller child and rushed up the stairs. Dr. Scholtes followed closely behind with Lyle. She looked unconscious, the telltale blue cast staining her face and hands. "Go help Shorty," he ordered.

I ran to the bus parked haphazardly at the curb. Shorty and I didn't even greet each other as he lifted another child from the front seat.

"The rest are in back," he shouted. I continued around to the rear of the bus and was shocked by what I saw through the open door.

"Thomas?"

"Lucile!" The scene inside the bus was horrifying. Ten more victims strewn across seats and up the aisle, Thomas crouched on the floor surrounded by bodies, unable to move without stepping on somebody. "Grab her," he said, pointing to a woman closest to the door. I pulled on the woman's coat but could hardly budge her. "Get her under the arms and slide her back enough to let me out," he said. I don't know how, but I did it and Thomas jumped into the empty spot and then out the back of the bus. He took the woman from me and cradled her in his arms.

"You shouldn't be here," he said. "I've got this."

"I'm working as a nurse."

"It's too dangerous," he said.

"There's no one else." I recognized the woman he was holding as the mother of one of my students. "Get her inside," I said. Thomas stared at me without moving. "I'm fine. Go!"

Dr. Scholtes and Vera arrived back at the bus just as Thomas finally headed toward the door. The four of us made several trips each up and down the stairs, filling the first ward of ten beds, then moving over to a second one next door. Grace and Nellie stood plastered against the wall, watching the parade of bodies, looking like they might collapse if they tried to step away. Dr. Scholtes shooed them and Thomas out the door and grabbed a sign that was painted weeks before and stored in a closet. He hung it on the porch before closing and locking the door.

QUARANTINE. NO VISITORS.

It was chaos inside the school for an hour or more afterwards. Before we could begin to take stock, Dr. Trueman, another of Munising's physicians, showed up with the sixteenth and final patient of the day. We were relieved when he stayed to help us get everyone settled.

Vera and I were each paired with one of the doctors and went bed-to-bed trying to make the patients as comfortable as possible. All of them arrived wrapped in layers of sheets and quilts, the unrelenting fever causing most to soak through their bedclothes on the short ride over. While the doctors assessed vital signs, we unwrapped each one from their blanketed cocoons, stripping off sweaty nightgowns and pajamas that could leave them dangerously chilled if not removed. There was no time for modesty as I tugged at buttons and drawstrings to free limbs and torsos from the damp, clinging fabric. Most were in no condition to help and it was hard to maneuver the dead weight of their bodies into clean clothing and underneath fresh linens. Several patients had nosebleeds and the liquid pouring out was watery and pink, unlike the bright red variety my brother Elton so often got. I did my best to clean them up as we moved around the room but the thin, bloody mucous dried quickly on their faces and would need to be soaked off later with a warm washcloth. Most of them grumbled as we touched their aching bodies and I followed the doctor's lead in not responding to every sound, though it pained me to withhold any bit of comfort. Each one curled reflexively into a fetal position after we finished tending to them. It became a hallmark of the illness, giving us just a glimpse into how terribly they were suffering.

"How's Lyle doing?" I asked Vera when we were finally able to take a break.

"There's a lot of fluid in her lungs. But Dr. Trueman said that about almost everybody. Fever's 105."

"Mrs. Doty must be out of her mind," I said.

"It's more horrible than I pictured Lucile." I was at least slightly more prepared having discovered Anna. "Look at them," she said. "They're dying." Vera went pale and steadied herself against the wall. I guided her to a nearby window, opened it, and got her a chair. She started to cry and I knelt beside her rubbing her back. I wanted to tell her it was all right, but didn't dare risk such an obvious lie.

"We'll get through this," I said instead. But my words did nothing to stop the tears that needed to come out. There was a strong breeze blowing in the window and I lowered my mask to take a few long, deep breaths. I knew that the thin gauze, even several layers thick, didn't offer much protection against what was happening. If it did, people like Lyle Doty wouldn't be sick. I never once saw anyone in that family without a mask on since word of the epidemic first surfaced and Mrs. Doty had been a firm supporter of the mayor's restrictions all along. She had done everything right to protect her loved ones from the illness and it still found its way into her home. I knew then that none of us were safe.

Vera calmed herself and we returned to the wards to set about the task of truly running a working hospital. After weeks of planning and preparation the old school finally looked, sounded, and smelled like the real thing and the make-believe nurse's roles we'd practiced that morning seemed like a crazy joke. My sense of responsibility for the sixteen deathly ill people in our care was overwhelming—not unlike the feeling I had the first time I stepped into a classroom full of children, ready to learn mathematics. At least with teaching there were books to rely on and numbers especially had precise properties and followed logical functions. But with the epidemic, nothing made sense and there was no way to understand what was happening. Simply getting through it was the only possible goal after all.

Dr. Scholtes stayed until Nurse Gardner showed up at 10 pm for her shift. Despite a full day of rest, she looked tired and peaked. I wondered if she was up to caring for such a large number of patients alone. Vera and I both offered to spend part of the night with her but Caroline and the doctor insisted we retire to the kitchen.

"Promise you'll wake me up if you need help," I told her.

"I promise," she said, offering her best smile, which didn't even soften the pallid cast of her face one bit.

I went to sleep so fast I didn't feel myself slipping away— still in my clothes, without eating a thing or brushing my teeth, my hair pinned up. When I awoke over ten hours later it was well past the time we'd set for relieving Nurse Gardner. I woke Vera and grabbed a clean mask, rushing out to scold her for letting us oversleep.

"Where's Caroline?" I asked Dr. Scholtes, the first and only person I encountered in an empty room on the first floor. He was sitting in a chair looking through some papers.

"I had to send her home. She's completely exhausted." He removed his glasses and rubbed his eyes.

"Is she sick?" I asked.

"No. Not yet. But I told her she can't come back for several days." He wasn't in much better shape. Although somehow always clean-shaven, I was quite sure the doctor had worn the same suit coat for the last week and his hair certainly hadn't seen a comb or brush in days.

"Who will cover her shifts?" I asked, knowing there was no one.

"Me. One of the other doctors. I'll figure it out."

"I can do it," I said. "That's if you think I could handle it."

"I want to avoid that if I can. I need you here during the day so I can be out checking on people."

"We both know you don't have many options," I reminded him. "And if you don't mind me saying it Doctor, you should get some rest too."

"That my dear, is not possible," he said. "I'm quite sure we'll discover plenty of new cases today."

"How are people handling it?" I asked, nodding toward the street outside.

"There's panic brewing. The city is completely deserted this morning. Most of the stores gave up and finally closed."

"That's good at least," I said, but perhaps too cheerfully, trying to pick up his spirits. Dr. Scholtes put his glasses in his lap, his head back, and closed his eyes. "I'll go get cleaned up and we'll start checking on everyone," I told him.

"Thank you, Lucile," he mumbled. Vera and I let Dr. Scholtes sleep in that chair for several hours. He wasn't happy about it when he woke up but he looked better and really only complained for a minute before heading right back out.

Our work tending to patients was much more difficult than it had been the day before. Besides the constant temperature taking and sheet changing, I quickly came to know the true horrors of the epidemic. Fevers ran between 102 and 105 degrees and left everyone nearly crazy with delirium. The ones babbling nonsensically were the least of our problem—it was the patients who cried out in distress over some vision or hallucination that kept us on edge. These outbursts were random and seemed to occur as the fever broke. On more than one occasion it took both Vera and I, using all of our strength, to keep one of the men or a frightened mother from getting up and leaving. Daylight hurt the patient's bloodshot eyes, making it necessary to drape heavy blankets over the windows to protect them from the glare. We had to keep kerosene lamps positioned on the fringes of the rooms where no one could accidentally knock them over, going to the bathroom or running from their fevers. An eerie glow washed across the sea of beds and it often took a few seconds to determine where help was needed when a call came out from the darkness.

One of the most difficult tasks was trying to get the patients to drink a few sips of water or juice, to prevent dehydration. Most of them had trouble breathing and were left to gasp at the air with open mouths, their lips cracking, their tongues dry and swollen. Holding a cup to their mouths usually resulted in whatever we poured in running out the sides and onto the sheets and blankets that we worked so hard to keep clean and dry. Those who managed to swallow anything were just as likely to spit it up or choke, triggering a coughing fit that went on for several minutes. It was the coughing that was the worst of all the symptoms.

"It's like they're drowning," Dr. Scholtes told me.

His simple explanation painted a truly terrifying picture of how these people were suffocating. As I understood it, the body tries to rid itself of germs as fast as it can and the lungs do their part by filling with fluid to flush tissues clean. This strain of influenza was stronger than most and the body's reaction was swift and intense, leaving many people's lungs completely overwhelmed with fluid. This is what caused the distinctive rattling noise that I couldn't get used to. The intense coughing was common, but rarely productive and did little to clear the lungs or ease breathing. The bouts were often so fierce that many patients woke up from the deepest sleep hacking uncontrollably, their bodies convulsing for several minutes before they dropped back into a coma-like stupor. When their condition improved the first thing everyone complained about was how sore their sides and chests were. Dr. Scholtes predicted that more than one would end up with a cracked rib or two as a result—a painful reminder of what they'd gone through even after they were mostly recovered.

During one of my numerous trips up and down the stairs I noticed a masked woman standing alone on the walk leading up to the school. I knew right away that it was Clara Doty. We were under strict orders not to open the main door for anyone but without hesitating I motioned for her to go around to the back. She was waiting for me at the bottom of the wooden staircase jutting off the kitchen. I turned the lock and opened the door slowly, quietly, sticking my head out to greet her but still keeping the door mostly closed.

"How is she?" Clara demanded, in full voice.

"Shhhhh," I said, slipping through the gap in the door. "There hasn't been much change." She marched right up the stairs to meet me on the landing.

"What does that mean?" Her voice getting louder. The only glimmer in her tired, drooping eyes was panic.

"Clara, please! You have to be quiet. You're not supposed to be here and I certainly shouldn't be talking to you." She was standing so close I could see tears falling from her eyes, rolling behind her mask, absorbed into the gauze before they could get very far. She quieted down, but didn't retreat an inch. "Her condition hasn't gotten any worse," I told her. It was not the report she wanted to hear.

"Has the fever gone down? How's her breathing?" she whispered in the plaintive tones of a desperate mother. She needed something to hold onto in her daughter's absence.

"It can take several days for the fever to break," I said. "The fact that it's not getting worse really is a good sign. She's young and she's strong," I added. Clara finally took a step back down the stairs. "I'll take good care of her. I promise."

"I know. I know you will, Lucile." She pulled a wadded-up

handkerchief from her sleeve. "Can I see her through a window perhaps?" I shook my head.

"She's on the second floor."

"Oh," she whimpered, her mask soaked in tears. It was heartbreaking to see a woman I'd only known to be strong looking so shaken and afraid.

"I should get back inside," I said. "But I'll check on Lyle first thing."

"Please, give her this?" Clara pulled a photograph from her coat pocket. It was the Doty family—Lyle sitting between her parents, posed on the lovely wicker divan on their front porch, dressed for summer, bathed in sunlight and squinting at the camera—relaxed and happy.

"Of course," I said.

"Thank you, Lucile. It makes me feel so much better with you here." Clara took a step up towards me again, her hand outstretched, looking for a handshake or a hug. I stood frozen until she realized her error. It was the simple common courtesies and gestures of intimacy that were the hardest to give up, but for those few weeks they could literally make the difference between life or death. "I'll just say goodbye then," she said.

"Goodbye." I turned to go inside.

"One last question, Dear," Clara said. "Where is the room she's in, exactly?"

"On the side," I said, motioning out the back of the school and to the right; she quickly disappeared around the corner. I heard the singing start before I even made it upstairs.

"*Sleep my child and peace attend thee, all through the night.*
Guardian angels God will send thee, all through the night.
Soft the drowsy hours are creeping, hill and vale in slumber sleeping.

I my loving vigil keeping, all through the night."

I rushed to Lyle's room and threw open the window and there was her mother, perched in the middle of a snow bank, mask slung below her chin, tears rolling down her cheeks, singing her only child a lullaby. I went to Lyle's bed with the photograph. She was sleeping peacefully and I tucked it into one of her hands as the final stanza drifted in across the room.

"Angels watching ever round thee, all through the night.

In thy slumbers close surround thee, all through the night.

They will of all fears disarm thee no forebodings should alarm thee.

They will let no peril harm thee, all...through...the night."

It was an expression of motherly love unlike anything I had ever experienced or would ever forget.

By late that afternoon there were seven additional patients admitted to the hospital and Dr. Scholtes pulled me aside, accepting my offer to work overnight. I was sent to the kitchen for an early supper and to rest as much as possible before relieving Vera at 11 pm. Despite the early hour, I fell asleep quickly and hard. I dreamed of canoe rides and Sunday dinners at the farm and as is often the case in dreams, the porch I knew so well from home merged with the Doty's porch in Munising. Howard was sitting on the same wicker furniture as in the picture but I couldn't speak to him. He kept glancing at his watch, waiting for someone. Reaching into his shirt pocket he removed the picture of me I'd given him the day he left, stared at it and smiled, giving it the lightest of kisses before putting it back. He looked healthy and peaceful and I wanted to stay asleep, staring at him forever.

Chapter 19

"LUCILE." IT WAS Vera.

No, not yet.

"Lucile. Wake up," she whispered, shaking my shoulder gently. I was still dreaming of Howard but roused quickly once I remembered where I was, though I dreaded what awaited.

"Did I oversleep?" I mumbled.

"No. It's almost eleven," she told me. "Just take your time." Vera stayed put on the edge of my cot. "I have some news," she said. "Don't worry, it's not about Howard." She was twisting one of the curls on the side of her head. It was a habit I'd witnessed dozens of times in school, before a test or when she thought she might get called up to the board.

"What is it?" I asked, sitting up and stretching, my thoughts still fuzzy.

"They brought another patient in and he's not doing well at all."

"Who?" She hesitated before answering. "Tell me."

"Charlie," she said.

"How bad?" I reached for my shoes.

"Pneumonia."

"Where is he?" I demanded. I headed out the door without waiting for an answer. I could find him on my own easily enough. I ran to the foot of the stairs and checked the first classroom closest to the front door. Empty. Charlie was in the room across the hall, lying alone at the end of a row of unmade cots. Dr. Scholtes and Dr. Tearnan were examining him when I barged in. Dr. Scholtes held up a single finger and I stopped several feet back. Dr. Tearnan was bent over the cot, a stethoscope planted in his ears, moving the chest piece back and forth under Charlie's pajama shirt.

"Yes, yes. Both lungs, I agree," he said, standing up, hands on his hips, staring down at my friend. "We can keep him comfortable but that's probably about it."

"That's what I thought too," Dr. Scholtes said. There wasn't a hint of hope in his reply. I paced behind them, inching closer to the bed with each turn.

"What a shame," Dr. Tearnan said. He draped his stethoscope around the back of his neck before turning to leave. "Oh, hello."

"May I see him?" I asked. Dr. Tearnan looked to his colleague for the answer. Dr. Scholtes gave his approval with a dip of his chin. "I'm his friend," I added as Dr. Tearnan walked past me. Dr. Scholtes blocked my way before I could get any closer.

"Prepare yourself Lucile," he said, stepping aside, but remaining close. I gasped. Charlie looked worse than anyone I had ever seen before. Worse than Anna or Lyle. He already looked dead.

"Cyanosis," Dr. Scholtes said. I wasn't even sure what that was but I knew it was bad. Charlie's pajama shirt was still unbuttoned and I could see that his chest was black and blue, like he'd been beaten about the torso. The skin on his face and hands was the same mottled color, his lips and fingernails solid blue. There were several dark purple spots on his cheeks. The rattling noise wasn't as noticeable, but only because Charlie was barely breathing. His breaths were so shallow and infrequent that I couldn't see his chest rise and fall, even standing that close. I reached down for a hand. It was cold, almost stiff, like his body was surrendering but taking its time to retreat.

"Can he hear us?" I asked, my back to the doctor.

"I doubt it," he replied. "But I can't be sure."

"Is he going to make it?" I kept looking at my friend.

"No. I don't believe so."

"Charlie," I whispered. Not because I thought he'd respond, but out of sheer disbelief. "Charlie," I repeated. I was trying to convince myself that it was even him, the same man who so eagerly greeted me every morning since I'd arrived in Munising.

"Charlie," I said one last time. I had no idea a body could be treated so brutally by an illness that no one had ever even thought to be afraid of before then.

"Lucile," Dr. Scholtes said, gently squeezing my shoulder. "I need to go over a few things before I leave for the night." I slipped Charlie's hand under the covers before following the doctor out of the room. I didn't look back at him. I couldn't bear it.

The doctor informed me there were twenty-four patients to care for in the hospital—twenty-three upstairs in various stages of illness and recovery and Charlie alone on the first floor, somewhere near death. I knew what to do. Vera would be just a holler away in the kitchen and the doctor would be back by 6 am.

"What about Charlie?" I asked when Dr. Scholtes slipped

his coat on. His silent stare told me all I needed to know but I refused to look away and give him permission to say there wasn't anything that could be done.

"Fluid. Aspirin. Keep him comfortable," he finally offered. "But only after you've checked on everyone else first," he stated plainly. "If he succumbs, call me right away."

"He might die tonight?" I said. I could feel all the blood rush out of my arms and legs in an instant. I steadied myself on the nearby newel post.

"It's very possible. Do you need me to stay?" he asked, though he kept buttoning his coat.

"No. I guess not." He nodded and walked toward the door. "Does his family know?"

"I'm afraid not. We can't get hold of anyone."

"Where is he from?" I said, suddenly feeling guilty that I didn't remember the answer myself.

"Around Marquette, I believe." I wondered, with utter disbelief, if that was where his funeral would be. "Goodnight, Lucile."

"Goodnight Doctor."

I went to find Vera the second I closed and locked the door. She had already worked twice as long as I would that night and was sound asleep. This was mine to face alone.

I quickly had to establish a routine that felt both fair to all the patients and efficient. I found that it took me about forty-five minutes to tend to everyone upstairs. I was lucky that some of them were resting quietly and did not require my attention each time I checked on them, though that could change at any second. Lyle was still there and would be ready to go home soon but had a low-grade fever and remained very weak. It was a real boost to my mood and stamina to feed her a bowl of soup, give her a quick sponge bath, and literally watch the color return to her cheeks as the night wore on. The poor girl's hair was matted to her head and she begged me to brush it out for her. I had to decline, but promised to do it in the morning, after my shift.

When my rounds upstairs were done, I was able to spend at least fifteen minutes with Charlie every hour. His body remained overwhelmed with fever and he seemed to be unconscious, always in the same position I'd left him in. At first, I just sat there and stared at him, struggling to accept Dr. Scholtes' prognosis. It took a time or two before I could look past the ravages caused by the influenza and see my good friend underneath. After that I moved closer and began to talk to him. I thanked him for being so kind to me from the first day I arrived and explained how much his support where Howard was concerned meant. I found an old newspaper and read him the headlines though it was several days old and he'd probably already seen it before falling ill. I noticed that he had a bright red rash around his nose and mouth from the damp gauze so I removed the mask. He was alone in the room and his comfort was more important to me than protecting myself from exposure. I was surrounded by the epidemic and would be for days—it felt like a small risk to take for someone so dear.

I did allow myself one short break that night, though it wasn't planned. I was drawn outside well after midnight by a clamor that erupted all over town. There was yelling and cheering, what sounded like the dull bang of pots and pans being struck with wooden spoons, and the whistles from the mills shrieking randomly into the night.

"What in the world?" I mumbled.

The noise continued for ten minutes or more and I'm sure

the night duty officer disbanded the culprits as fast as he could. I went back inside and stood by the stove in the room where Charlie was resting before getting back to work. I watched from the front windows, waiting to see if anyone approached the school or even just passed by, but no one did. I considered calling one of the girls at the switchboard to find out what was going on, but didn't want to give the wrong impression when I was supposed to be caring for very sick people and not worrying about a little commotion on the streets.

Charlie's condition deteriorated rapidly sometime after four in the morning. His already futile attempts to breathe became even more sporadic, if you could even call the short gasps he took every fifteen or twenty seconds breathing. His cheeks were sunken and turned dark purple and holding his hand was no longer possible—each one curled into a tight ball, his own fingernails digging into the fleshy part of his palms. I piled three or four blankets on top of him but there was no stopping the shaking. I quit going upstairs altogether after five o'clock and my last check on the patients there was only a brief pause in the doorway to scan the room. I raced back to Charlie's bedside, truly believing he might die in my short absence. I was desperate and determined to make sure that if he passed during my shift, he would not be alone.

I ended up sitting next to him on the cot, resting my body fully against his so that he knew someone was there. I stroked his hair with my fingers, lightly brushing his bangs across his forehead like I'd seen Mother do with my brothers. It only felt uncomfortable for the first moment or two. I knew Charlie was closer to death than to life by that time and there was no room left for formality.

"It's okay Charlie," I whispered. I kept running my fingers

through his hair. "It's me Lucile. I'm here." The time in between his breaths became so long that it was nearly impossible to know which one might be his last. I found myself holding my own breath in between his as I sat there beside him, waiting for his suffering to end.

"It's okay," I repeated again and again. His whole body trembled when his lungs finally took in air for the last time. I waited several minutes and when an exhale never followed, I knew he was gone. I looked at my watch—5:47. With his passing, I was instantly gripped by panic. I needed to cry, but couldn't—wanted to scream, but didn't know if I would stop. Charlie's death suddenly exposed my worst fear. The one I had been holding back for weeks.

Is Howard dead? Did he die alone?

The likelihood gnawed at my insides and I thought I was going to be sick. If influenza could kill like this in only a day or two what chance did Howard have battling an enemy that was deliberately trying to kill him? The admission left me frozen in place next to my dear friend's ravaged body.

I was still sitting there when I heard the lock on the front door turn and someone walk in. I stood up immediately and covered Charlie's face with the sheet from his bed, covering my own with my mask that I'd lowered once he passed.

"Lucile! Vera! Come quickly," Dr. Scholtes bellowed from around the corner. I watched unnoticed from the darkened classroom as he strode into view, dropping his medical bag at the foot of the stairs and slinging his coat over the banister. He had washed his hair and wore a freshly starched shirt. I felt sure his unrestrained arrival could only mean one thing—more patients.

"There you are," he said, spying me in the shadows. There

was only a tiny bit of light seeping in around the blankets on the windows. "Where's Vera?" The kitchen door opened and she joined him in the hallway, looking rumpled and barely awake.

"It's over," he said. "The war, it's over!" I don't know if it was Charlie dying or the enormity of the news but I couldn't even take in what he was saying. It sounded like he was speaking a foreign language. Words that I'd never heard before.

"What? It can't be," Vera said. She locked eyes on me. "Lucile, did you hear? The war's over!" I knew that I was supposed to smile, so I did.

"They signed an armistice last night. The fighting stopped in France at 11 am. Five o'clock our time," he explained. I wanted to feel happy and relieved but only felt the gnawing emptiness. I watched in horror as Vera hugged Dr. Scholtes and gave him a quick peck on the cheek. Neither one of them was wearing a mask.

There's a war still raging here.

"I can't believe it!" Vera squealed, crossing over to me.

"It's wonderful news," I said, taking her hands in mine but resisting her attempt to pull me into a hug. "The best possible news," I repeated. I looked at each of them, waiting for a break in the excitement to tell them about Charlie. Dr. Scholtes came into the room behind Vera and noticed his body over my shoulder. Vera followed his gaze to the bed.

"Did Charlie pass?" she whispered, squeezing my hand like a vise.

"Yes," I said. Dr. Scholtes went to the cot and reached under the sheet, checking for a pulse.

"When did he expire?" he asked. *Expire?* I could have cursed him for being so impersonal.

"Almost a half hour ago—5:47," I said. Vera was crying softly into my shoulder.

"Would one of you call for the car from Bowerman's please? Tell them to come around back," he said. He pulled all the blankets off the bed and dropped them into a heap on the floor, leaving only the sheet to cover Charlie. "We need to get the body out of here as quickly as possible."

"I'll do it," Vera said. She released my hand and whispered, "I'll be right back. You should rest." I nodded but knew sleep was a long way off.

"Lucile, will you please go upstairs and check on the others for me? I have to be down here when they arrive to make the collection." I went to leave the room without saying a word.

"Lucile?" Dr. Scholtes said. I stopped but didn't turn around. "You know there wasn't anything you could do to save him?"

"I know," I told him, because it was what he wanted to hear. My fiancé was missing, my good friend dead. The war was over and the epidemic had Munising in its grip. That was all I really knew.

When Vera came upstairs to relieve me, I retreated to the kitchen to fix a cup of tea, not knowing the men from the mortuary had arrived and were in the other room. Before the kettle even boiled, they barged in from the hall carrying Charlie's body on a stretcher. It was wrapped snugly in a sheet, the pink stain from his nose and mouth spreading out across the white fabric. The teakettle started to wail as I stood to the side, watching the procession pass before me. Dr. Scholtes followed the men out the door.

"Burn everything after you get him in the coffin," he told them. "He must be buried today."

As soon as they were gone, I looked at the stove. A plume of steam was pouring from the kettle's spout, billowing out into the room like fog blowing in off the lake. The whistle hurt my ears and I finally grabbed it, lifting it up and over the teacup I'd set out on the counter, pouring the scalding water into a pail on the floor instead. I set the pail in the sink, tempering it with several pumps of ice-cold well water. I took it, a scrub brush, some rags, and a bottle of disinfectant into the room where death still lingered. There was work to be done.

I attacked that room like only a good farmwoman can— as much as I tried to ignore it, I had more than a bit of my mother in me. First, I went to the windows and pulled the blankets down, opening each one before moving onto the next. The cot Charlie laid in was already stripped but I flipped the thin mattress and set a mucous stained pillow by the door to be burned. Then I started to clean.

I dumped twice as much Lysol as needed into the bucket and the cloying, medicinal smell burned my nostrils as it swirled into the hot water. Taking a rag, I sloshed the amber colored solution everywhere, methodically wiping down each surface in the room, moving clockwise from the door—walls, window-sills, blackboards, and all of the trim moldings—from floor to ceiling. Using a chair to stand on, nothing went untouched and I had to return to the kitchen three times to change the dirty water. I sweated through my blouse before even making it halfway around the room, despite the cold air pouring in the open windows. I finished by wiping down the cots, the chair where I'd kept my vigil, and the floors, working my way from the farthest corner of the room over to the doorway. I stared at the hands moving back and forth in front of me but didn't recognize them. They were fiery red and deeply wrinkled. The pain hadn't even registered with me yet.

I dropped into bed sometime after noon but had trouble dozing off. The overcast sky was still too bright for sleep and whenever I closed my eyes I had to relive Charlie's final moments. Vera came in regularly for tea, juice, or soup for the patients who were doing better and I left my back to the room so I didn't have to talk to her every time. I don't know when my body finally relented but once it did I slept straight through the night, waking just before sunrise. I got dressed in the dark and snuck out the back door.

The blue-black sky was absolutely clear and it was colder in Munising than any November day I'd ever experienced back home. It was a relief to be alone on the streets surrounded by darkened houses, drawn tightly against the epidemic. Many recent outings with Vera garnered scared and angry looks from passersby. It started when we were assigned to do the health surveys but grew much worse after volunteering at the emergency hospital. Some people simply avoided making eye contact but others veered off course to keep from coming near us. I also caught several women peeking out through closed curtains when we passed by their homes, making sure we didn't stop and linger on the front walk. A few generous citizens brought donations of food or supplies to the school but would knock and run away before anyone could answer. I understood their fear and tried not to be hurt by their actions but I was helping when others wouldn't, caring for their loved ones, trying to do the right thing. I didn't tell my family about my work as a volunteer nurse. It would have caused a bitter fight with Mother, and Father would have certainly forbidden me from doing it. I worried about getting sick mostly for them and wondered if

I ever would have taken such a risk if Howard wasn't injured and missing. That walk gave me the first real break I had known in days. I took in deep lungfuls of frigid air and kept my eyes focused on the dark void at the base of the hill, where I knew the lake stood. I could hear the waves crashing rhythmically onto shore and was reminded that some things were still the same even though the world I found myself in was barely recognizable.

When I returned to the hospital there was a man unloading bags of food, paper wrapped bundles of sheets and blankets, and stacks of firewood from a car backed up to the rear of the school. I immediately recognized that it was Thomas and stood out of his sight, wondering if I should let him finish the delivery and leave without approaching. I was cold and the front of the building was locked up tight. I would have avoided him if I could but it was becoming harder and harder to do that.

"Hello Thomas," I said, walking into view.

"Lucile!" He startled and almost dropped the armful of kindling he was carrying. "I didn't think I'd run into anybody this early." He paused. "But it's good to see you."

"Nice to see you too," I said. "I was just getting some fresh air before my shift."

"How many patients you got in there today?"

"I don't know exactly. Over twenty." We both just stared at each other for longer than was comfortable.

"Well, I'll be out of your way here in a minute." He continued to unload the wood—back and forth, stack after stack. I watched him for a moment hoping for something else to say, but the silence between us remained unyielding.

"I should get inside," I said, taking a bag of groceries in

each hand. I went halfway up to the door before realizing I couldn't open it. Thomas pounded up the stairs behind me.

"I got it." He stopped a step or two below, leaning in against me and reaching around to the door. "Lucile, you can't avoid me for the entire school year you know," he said, before pushing it open.

"I'm not avoiding you." Thomas stayed close when I turned around. The way we were arranged on the stairs left us face-to-face, mask-to-mask. He was looking right at me as I lied.

"I know I shouldn't say it and I don't mean to make you feel uncomfortable, but I just can't forget that night at the fair. I've tried to stop thinking about it, but it's no use."

"Me too," I said, though my thoughts were more of guilt, than pleasure. His dark eyes remained fixed on mine.

"I've been so worried since I saw you here the other day. It's such a risk you're taking to help out like this."

"We're all just doing our part," I said. He nodded slowly but didn't release his gaze. I took a deep breath. "Thomas, I hope you don't think I'm the kind of woman that takes such things so lightly. I'm engaged. I've never done anything like that before. I swear to you."

"Lucile, I know exactly the kind of woman you are, which is why I can't stop thinking about you." He was so close by then that I could hear the drag of his breath through the gauze. It seemed that only our masks prevented us from almost kissing again.

"You shouldn't say that," I whispered. "Nothing can happen."

"Well, I hope you'll forgive me then, for wishing it was different." I'm not sure if it was his stare, the sound of his voice or the pull of his body next to mine, but my nerves got the best of me and I blurted out the truth.

"Howard's been injured," I said. "I'm waiting to get word if he's okay."

"What?" He retreated to his own step immediately.

"My fiancé. Howard. He's been hurt." I hadn't even told Thomas his name.

"That's terrible news," he said, without a bit of hesitation. "I had no idea."

"I know you didn't. But I'm sure you'll understand that all my thoughts and prayers are with him right now."

"Of course. As they should be. I'm sure you'll get good news very soon."

Thomas immediately headed back to the car.

"Thank you," I said. I lifted my arms with the two bags of groceries. "Thanks for everything, Thomas."

"My pleasure, Lucile. You let me know if you need anything," he said. "Anything at all."

I rushed inside the kitchen and ducked around the corner where I couldn't be seen. I had to bury my face in between the bags of groceries to try to muffle the sobs I'd been holding in for days. It was the war and epidemic. It was Charlie, Thomas and Howard; guilt and fear. It was desperately wanting to go home but refusing to give up. I'd been doing my best to cope with all of the strain and uncertainty, but I was close to breaking if there wasn't some sort of reprieve. Some sign that my world wasn't actually coming to an end.

After my experience with Charlie, the doctors determined that it was too much to ask one of us young women to stay at the hospital alone overnight. Instead, they took turns staying up and Vera and I continued to care for patients during the day until Nurse Gardner was able to return. Lyle Doty went home very soon after Charlie died and was gone when I made my rounds the next morning. Vera told me that both of the Dotys came to pick her up and agreed to don two masks each to be allowed to come inside and personally thank everyone that worked there.

"They asked about you," Vera told me. "I had to swear to them that you weren't sick, but only resting. Mrs. Doty was ready to burst into the kitchen to see for herself until Dr. Scholtes convinced her you were fine."

The wards upstairs remained full and there was always at least one new admission for every person we sent home. People were recovering slowly and it took days for the fever and cough to subside. The number of new cases was more than double that of the week before and Dr. Scholtes estimated that there were at least 50 cases across the city, probably more. He and Mayor Sullivan were worried that if the situation got any worse, Munising would suffer the same fate as Petoskey to the south—a mandatory quarantine enforced by the state. It didn't sound like the worst idea to me. Grand Island had been completely cut off for over a week and all eight cases that developed there recovered and no new ones had yet to surface. Nearby Newberry, which was slow to enact any bans at all, was suffering terribly with dozens of deaths as a result.

Mayor Sullivan was a frequent visitor to the hospital and convened several meetings with the doctors in one of the empty classrooms on the first floor. We couldn't hear what they were saying and certainly didn't try to eavesdrop but I've never seen such a somber group of men as I did emerge from that room. They would disperse out the door and up the stairs in complete silence, the full brunt of their worry and exhaustion conveyed in furrowed brows and vacant, sleepless stares. Dr. Scholtes did tell us that an influenza vaccine was expected soon and shots would be given free to anyone wanting them. His lack of enthusiasm led me to believe that they probably wouldn't help.

Vera and I were taking a break and out on a walk that Wednesday, November 13th, late in the afternoon. I was in the middle of telling her some story or another when she nodded at someone across the street. It was George Wright, the city's longtime mail carrier, and he was waving at us enthusiastically. Besides the teachers he was the only person still allowed to go out on the streets and door to door during the epidemic. Accustomed to plying his route alone, Mr. Wright welcomed the camaraderie that developed among us all. He made it a point to know everyone by name, despite never seeing more than our eyes and I wondered if we would even recognize each other once the masks came off. Exchanging greetings with him had become such a regular part of our routine that Vera and I did not break stride, even though his gestures were more animated that day.

"Lucile," he yelled.

"What does he want?" Vera said. We turned to look and saw him waving something in his hand as he raced down the sidewalk.

"Lucile, wait," he yelled again, finally catching up. "These are for you." He held out a letter and a postcard. Flushed and sweating, a smile filled his face that was so big it reached beyond the sagging corners of his gauze mask. The postcard had a picture of a soldier on horseback in the midst of battle, a sword raised high overhead. I realized it had to be from Howard but was so weary from waiting, so fearful that it might not be from him, that I hesitated to accept the mail. "Forgive me for noticing," George said, "but I knew you'd want these right away." He pushed them both into my hand.

I turned the postcard over and was surprised to find a message written entirely in French. I was too shaky to stand there and translate it then, but knew the handwriting to be Howard's. His very own signature waiting for me at the end of the simple, two sentence greeting. It was all I needed to see.

"He's alive," I said. "Howard's alive."

I threw my arms around George's neck and hugged him so hard that he had to take a step back to keep his balance. Vera was waiting her turn to congratulate me, bouncing around to the side like a late August firefly.

"Oh Lucile!" she said as we embraced. "It's a miracle. Our prayers have been answered." There were times when her dramatic flair hit just the right note. Vera more than anyone, was the person who witnessed and shared with me, the entire ordeal first-hand. She dropped the bag of groceries she was carrying and held me close, with one hand gently cradling my head on her shoulder. I don't know if I was laughing or crying more, but we stood there for at least a minute. I needed to let the news that Howard was alive sink into the deepest parts of me—the places where I'd sequestered most of my doubt and fear in order to just move on while I waited to learn his fate.

"He's alive," I whispered repeatedly into her coat sleeve. "He's alive. He's alive. He's alive." Mr. Wright was half way down the block when I turned to thank him properly.

"Mr. Wright," I yelled. "How can I ever thank you?"

"Just doing my job, Lucile."

"How did you know?" I asked, waving the postcard in the air. I'd never told him about Howard or our circumstances.

"Mr. Samms talked to me right before he got sick. Told me

you might be getting something important and asked me to keep an eye out for it."

"Charlie," I said to myself. His name made me smile and tears spilled even faster from my eyes, dropping onto the precious card and letter I clutched tightly in my hands.

Chapter 20

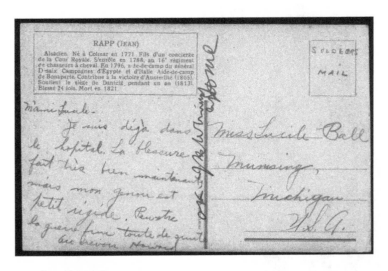

My friend Lucile,

I am already in the hospital. The wound is healing well, but my knee is a little stiff. Maybe the war will be over soon.

Goodbye,
Howard

October 6, 1918

Dear Lucile,

You will no doubt be somewhat surprised to hear from me in my present condition. I am in an American Red Cross Hospital in Paris, I was wounded but don't worry because it is not at all dangerous.

We went up to the front on (*censored*) and it was a bad battle but entirely successful for the Allies. In the early morning of (*censored*) we were marching along in the dark when a big shell suddenly burst near us. I heard it coming and dropped flat. A little mound of dirt saved me and I was congratulating myself all day on my good luck. Several other men were wounded and killed near me, many of whom I helped to dress.

About 6:30 in the evening that same day, we had moved up near the front again, when the Germans started shelling the road. We ducked into a little ravine, but a shell got a bunch of us—this time me. A shrapnel wound on the outside of my left leg, just below the knee. Fortunately, it neither broke the bone or kneecap although it took out a little piece of bone, which makes it very sore. I dressed it myself and waited there until 3:30 A.M. for an ambulance. On (*censored*) it was operated on and feels pretty good today. I count myself as lucky and don't regret a thing as long as I'm still able to come home to you. There is much talk of peace now and I certainly hope that this war will soon cease.

I'm sitting in such an awkward position that I guess I will not write any more. You can write to the same address and it will be forwarded. I hope to be home soon and there is nothing that could stop me from coming straight to Munising the moment I step off the ship that brings me there.

With all my love,
Howard

Chapter 21

THERE IS A fine line between elation and heartache. The feeling I had when I learned Howard was alive wasn't that different from when I first got word of his injury. Heart racing, hands trembling—I was out of breath and unable to think clearly. But instead of falling to the ground in a heap, I could barely stop myself from running through the streets shrieking for joy. It was difficult not being able to go around and tell everyone the good news though I did race to the Dotys' to call both of our families. Mr. Bridgman answered the telephone and when I told him Howard was alive he didn't mind shedding a few tears in front of me then.

After working one more day at the hospital, Dr. Scholtes asked to speak with me in the kitchen. He wanted to examine both Vera and I since we'd been working there for almost a week during the peak of the epidemic.

"Does that hurt?" he asked, moving his fingers across a small lump in my neck. I knew full well by then that swollen glands were a common symptom of influenza.

"No. Not really. It's a bit uncomfortable when you push on

it." He continued the exam in silence. I was tired, but other-wise felt normal.

"You've developed a goiter," he finally told me, explaining that an enlarged thyroid was not uncommon in women from the Midwest. "We'll keep an eye on it, but I want you to leave the hospital immediately. No sense taking any chances."

And like that, my stint as a nurse was over.

"Let me phone the inn and tell them I'm sending you back," he continued, excusing himself to make the call. Mr. Redfern, the owner, was afraid to take me in after my work at the emergency hospital—he thought it would hurt what little business he still had. Before he even returned with the news, Dr. Scholtes made a few other calls to secure a place for me to stay. "Mayor Sullivan has agreed to host you in his home," he said, after explaining the problem. "You may have to be quar-antined for up to a week, I'm afraid. Probably less. We'll see how you're feeling." I was shocked by the news.

"I guess that's best," was all I could say. Seven days sounded like an eternity to be cooped up in a strange house with some-one I barely knew and, my previous encounter with the mayor at the inn didn't offer me much reassurance.

"Stella knows you are coming right over and will be there to greet you," the doctor said. I had no idea who he was talk-ing about and gave him a puzzled look. "The mayor's sister," he added. An edge of panic rumbled across my stomach. I was so much better than I used to be as a child, but meeting new people—especially by myself—still left me quite uncomfort-able. "Here's their address," Dr. Scholtes said, handing me a piece of paper as he left the kitchen. "You should leave soon." I followed him out and went upstairs to find Vera.

"A week! You can't go there alone," she exclaimed when

I told her about the quarantine. "I know you've heard the rumors about his drinking."

"Vera! You're not helping," I snapped. I swung around in a huff and stomped away, keeping news of the mayor's sister to myself.

"I'm sure it will be fine," she said, following me closely. I rarely lost my patience and Vera knew that. Desperate to undo her careless remark, she talked the entire time as I packed my things, offering every trite reassurance she could think of. I considered taking the next available train home but if the goal were to keep me from exposing others to the flu then the doctor would never approve such a trip. Vera prattled on and her increasingly frantic tone made my head spin. She was usually remarkably relaxed and easy going—the exact opposite of me—traits I found mostly refreshing. But sometimes, I just wanted her to be quiet.

"Vera enough!" I finally said as I approached the front door. She looked startled by my tone if not my words and dropped her head to her chest.

"I'm sorry. I just can't believe you're going."

"I'll be fine. Besides, the mayor's sister lives with him."

"I would come with you if I could," she said, when her face suddenly lit up. "Wait here one minute," she told me. Vera ran back into the kitchen and returned seconds later with a stack of papers.

"Take these," she said. It was a pile of word cross puzzles she had carefully cut out of inn's daily newspapers. There were dozens of them. She loved to fill them in at night before bed or when a rainy day kept us inside for too long. Aunt Rose was a fan too, but I hadn't ever taken to them.

"Thank you," I said. Those puzzles were a daily treat for

her, the way someone else might anticipate opening a present or how I looked forward to dessert. I was flooded with guilt for snapping at her. "I'll miss you," I confessed, and I meant it. We'd been faithful friends for over ten years, spending every day together for the last two and a half months.

"I'll miss you too, Lucile." Vera reached up and unhooked her mask from both ears, letting it fall down around her neck. She was crying. "Take care of yourself," she said. I undid my mask too.

"You're a good friend Miss Smith." She nodded but didn't respond. I had to cock my head to the side and look up into her face to get her to look at me. I had one more thing to say. "I couldn't have gotten through the last few weeks without you, Vera." My words were slow and deliberate and brought a smile to her face. I pulled her into a tight hug and we said goodbye.

It took just a few minutes to walk the four blocks to the Sullivan's place at the corner of Onota and Chestnut. I had passed the plain three-story house a number of times before without ever realizing the mayor lived there. I would have envisioned his home to be counted among Munising's grandest, instead of the modest, unkempt one in front of me. A small porch had been added on to create an entranceway of sorts, but looked every bit the ramshackle addition that it was. The whole house needed a coat of paint and the large corner lot was devoid of any landscaping, except for the winter-bare trees on the berm. I double-checked the house number and stood frozen on the sidewalk, staring at my dingy accommodations for the week when the front door flung open. A woman waved me in but disappeared back into the house. I climbed the stairs and waited at the screen door. I could see the mayor's sister running around the kitchen at the end of a long hallway. Stella

Sullivan was younger than the spinster I'd imagined, with the most beautiful red hair flowing down her back. She raced to the door as soon as she noticed me standing there, still carrying a large mixing bowl filled with apples, oranges, and bananas.

"Please, please, come in," she said. "I didn't mean to leave you out in the cold." She looked around for a place to deposit the fruit, finally setting it on the floor. She took my bag and tossed it on the bottom step leading upstairs.

"You must be Lucile," she said, wiping her hands on the apron hanging at her waist. "I'm Stella Sullivan."

"Nice to meet you," I said. We shook, her hand sweatier than my own.

"Lucile or Lucy?"

"Pardon me?"

"What do you like to be called?"

"Lucile."

"Lucile it is," she proclaimed. "It suits you." I smiled and nodded politely. We stood staring at one another for several seconds. "Let me take your coat," Stella said. When I handed it to her I noticed she was looking at my mask. "You must be tired of wearing that." She seemed to be suggesting that I remove it.

"I've gotten used to it," I said. Vera and I had even taken to sleeping with them.

"Tom says they don't really help, except to make people *feel* safer."

"They can't hurt," I replied.

"True enough." She stood facing me, studying my face. "Let's get you upstairs. I'm sure you could use a nap." Stella collected my bag and led me up the narrow staircase right into a tiny bedroom.

"I changed the sheets as soon as I heard you were coming. No time to press them I'm sorry to say, but they are clean and there are fresh towels right here," she said patting a stack on the dresser. She pointed to a wash set in the corner. "That water should still be warm if you need to freshen up and there's another blanket in the closet if you want it." Stella had the door halfway shut before saying one last thing. "Lucile, Tom told me how you were one of the only people willing to help out at the hospital. I don't think I would have been brave enough to do that." She smiled. "You rest as long as you need to and don't worry about a thing." I was so touched by her genuinely kind words.

I looked around the room more closely before slipping off my shoes and sitting on the bed. I was surprised to find everything so neat and lovely. The mirror across the room revealed why Stella had been so adamant about a nap—I was pale and drawn and not even the mask could hide the dark circles surrounding my eyes. I fell back onto the mattress and slipped under the coverlet with all my clothes on. The last thing I did before snuggling into one of the thick down pillows was finally remove that mask. What a treat it was to drift off with my face resting directly on the cool cotton pillowcase—a feeling I'd always loved.

It was six in the evening by the time I woke up. My clothes were so wrinkled I had to slip into the only other dress I had with me before going downstairs. I cleaned up as best I could but there wasn't much I could do to my hair without washing it. Being away from the hospital for the first time in a week, I was horrified to realize that everything about me smelled like antiseptic.

"We're in the dining room," Mayor Sullivan called out

the moment I stepped on the creaky stairs. I could hear him and Stella talking in hushed tones and the most marvelous aroma filled the entire house. The first thing that struck me when I found them was just how much they resembled each other, though Stella's shimmering locks and rosy cheeks went a long way toward softening the somewhat masculine profile she shared with her brother.

"Lucile," the mayor said, greeting me with a hug that I might normally reserve for Aunt Rose or Vera. "Welcome!"

"Were you able to rest?" Stella asked. She pulled out the chair at the head of the table and motioned for me to sit. The room had a soft amber glow, lit by a dozen or more candles scattered about. A Victrola in the corner played music, something classical. The Sullivans were dressed to the nines, much nicer than I was.

"Oh yes. I slept like a log. Thank you both so much for taking me in. I know this quarantine must be a terrible inconvenience, especially for you, Mayor."

"Ah, ah…" he said.

"T.G.," I said. Stella returned from the sideboard with a glass of wine.

"We're happy to have you," T.G. continued, raising his glass and waiting for Stella and I to join him. "Cheers!"

"Sláinte!" Stella said—an old Irish toast to good health I had heard being called out from the bar at the inn almost every night, before the epidemic closed it down.

"Cheers," I said. I took a tiny sip and enjoyed the flavor. I had only ever tasted a bit of sherry at Aunt Rose's.

I have to say that the rest of the evening unfolded better than I could have ever expected. Stella was a fine cook and though her food was simple it was perfectly prepared and served in ample proportions. The conversation was lively and lighthearted, just right for three people only getting to know each other. T.G. kept the Victrola turning, showing off his impressive collection of Irish folk music from lively jigs played on the accordion and fiddle, to mournful ballads accompanied by the pure wail of a lone oboe. I learned that neither of the Sullivans had ever married, though Stella only came to live with T.G. after her fiancé was killed in a railroad accident.

"I never found the right man after that," she said, sounding at peace with her fate, but I could see her picturing the one she'd lost as she told their story.

Although I couldn't imagine ever sharing a home with my brothers as an adult, these two seemed to really enjoy each other's company and the conversation flowed easily all night long. I told them about Howard and how I'd only recently learned he was safe and that I hoped to get news soon of his homecoming, which was imminent with the end of the war.

"I'll be sure to have George bring your mail to the house this week," Stella said. She reached across the table to give me a pat on the hand, a smile, and a wink. The Sullivans were good people and I knew that night, before turning in, that I would be very comfortable in their home for however long the quarantine lasted.

"I'm suddenly so tired," I reported. It might have been the wine but I was shocked to look at my watch and see that it was after midnight. I laughed at the late hour. "Well, it's certainly past my bedtime," I said, standing up to help stack the dishes.

"Lucile," Stella scolded. "I won't have a guest clearing the table." She was smiling, but her request was absolutely serious. "Tom will take care of all this later," she roared, sweeping her hand across the mounds of dishes and left-over food. T.G.

laughed too but not as enthusiastically as his sister. I couldn't tell if she was joking or not.

"Well then," I said, putting my plate back down, "starting tomorrow I must insist that I am no longer considered a guest." I looked at Stella. "Agreed?" I said. She nodded. "T.G.?"

"Agreed," he replied.

It was only after retiring to my room that I realized we hadn't discussed the epidemic even once, all night long. It was exactly what I needed but I couldn't believe the restraint shown by the mayor when I learned of the mounting pressure he faced as influenza continued to ravage the city. T.G. was sitting across from me in the parlor the next evening when I picked up the Munising News.

WARNING ISSUED BY THE STATE BOARD:
Letter to the Mayor Advises More Vigorous Action

He must have known about the article but didn't look up once from his book as I read it. The state was secretly sending investigators to monitor how different cities were managing the epidemic. Evidence of unnecessary gatherings and co-mingling was reportedly found in Munising and this, combined with the fact that the number of cases of influenza in town had doubled, left the state health officer issuing threats.

I would advise you to take more vigorous action to curtail the spread of influenza in your city, Mayor. Rest assured, if you and your health officer do not protect the general public, I shall.

"Utter piffle!" I said, crinkling the paper into my lap. "This isn't your fault." The mayor looked at me out over the top of his glasses, completely immune to my outrage.

"You know that and I know that, but Dr. Hill sees it differently," was all he said.

"You and Dr. Scholtes have done as much as anyone could," I declared. "More!" He closed his book and removed his glasses. "What do they expect you to do, arrest anyone out on the street?"

"I believe that's exactly what they want," he replied.

"That's ridiculous," I shouted. "I've been in people's homes every day for weeks. Most of them didn't even believe that the threat was real. They were going to do as they pleased no matter what anyone said. The jail would have filled up in an hour."

"Agreed. Their big-city rules don't always work the same up here."

"Somebody needs to explain that to Dr. Hill." I was ready to volunteer for the job myself.

"He's just blowin' smoke because he's got people above him breathing down his neck too. The proof is in our numbers Lucile—one death and very little pneumonia. There isn't anything for Dr. Hill to worry about in Munising. He'll move on soon enough."

"What if it gets worse?" I asked. I wasn't sure if he realized I had held the hand of the one person who died.

"It could, of course, but I think this may be the peak," he declared with a remarkable air of confidence. I don't know where he got his information and perhaps it was just a wild guess or even wishful thinking, but I wanted to believe him. The epidemic couldn't go on forever.

My stay with the Sullivans continued to be most enjoyable. I found several good books among the hundreds lining two massive bookcases in the parlor and we played a lot of cards too—Flinch, Rook, Euchre, and of course my favorite,

Cribbage. I was also introduced to another game called Oh Hell! that combined two of Mother's most avowed sins—gambling and swearing. I loved it! Stella and I slowly worked our way through the stack of word cross puzzles, especially during the day, as the mayor ran the city from his office at the house. He held secret meetings with Dr. Scholtes on the enclosed back porch, certain that the cold temperatures and fresh air met the basic requirements of our quarantine. Each and every night culminated with a glass or two of wine, another fine meal, and more lively tunes played until midnight or later. What others must have thought to hear the muffled music and see our dancing shadows from behind the curtains, all while the black and red sign remained tacked across the front door.

As promised, Stella did have George Wright watching out for any mail bearing my name, though nothing from Howard came that week. She also had all of my things from the inn packed up and brought over the day after my arrival. It turned out she had a contact on the outside that was running errands on our behalf.

"I got some of those chips you like from Peters' Grocery," Stella announced one day as we were making egg salad sandwiches for lunch.

"How did you manage that?" I said. There was no delivery service available and Stella obviously hadn't fetched them herself.

"Your friend Clara dropped them off," she said.

"Clara Doty?"

"Yes indeed. She's the reason we've been eating so well. Been by every day with groceries since she heard you were staying with us. She thinks the world of you, Lucile."

"How nice," I said. "How's Lyle doing?"

"Her recovery's been slow, but she's going to be fine." I was so relieved to hear it.

Mrs. Doty was not our only company that week. As a special treat, she smuggled in a local Swedish woman late one evening to give us all relaxing rubdowns. Beata Siabiaskofski was the wife of a Russian immigrant known about town as Hatless Harry for his refusal to protect his head all winter, no matter how cold it got. It was wonderful to experience my first massage and Beata refused to let Mrs. Doty pay after she discovered that her son Erwin was one of my students. Vera also came by every day and we exchanged notes through the mail slot when we were certain no one was looking. She was my source of information that entire week, reporting only on the things that interested me most, more thorough than any newspaper.

Grace and Lola got the flu, she wrote. *Mild cases. Don't worry.*

How's everyone else? Nellie still threatening to leave? I replied. I left the tiny foyer to drag the piano bench in to sit on while she responded. The neighborhood streets were usually quite deserted and our gabfests had grown rather long. A note was waiting face-up on the floor when I returned.

No. But Thomas went home. I dropped to my knees, using the bench as a table instead.

Why? I scribbled, passing it back as fast as I could. I stared at the metal flap in the door, looking for any sign of movement, listening for a hint of the noise it made as something passed through. Click-clack.

Mother died. Sister very sick too. He was from Detroit, where the epidemic had been rampant for weeks.

Poor Thomas! How long will he be gone? Click-clack. My mind was racing to think of how to contact him. Vera might be suspicious, but I could always send her away with a letter. Click-clack.

Left this morning. Not coming back. I sat on the floor with my back against the door, the mail slot just to the side of my face. When I didn't respond right away Vera sent another comment through on a different piece of paper. Click-clack.

So sad. But probably for the best??

I hadn't told Vera I'd settled things with Thomas that day behind the emergency hospital and she and I had discussed, on more than one occasion, how awkward it would be to have Howard come to Munising with Thomas there. We had plotted about all the ways we could keep the two of them apart, but I always knew that Thomas wouldn't interfere with Howard if they ever met. I didn't have it in me to explain the entire situation to Vera. Not on little scraps of paper. Not one sentence at a time.

Yes, you are probably right. But still terribly sad, I wrote. Click-clack.

I realized that I would never see Thomas Fremont again and it made my heart ache even though I knew we were only ever meant to be friends.

Vera was relieved of her duties and began her own quarantine the day before mine was finished. I returned to the Beach Inn that Thursday and felt more than a little lonely without either of my close friends to rely on. It was hard not to look for Charlie whenever I came in the front door or down the stairs, and the pile of old newspapers stacked on the front desk made it seem like he'd merely stepped away. I resumed my duties as a health clerk and following my stint at the hospital, found it easier than I remembered. The tone of the visits was quite different—people were feeling scared and cautious, grateful for any bit of information we could provide about the epidemic. Free inoculations were being given at the courthouse every afternoon from two to four and it was our job to spread the word. We even had to do a survey on Thanksgiving and nearly every family we visited sent us away with some small gift or treat. Vera was back by then and the Dotys hosted us for dinner later in the day, though we had to get special permission from the mayor and Dr. Scholtes to join them, which wasn't a problem, of course.

The next day, Superintendent Abell announced in the Munising News that if health conditions continued to be favorable the schools would reopen December 9th. He cancelled all holiday breaks and school vacations other than Christmas and New Year's Day in order to make up for some of the lost school year. Students and families were charged with pursuing a rigorous course of home study to prepare for the return to school, though I knew from my visits that there was little schoolwork being done. I was eager to get back in the classroom and start teaching again and the idea of life resuming a normal pace was more than a little appealing. I thought of Howard often and while it was frustrating to remain out of touch, I refused to complain about the situation no matter how long our reunion took. To even have a future with Howard, when so many other couples were denied the chance, was a gift and I knew it. I wasn't sure if my letters were getting to him so I just kept writing as if they did. Unlike my family, I told him everything about the epidemic and I knew that he would understand my decision to volunteer despite the obvious risks. We had always shared the same desire to find useful work and help others. Safely ensconced back at the inn with Vera, ready to return to work, knowing Howard was safe, it felt like we had beaten influenza.

It was the Thursday before the schools were due to reopen when Vera and I returned to the inn to find it filled with people. The sight of the mayor, all of the city's doctors, Superintendent Abell, and Nurse Gardner milling about left no doubt—the epidemic was back.

"There are 300 cases in Gwinn and Princeton with five deaths," Dr. Scholtes announced to the group. "Both towns are quarantined," he added. "Marquette reports 383 cases and twenty-one deaths with 58 new cases this week alone." Everyone in the room was utterly still as he recited the statistics. A quick and informal vote was taken and the city's flu ban was extended indefinitely by a unanimous show of hands. Taverns, soft drink parlors, theaters, churches, and the schools would all remain closed—no more than five people would be allowed, by law, to gather in common areas of hotels, boarding houses, and retail stores. All businesses were ordered to close at 6 PM and children were required to stay in the immediate vicinity of their homes and would need a note if sent to run an errand.

"There will be no exceptions this time," Mayor Sullivan bellowed over the crowd before adjourning the meeting. "None," he repeated, making clear and specific eye contact with the Chief of Police. Vera and I were chatting with Nurse Gardner in the lobby when the mayor approached.

"By official proclamation, I'm sending you ladies home for the holidays," he said.

"T.G. we are in no rush to leave if we're needed here," I said, knowing that Vera agreed.

"I think we can arrange the patrols to make do

without them. Can't we, Caroline?" he replied, nodding toward Nurse Gardner.

"That shouldn't be a problem," she said. "You girls have done more than enough already." The mayor leaned in and whispered.

"Trust me, the schools won't be opening before Christmas. Go home. See your families. Get some rest."

We left Munising on the first train heading south that very same evening. The journey home took a day and a half since we departed so quickly, left to patch together a series of connections that had us criss-crossing the state in all directions to get to Albion. I wondered what it would be like to see my family after everything that had happened. I was hardly the same person who'd never even left home before, just a few months prior.

The hardest part about leaving Munising was knowing that Howard would continue to post his letters to me there. It was no use trying to alert him since by the time he received word of my trip home I'd likely be back in Munising. That meant it would be at least three weeks before I could possibly hear from him again. As I stared out the window of the train for countless hours I must admit there was a tiny part of me fantasizing of a reunion with Howard in Albion. What a wonderful Christmas present that would be. Even though I knew it was impossible, I let my mind play the scene over and over in my head as I drew closer to home. There were no tears when we saw each other—just an easy long embrace, an even longer kiss, and the deepest certainty that having survived war and disease, the future would be ours for the taking.

Chapter 22

Christmas

Blois, France

Dearest Lucile,

As I sit here this Christmas morning my mind easily drifts back to one year ago when I was enjoying myself with you in Albion. Although far away, I am not unhappy for I feel fortunate to spend the day at all and am enjoying a little Christmas cheer. Last night we received our "Christmas box"—a couple bars of chocolate and some cigarettes—the latter of which I promptly exchanged for more chocolate. After that we watched movies and had a short program of caroling, which I volunteered to help plan. I wish you could have heard us sing and then give three cheers for Jesus Christ, whose birthday we commemorated. There was nothing sacrilegious or irreverent about it. There were probably 2000 men in the courtyard and it was really quite moving.

I suppose you are planning and dreaming dreams every day, as I am. I do not know whether to try to finish my schooling or get directly into work when I am released. The war has disturbed my mind in more than one way so that I'm not sure what I want to do. My experience here in first aid work has aroused a desire for the medical profession but that would require considerably more schooling. I trust that plans will materialize upon my return. My stint overseas has only shown me more clearly an intense longing for the kinder, sweeter things in life. By kind and sweet, I do not mean weak, for strength is a virtue I have learned here. It seems that this life will test me out and I have now seen the law of "survival of the fittest" at work. I do not know how fit I am but at least I have survived and that is good enough for me.

When you receive this note the holiday season will have passed and you will again be dispelling the clouds of ignorance which envelope the minds of youth. I have often formed a picture of you at work this year and know that you are an excellent teacher. It suits you so much.

A bunch of soldiers left this morning for the U.S.A. How those who remained longed to go but we must wait our turn. I am well and I hope you are too. I trust that the influenza I read so much about has left you and our families untouched. Without any word from home yet, it is hard to be sure.

With love and high hopes,
Howard

132 BLOIS. — Le Square Victor Hugo — LL

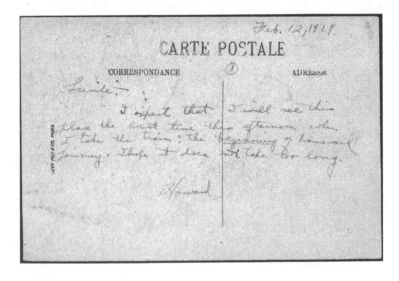

February 12, 1919

Lucile –

I expect that I will see this place the last time this afternoon, when I take the train; the <u>beginning</u> of homeward journey. I hope it does not take too long.

Howard

February 19, 1919
Base Hospital 119
Savenay, France

Dear Lucile,

Unless the very unexpected occurs, I am writing you my last letter from France. You may have it for a souvenir! Upon my return, it is my intention to never have to write you a letter again.

We are in a huge camp here, which includes 3 large hospitals. Trains are coming and going at all times with their loads of soldiers who have "done their bit" and are anxious to go to their beloved homeland, now more than ever.

As I leave France, I have no regrets. I love the French people and it is my earnest hope and ambition that we may return to some of these scenes again under much more favorable circumstances. How glad I am to be "homeward bound". Anywhere that you are will do.

With love,
Howard

Chapter 23

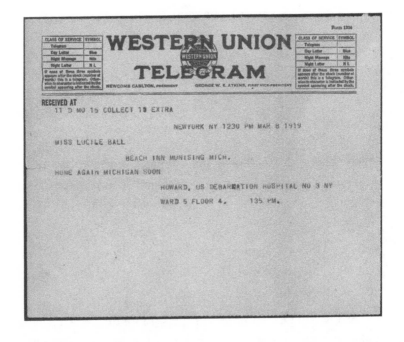

I KNEW SOMETHING was going on when I saw Clara Doty peeking into my classroom. It was well after noon and Lyle had had math that morning, so I presumed her mother was looking for me. I caught just the briefest glimpse of one of the large and frivolous hats she favored right before Principal Smith walked in.

"Excuse me everyone," he said, crossing to the middle of the room, right to where I was standing in front. "I need to relieve Miss Ball for a moment so she can take a message in the hall." He spied the jumble of numbers and equations on the board behind us. "Perhaps you can all just have a quiet break until she returns. She won't be long," he concluded, dismissing me with a smile and a nod.

"Bill Evans from Western Union just delivered this to the house," Clara said before I could even shut the classroom door. She handed me a telegram. It was in a sealed envelope, my name typed and showing through the transparent window on the front. "I had to bring it over right away."

"Thank you," I whispered.

"It's got to be from Howard," she exclaimed. "He must finally be in the States!"

She was right. I'd been anticipating the telegram's arrival. I learned of Howard's departure from France just a few days earlier and, given the delay in the mail combined with the time it would take him to cross the Atlantic, I'd calculated that news of his safe passage would be arriving soon.

"Yes, I've been expecting it. I should have told you that. Thank you so much for bringing it over."

"Of course, dear" she said, looking at me like I'd fully lost my mind. "Aren't you going to open it? You've waited so long."

"I will Clara. Later. The moment school lets out." I nodded towards my classroom. Her face went blank as she watched the envelope disappear into my dress pocket.

"All right then," she said, though I knew she was disappointed.

"It's wonderful to know that it came," I offered. "Thank you again." I gave her a hug. "I'll see you this afternoon." She held me by the shoulders before letting go.

"I'm so happy for you Lucile. We can't wait to meet your young man," she said, turning to leave. I waited for the top of her hat to disappear into the stairwell at the end of the hall. Keeping my back to the door, I carefully slipped the envelope out of my pocket and clutched it to my chest, closed my eyes, and drew in the deepest breath of relief. The one that had eluded me since the day Howard departed.

"Welcome home, my love," I whispered. "Welcome home."

When I first learned of Howard's injury I never could have imagined it would take the Army five months to bring him back to me. During that time, I received only a handful of letters and the ones that did make it through came in no particular order—often weeks apart—which made it impossible to piece together exactly what was happening. Howard made no reference to any of the details I shared in my letters to him and the fact that the telegram was addressed to the Beach Inn meant that he probably hadn't received any of them.

Clara and Pa Doty invited me to stay at their house upon my return to Munising after the holidays and Vera continued on at the Methodist parsonage, where she had stayed during her quarantine. What a treat it was to further my friendship with the Doty family and I so enjoyed living in such a beautiful home—gleaming hardwood floors covered with ornate oriental rugs, thickly padded window seats overlooking the lake, silk draperies, down comforters, every latest appliance and fixture in the kitchen and bath, and a maid to clean and do the laundry three days a week! It was such a far cry from my life on the farm or from any of the finer things Aunt Rose had ever exposed me to over the years.

The epidemic still had a grip on Munising when we returned, though everyone had settled into a routine that was somewhere between the full restrictions seen early on and the beginning of something that at least resembled normal. The schools were open but attendance was voluntary, with barely half the students present. The emergency hospital was still up and running with a different nurse in charge, allowing Caroline Gardner to resume her duties at the school. Most businesses were open but continued to allow just a few people inside at a time and places of entertainment could only operate for limited evening hours, with all the chairs and stools removed to prevent loitering. Houses with active cases of influenza were quarantined for up to two weeks and pleasure parties or public meetings were discouraged, requiring approval by the mayor.

It was quite a shock for everyone when Dr. Scholtes stepped down as the health officer after questions about the city's handling of the epidemic continued to surface. I saw him shortly before he quit, looking more haggard than I imagined a man could ever be without actually collapsing. The doctor was cleared of any wrongdoing later that same week and if it weren't for the blow to his reputation I'm quite sure he would have felt nothing but relief to be done with the job. The epidemic disappeared as February dawned, ending just as swiftly as it began. It was amazing to watch Munising literally come back to life once the threat passed.

The bitterly cold temperatures—typical for that time of year—did little to keep the streets from filling up as soon as all the bans were lifted. The sidewalks, narrowed by nine and ten-foot tall snow banks, were packed with people and everyone was in a buoyant mood. Large crowds gathered on the corners and in front of the bigger stores. Friends who hadn't seen each other in months stood there mingling like it was a sunny, spring afternoon, their gauze masks replaced by woolen scarves. I joined Clara at her knitting circle twice a week, Vera and I took in every show and movie at the Delft Theater, and all of the teachers often bundled up to enjoy one of the many wintertime activities so popular in the area. On several occasions, we borrowed the Doty's horse and sleigh to venture out as far as we could from town and snowshoe up into the hills or over to the lakeshore. I was so impressed by the stark beauty of a winter waterfall frozen midstream or the birds-eye view of the Pictured Rocks shrouded in white and dripping with giant icicles, many of them twice as tall as me. There were hours spent tobogganing down Lennox Hill in the shadow of the water tower or Sunday afternoons skating out as far as we cared to on the frozen bay. The Dotys were so generous to allow me to invite my friends back to the house to warm up by the fire and Clara always had a pan of hot cocoa waiting for us on the stove. I never enjoyed winter as much as I did in Munising, but I didn't know if life was always so busy and active that time of year or if being cooped up by the epidemic had left people more willing to venture out into the snow and cold.

"Miss Bridgman?" I was walking home from the movies by myself one afternoon when I heard a man approach. I turned to see him running to catch up with me. He looked familiar but it wasn't until he got closer that I realized who it was.

"Mr. Schultz," I said. I hadn't seen Anna's husband since the day I'd found her in bed with the flu. Dr. Scholtes never told me if anyone had spoken to the man about his temper.

"Can I talk to you? It'll only take a minute."

"Yes, I suppose." I was glad we weren't alone on the sidewalk. I noticed Anna standing across the street. She appeared to be window-shopping but I could tell she was only pretending, giving her husband privacy to handle his business with me.

"I wanted to say I'm real sorry for how I acted that day, for grabbing you like I did. I didn't mean to scare you."

"I know that, but thank you for saying so."

"She got so sick, so fast. I thought she was dying." I couldn't tell if it was love or remorse but the man looked near tears. "I really do feel bad about being so rough on you."

"I accept your apology Mr. Schultz. No harm done." He glanced across to his wife. They shared a smile. I waved to Anna and she waved back.

"That's real decent of you, Ma'am. Anna said you were nice."

"I'm just glad everything turned out all right," I told him. I think most everyone felt that way, at least in Munising, where the death toll remained miraculously low—just four by then. Memories of the epidemic faded quickly and I was happy to resume my life again and prepare for a reunion with Howard.

I opened the telegram by myself, standing at the edge of the lake down by the city dock. The snow all around could only be measured in feet, the temperature in single digits. Even though it was early March there was no sign of winter's end anywhere. A wind off the lake stabbed at my cheeks and I quickly removed my gloves to open the tissue thin envelope and unfold the paper inside.

HOME AGAIN MICHIGAN SOON

Four short words sent from New York City, uttered from Howard's mouth on the very same day that I was reading them. We hadn't been this close in over eleven months, together again in the same country, separated not by a vast ocean but only by land and the time it would take a train to traverse it. Our letters could now pass back and forth in mere days, not weeks. Perhaps we might even arrange a phone conversation and I could let his voice linger in my ears as further proof that he was really coming back to me.

I was overcome with emotion, but the feeling was bitter-sweet for as close as Howard was it felt almost cruel to still not be able to see him. I didn't know if I could wait any longer to take in his sturdy frame, that head of neatly combed hair, or those steely blue-grey eyes that looked at me with such love. Before the telegram had arrived, it was only about survival. But now—there was hope, and excitement, and the promise of endless possibilities.

Chapter 24

March 8, 1919

My Dear Lucile,

I am feeling pretty tired and a little sick today. The trip across was rough and tedious. My wound is almost healed but the knee joint is not well. I am told that use is the only thing that will help it. I need some good work outdoors to regain my former stamina and vigor. I am so fortunate and happy to be in the U.S.A., which I love more than ever and hope will be a land of opportunity for me.

We certainly received a royal welcome this morning. I am living in a large building (formerly a department store) that seems like heaven! And "eats" the likes of which I only dreamed of in France. After being re-clothed we are given four or five days to see the city and then will be sent to our hometown or, in my case, the nearest hospital. I hope to go to Camp Custer. Say nothing to your folks and I will surprise them and all of our Albion friends. Lucile, that reminds me—do you have a spring vacation and when might that be?

I apologize for my writing. This is the best pen that I could borrow. Mine is somewhere in France. If you write a letter (or two!) I will still be here to get them. Sent you a telegram C.O.D. I was sorry to have to do it, but I am broke. No pay for a long time, but we will get back pay here. It seems good to write a letter again that I know will be read by no one but you. It has been a long time, my love. The only thing that makes waiting a little longer to see you possible, is knowing that we will never be separated like this again.

Much love XX,
Howard

March 14, 1919

Dear Lucile,

I feel like a new person this morning after receiving your most welcome letter! You cannot imagine how depressing it was to go without news from all my loved ones for so long. I received only one letter, that from you, since September 17. I did not truly doubt that everything was all right, but I did wonder sometimes. There was too much time to wonder.

I am leading a fast life here attending theatre parties, going on sightseeing trips, etc. A little of this life is interesting and fun but give me a small city or the country. Being in the army has only aggravated my desire for freedom and outdoor life.

Yes, how much I want to have a long talk with you too! I have coined a thousand plans, but just now I feel the need for more education. Some colleges are offering good opportunities to "returned heroes"!! But, what "line" shall it be? My ideas have changed in the past year and I have more of a desire to make money than I used to. Not for the money but for what it will command in life. Also, I feel we should travel! I want to take you many places, especially a few where I have now been. How big and wonderful this world is but how little we see in our own backyard. While there is money for such luxuries in business, I have not had either the training or inclination for that kind of work. I don't know whether to continue at Albion and work toward a Master's Degree or go to a different institution to find some new ideas. I worry sometimes that I am not as fine a scholar as I should be to "climb higher".

I do not want to wait long before we start a little home. Your suggestions or plans of the heart for us are welcome to me too! I feel so much confidence in you Lucile. You have a splendid "home training" along lines that were denied to me with my mother's death. And now you also know a bit about being on your own and experiencing life.

I understand from your letter that you have no spring break in which to visit Albion, due to the time lost to the influenza outbreak. How I would love to meet you again there for the first time, but no matter. As soon as I am in Michigan and can get furlough or my discharge, I will come to wherever you are. Continue to write me here and the letters will be forwarded. They will take longer to reach me but that only means I'm moving closer to you.

Your lover,
Howard

March 23, 1919
Camp Custer

My Lucile,

It is six o'clock and I just arrived in camp from a 48-hour pass to Albion. Believe me, it is a change coming back from friends and family to the west end of Custer, where I know no one. But I am accustomed to changes in the army. What a beautiful evening it is for canoeing on the little lake here near the hospital. After this letter is finished, and my mind is full of thoughts of you, I shall take a ride in one of the rowboats for old time's sake.

Lucile—you cannot imagine the emotions that thrilled me as I saw some of my friends again or as I walked through all the familiar places so dear to us. I could scarcely control myself when I joined the college prayer meeting Thursday evening. My heart was beating so hard and so fast. The same as when I drove into your yard and walked into your house after the last year's experiences. I stayed with your family last night and your brothers and I went for a walk and did a little shooting this morning. Then I looked through the picture album you made for me. What a treat it was to catch a glimpse of your full life while I was gone. I went to dinner with Rose and met all her fine friends. I enjoyed myself so much but must get accustomed to such life again. I also stopped by the frat house and was urged to entertain the boys with a few stories. I remember what Professor Hembdt used to say with a new understanding, "If you have had experiences, have paid the price, people will listen to you." I am finding it to be true.

Now Lucile, don't plan and don't be disappointed if I do not arrive soon, but I understand that we may leave for Detroit on Tuesday and my first effort there will be to get a 10-day furlough. There are so many changes in the army that I would not want you to count on it but I will come to you as soon as possible. I assure you of that.

Lucile—I must say it and know you will understand. I feel just a little sentimental. I am so hungry to put my arms around you I can hardly stand it sometimes, it seems. I have waited for that moment of reunion for a year and I can wait a little longer. Some have waited a greater time than us and others cannot even have their reunion here. I think of our friend Red Marlatt often. How fortunate we are Lucile, and oh how I want to find my work and succeed in life with you by my side. Let us take a walk together in the setting sun. Wouldn't it be grand?

Goodnight,

Howard

April 4, 1919

Camp Custer-Ward 27

Dearest Lucile,

I just returned from a good walk. I am a little tired, but feel so much better. I have been busy all week and am trying not to be too anxious. I had a bit of a reaction this afternoon and felt just a bit lonesome for you—a lot, actually. And, so I went for a walk in the cool of evening. It was so quiet except for the last few weary notes of the birds. The little lake I've mentioned was still and glassy, mirroring the sky and the sun, itself a ball of fire.

Tonight Lucile, I am an American citizen. At 2:45 today I renounced my allegiance to Canada and took the oath of the United States. It was an important moment but otherwise empty without you there to share it with. I think that is what prompted my reaction afterwards.

You will note that I was transferred to another ward. Some lucky boy left today and I am filling in his space. The nurse told me (again!) tonight that it would be my turn in a day or so. If not, I will get a 24-hour pass to go to Albion to relieve the monotony of waiting.

I have been thinking considerably about Physical Education as my career. It seems that I cannot forget it and find that I can arouse more enthusiasm about this than anything else. I wish the Hateful Hun had not hit a bone, but it may be possible that this wound will not hinder me in entering the profession. I have a letter and the catalog from the Dean of the Y.M.C.A. College in Chicago. He told me that there are many opportunities for men of education and training, even perhaps in foreign lands, which seems to interest me. To be frank Lucile, can you picture me as a teacher? I read so much about what a man can do if he wills it to be.

I will close these ramblings, Lucile. Oh, how I wish I were pulling into Munising this morning. That moment when I first lay eyes on you cannot come fast enough.

Much love,
Howard

Chapter 25

WHEN THE EPIDEMIC returned to Munising for the third time, it arrived swiftly and without warning.

It was April 18, 1919—the day before Howard's twenty-fourth birthday. The sky was clear and blue, the sun shining brightly, and even thermometers in the shade topped out at almost forty degrees for the first time in months. People on the streets were strolling around casually instead of darting from place to place—coats open, without hats or gloves—more certain than ever that summer would actually make it back to the U.P. again that year despite winter's wrath. Out of nowhere, 81 cases of influenza surfaced all at once, as if it had never really gone away. I first learned about the outbreak when Principal Smith showed up in my classroom to make an announcement. He was pale and out of breath, his tone grim, the message uncharacteristically stern.

"Go straight home," he told the students. "Don't stop for a soda and do not run into Peters' Grocery for penny candy. I mean it now!" The windows in my room were all open a crack and I could hear robins chirping outside as he spoke.

"Be sure to tell your parents the epidemic is back and that

they can read more about it in the News tonight. DO NOT come to school next week if you are sick. You will be sent home and your entire family quarantined!" His warning pushed several of the younger girls into hysterics.

Each room was dismissed one at a time and the students filed out of the building without saying a word, walking down the streets like a perfectly spaced wedding party passing down the aisle. The teachers gathered for a meeting once the students left and were told that the mayor was reinstating the door-to-door health survey immediately. There were 47 homes already under quarantine and the emergency hospital was reopening to take in fifteen of the most severe cases. There was even one death being reported. All the teachers received new gauze masks before leaving and it took all of my will to pull that thing over my mouth and nose again before stepping outside. After battling it once and presuming victory, the epidemic's resurgence terrified me and I couldn't help but wonder what it had in store for us.

"**RESTRICTIONS ON AGAIN**," read the headline in the newspaper that evening. Schools and churches remained open but would have to be disinfected each night. The Delft Theater was placed on a half-capacity schedule, businesses were again restricted to serving no more than five customers at a time, and all dances or large public gatherings were cancelled. An extra police officer was stationed at the post office to enforce the restrictions and another would be roaming the streets in plain clothes to report any and all violations. With several hundred cases and a number of deaths reported in nearby Marquette, I never heard anyone complain about the restrictions this time around. Not even once.

Vera and I spent the evening at Froebal School helping

to set up and restock the emergency hospital. We readied the cots and folded gauze for masks, sterilized dozens of thermometers, and unpacked the city's remaining supply of vaccine. I stayed on by myself until well past midnight making soup and squeezing oranges. The work was all too familiar, only this time I knew how futile the effort was—all we could really do for the flu victims was to keep them as comfortable as possible, wait for the fever to break, and the bloody coughing to subside. It was hard not to surrender to fear and desperation a second time around. As I walked in and out of the room where Charlie died I had to keep fighting off visions of myself lying in a bed, blue in the face, straining to breathe. I couldn't shake the thought of taking ill before Howard and I were reunited and I'd nearly worked myself into a panic by the time I left for the night. In the three short blocks to the Dotys' house I counted fifteen black on red quarantine placards, dooming me to a night of little sleep and runaway fear. I wondered if I should head home immediately so even if I did get sick, I might make it to Albion in time to see my family and my beloved Howard before the Spanish Lady finally got to me.

I was exiting Tredway's Pharmacy early the next morning carrying a bag of donated gauze, Vicks ointment and rubbing alcohol that I'd agreed to drop off at the emergency hospital before starting my reinstated rounds with Vera. I walked alone on Superior Street towards the school when an automobile turned up the road behind me. A quick glance over my shoulder revealed that it was Shorty in his bus. He was driving on the wrong side of the street and despite the early hour started honking the horn repeatedly. Shorty was a real joker and loved to goof around but I never cared for his sense of humor as much as others seemed to. I just kept walking, refusing to turn around and he continued to sound the horn, though he finally surrendered to my pace. I heard the brakes squeak and the door to the bus open, then close.

"Lucile."

I stopped walking the instant I heard Howard's voice. Anchored in place, my entire body trembling, I stared straight ahead as the empty bus pulled past me and disappeared around the corner. Each leaden heartbeat echoed in my ears and I broke into a cold sweat despite the frosty air surrounding me. I couldn't will myself to turn around, afraid that my mind was playing tricks.

"Lucile," Howard repeated. "It's me." I turned to look at him but could barely focus my eyes. He was dressed from head to toe in army green with a small duffle bag on his shoulder. His unshaven face gaunt and his eyes glued on me from behind his perfectly round spectacles. Tears were already running down his face.

"Howard."

I choked out his name as loudly as I could. My arms went limp, my purse and the bag of supplies fell to the ground. My legs refused to move, though I was desperate to reach him. I watched helplessly as he took the last ten steps of a yearlong journey back to me. He was limping slightly, though it didn't seem to slow him down, and once he was close enough I threw myself on top of him. Our first embrace was overwhelming. There was no way to press my body close enough to his to make up for the strain of all our days apart. After the initial, emotion-filled fumbling, our arms slipped perfectly into place as if only a bit of time had passed. Howard was the first to pull away. He reached up and unhooked the elastic of my mask from each ear and cupped my face in his bare hands, gently caressing my cheeks. His touch released a silent stream of tears.

"You're here," I said.

"I was going to send you a wire but I would have missed the train." He reached down and held my left hand up between us. "Let me see." He tugged at the fingertips of my glove until the engagement ring was revealed. "I wish I could have afforded something larger."

"It's perfect."

Then he kissed me. Initially it was soft and tentative, like a small bit of affection offered on the front porch when you know prying eyes are watching. But then came something more passionate—long, and slow, and full—the kind of kiss that lovers share when there has been a true meeting of hearts, as Howard so often said about us. It seemed like we were the only two people in the world, and I felt no shame or embarrassment welcoming my soldier-man home from war, where anyone could see. On his birthday, nonetheless.

"I love you, Lucile," Howard repeated over and over. He continued to hold and touch me so passionately, like a man stumbling upon a shady oasis, seeking shelter from the burning desert.

"I love you too," I said. "Thank God you're back."

We stood there for many minutes more—hugging and kissing, laughing and crying. It took a while for it to feel safe enough to let go. I had never known such complete and utter joy as I did seeing and holding Howard again.

Vera was waiting on the sidewalk in front of the hospital when we approached. I was late to meet her and the initial flash of impatience I saw on her face quickly evolved into confusion, then elation, when she realized who was with me.

"HOWARD!" she shrieked, undaunted by the early hour or the building full of influenza patients behind her. "I can't believe it! Is it really you?" she yelled, running to greet us. She hugged Howard with such enthusiasm that anyone watching would have been confused about which one of us was his fiancé.

"It's good to see you Vera," Howard exclaimed. They were friendly before the war but not close, each knowing how important the other was to me.

"You look good," she told him, stepping back and giving him a cursory inspection up and down. It wasn't even true if you examined him closely and knew him like I did. "How's the knee?" she asked.

"It's fine," Howard replied. What else would he say? "Thank you for asking."

"Lucile!" Vera shrieked again, suddenly. She smothered me with a hug and before letting go, whispered closely in my ear, "I'm so happy for you."

The commotion had drawn Nurse Gardener and Clara out onto the stoop.

"This is Howard," I said. He moved to climb the stairs and greet them.

"Nice to meet you," Caroline said, holding up a hand to stop him. "We've got some very sick people here," she explained. Clara had disappeared inside.

"I completely understand," Howard said. I had told him just a little about the epidemic's reappearance during our walk over. "Nice to meet you too." Clara came back outside and reached down, handing him a mask.

"You're going to need one of these," she said, "before our undercover officer catches you." She winked at me.

"You stay and visit," Caroline said to Clara. She turned to

Howard. "I hope to see you again. Welcome home." Then to me, "Lucile, it's good to see you smiling." Clara came down the stairs to join us.

"I'm Lucile's friend Clara Doty," she said. "Welcome to Munising."

"Thank you, Ma'am. It's such a pleasure to be here." It was surreal to see Howard standing there. The gauze mask only added to the folly.

"Where is Howard going to stay while he's here?" Clara asked. It hadn't even occurred to me.

"The Beach Inn, I suppose." I certainly wasn't having him rooming at one of the boarding houses with all the mill workers, especially with the flu back at it.

"Nonsense. He'll stay with us. It's already been decided," she concluded with a satisfied grin. "Take him home right now and get him settled."

"We have to make our rounds this morning," I said, looking at Vera.

"I can do it alone," she said, thrilled to have a stake in the master plan.

"Yes. That's how we'll do it. I'll take care of everything with Dr. O'Brien," Clara stated. "And you know T.G. wouldn't have it any other way."

"That's the mayor," I whispered to Howard. "Thank you both so much," I said to my two dear friends, taking Howard by the arm and leading him away. There was so much catching up to do, though with the initial rush of excitement fading I began to feel nervous as we made our way to the Doty's. The lake was looming in front of us and I gave him a brief orientation to the city, talked nonstop about the people he'd just met, and filled him in on all the restrictions related to the epidemic.

Howard listened closely but remained quiet. He explained that he planned to stay in Munising for five days before heading to Clio, to visit with his family. They had reunited earlier, during one of his furloughs from Custer.

When we arrived at the Doty's, I introduced Howard to Pa and Lyle, then we quickly excused ourselves to the tiny room adjacent to the kitchen—a former maid's quarters, turned guest room. Howard sat in a chair in the corner while I rushed around changing the sheets and unpacking his bag. I caught him drifting off several times but continued to fill the space between us with more and more nervous chatter. He insisted that he wanted to visit some more but I ignored him, removing his shoes and then his clothes until all he had on was an army issued union suit. He obliged me with no resistance, lifting arms and legs one at a time as I removed every last bit of his uniform. It was cathartic to reclaim him as a civilian, all for my own. I wanted to take that uniform outside and burn it, but left it folded on the dresser instead. He slid into bed and I bent down to cover him up, giving his forehead a light but lingering kiss.

"Just one touch of lips," he whispered. He looked at me with droopy eyes and a boyish smirk, a blink or two away from slumber.

"I don't know what I would have done..." I said.

"I'll never leave you, Lucile."

"Promise?" He nodded. "Sleep well," I said. When I turned for the door he gave the back of my dress a tug.

"Stay until I fall asleep. It's too soon to say goodbye." Indeed, it was.

I made sure the door was securely latched before tiptoeing around the foot of the bed. I felt Howard's gaze upon me and avoided looking at him, too nervous to catch the glimmer of desire that was certainly following me across the room. I sat on the furthest edge of the mattress and removed my shoes, making sure not to let them go clunk on the floor. The moment I laid down one of Howard's hand reached out for mine and pulled me toward him. I slid over until there was no space between us and rested my head on his chest. He smelled of witch hazel from his most recent shave and I could feel his breath on my hair with every exhale. I closed my eyes and matched my breathing to his and we stayed like that for an hour or more, very little of which was spent talking. There was some more kissing and touching and even a few tears as we held each other. I remained on top of the sheets and blankets but I can say there were moments between us that made me wish we were already married, that there wasn't any reason to stop being close. It was the first time I realized what it meant to be fully committed to a man and to want to be his wife in every way.

Howard fell asleep with my head nuzzled under his chin and my arms wrapped around his torso. I stayed with him for as long as I dared and slipped out of the room unnoticed. He slept all the way through until morning and arrived in the kitchen for breakfast, freshly scrubbed and dressed in his own clothes. He looked much more like the energetic college student I'd said goodbye to than the battered soldier I greeted the day before—except for the limp.

"Good morning!" I exclaimed. "How did you sleep?" I crossed the room and gave him a very respectable kiss on the cheek. Clara and Lyle were in the kitchen too, helping me put the finishing touches on a very large breakfast I'd been silently preparing since before sunrise.

"I slept well," he said, pulling out his pocket watch. "VERY well according to this old thing." Pa walked in upon hearing our voices and Howard reached out to shake his hand right away.

"Good morning sir," he said. Pa nodded and took his place at the kitchen table, motioning for Howard to join him. Clara arrived and filled Pa's coffee cup, putting a spoonful of sugar and a generous pour of cream into the dark brew. She even stirred it for him.

"How do you take your coffee?" she said, waiting for Howard's order.

"Black, thank you."

"What?" I said. He was always a sugar—no cream man, like my father. Lots of sugar as a matter of fact.

"That's how I had to drink it over there," he said. "Just got used to it that way." It was a small thing, but the first of many hardships he'd endured that would come to be revealed.

"Don't be shy now," Clara said, pouring Howard's coffee. There were mounds of food piled in the middle of the table, enough to feed at least a dozen people, and a belated birthday cake to top it all off. We all filled our plates, with Clara serving herself last. "Pa would you mind?" she said. We bowed our heads. Howard reached underneath the table and took my hand.

"Dear Lord, we thank you for this food and the company we are about to share. We are especially thankful that you brought Howard home safely to our dear friend Lucile. Please bring them patience as they open their hearts again to each other and watch over us all until this terrible epidemic passes for good." Pa glanced up at his wife, who nodded her approval. "Amen," he said.

"Amen," the rest of us repeated.

We lingered over breakfast for however long it took four adults to drink three full pots of coffee. The Dotys were as charming and boisterous as usual and loved having someone new to regale with tales of their beloved city. I tried diverting the conversation once or twice but Howard insisted they continue and seemed genuinely excited to hear all about this place I'd discovered, described in all the letters that he never received. Stories about lumber mills and pictured rocks soon turned into a detailed account of the epidemic's onslaught, all against a backdrop of Lyle practicing piano in the parlor.

The Dotys spoke about its slow arrival, that the teachers were pressed into service, and how the Froebal School was converted into a hospital, filling up overnight when the flu finally hit.

"I don't know what this town would have done without Lucile," Clara said. "What we would have done," her voice trailed off, as if her breath had been stolen.

"Our Lyle came down with it," Pa told Howard.

"And Lucile was there to take care of her," Clara said. "Saved her life."

"Clara." I looked at Howard. "I did what I could. It wasn't much. Really." Her dramatic depiction of events embarrassed me.

"Don't listen to her, Howard." Clara was talking to him but looking at me, her voice took an unusually serious tone, growing louder and more forceful as she spoke.

"Who do you think called all those nurses that we had to shame into signing up on the volunteer list to begin with? Hmmm?" She paused to catch her breath. "I did. I called them.

And every last one turned me down, even as I begged for help over at that hospital. EVERY...LAST...ONE!"

I shifted in my chair, wishing she'd stop staring at me. Howard sat back from the table, eyes wide, mouth hanging open.

"I saw how people avoided that place. Left food on the stoop and ran away. Looked at you and Vera like you had the plague or something when you were locked in there taking care of their friends, their family. It was shameful."

"Shameful," Pa grumbled.

"I would have volunteered myself but I had Lyle home from school with nowhere safe to go," her voice cracked. She finally looked away as the first tear rolled down her cheek. "Then she got sick." Clara looked at Howard. "Sicker than anybody you've ever seen." Not an easy sentiment to assert so confidently to a limping soldier just back from the front lines, the roar of guns still ringing in his ears.

"When the doctor told us they had to take her..." She began to weep and wiped at her face roughly with a napkin, shaking her head and waving for Pa to continue.

"They had to pry Lyle out of your arms," Pa said. He was whispering, speaking to his wife as if they were alone. "You hadn't slept in days. You weren't yourself." Pa's normally booming voice cracked too. He looked at Howard and then me.

"I had to hold her back when the doctor took Lyle out to the car. We were so relieved to know that you were there with her, Lucile. You have no idea." Pa let out a whimper as he tried to stop the tears. The room went silent except for the sounds of a pretty little etude drifting in from two rooms away.

"I couldn't believe it when they brought her in. I didn't know that someone that young could be so ill," I said. I broke down too. "We had twenty-four patients all at once. It was the same night my friend Charlie died. I did the best I could," I told Howard. He passed me his handkerchief and left his hand resting on mine.

"We never thanked you properly," Pa said.

"It's not necessary. I was glad to see her through it." I meant it, but couldn't look at either one of them as I spoke.

Pa remained silent until my nervous eyes settled on him and even then, he paused a tick or two more. "We can't *ever* thank you enough," he said.

"You'll always have a special place in our hearts," Clara added, only she stood and came around the table, clenching me against her as she wept.

"She's a good woman, Howard. A real keeper," Pa said.

"I've known that for a while now, sir," he replied. I looked over at Howard and caught him staring at me. He made no attempt to hide his gaze or look away, just like the day he first spied me across that college classroom—a stranger to behold. His face was filled with shock and worry, confusion and pride, all mixed up into an expression I'd never seen before.

"I didn't know," he whispered when I paused by his chair, clearing dishes from the table.

"You couldn't have done anything," I said.

"No, but not knowing is always harder." His words hit me like bullets and I understood exactly what he meant. It sickened me to know he'd suffered alone, for so long.

And that is how the next several days continued to unfold, each of us taking turns sharing stories about our time apart. The details never came out all at once but rather in bits and pieces, randomly and casually, in among the people and activities of the day. We kept busy during his stay and it was a good way to get reacquainted without trying too hard or expecting too much. Howard seemed nervous much of the time and had difficulty relaxing or sitting still. I could tell he was often holding back as much or more than he was telling about his experiences overseas but it was easy to be patient, knowing just a little of what he'd endured.

Not only did the mayor fully relieve me of my health survey duties while Howard was in town, but I was also surprised to receive a call from Principal Smith that Sunday evening. Upon hearing about Howard's arrival, all of the other high school teachers insisted on covering my classes.

"Take as much time as you want, Lucile. There are more important things than work," he said. "And don't even think about showing up, the other teachers won't allow it," he joked. It was one of the kindest things anyone had ever done for me.

With three days at our disposal I set about showing Howard everything I loved about Munising and thanks to the influenza restrictions, we nearly had the city to ourselves. There were matinees at the empty Delft Theater, a motor tour of the area's waterfalls in Mr. Doty's car, Sunday night dinner at the Beach Inn, and several stops at the grocery for potato chips. We visited the school one afternoon so he could meet all of my friends, Nurse Gardner, and Principal Smith. Everyone was so gracious and all of my students clamored to meet "Miss Ball's fiancé".

"You've made quite an impression on everyone," Howard told me afterward. "But then, I'm not surprised."

Much of our time together was spent outdoors at Howard's request. We hiked to the Pictured Rocks and he was as awed by them as I was. We also spent an entire day all by ourselves on Grand Island. The weather was especially sunny and warm. Not only were we able to spot the island's famed and elusive white deer but we also hiked all the way out to the East Channel lighthouse, which faced Munising Bay and the city shoreline, for a late picnic lunch. That was where I finally got up the nerve to ask Howard about his injury.

"Can I see it?" I said, watching as he rubbed his knee. He'd been massaging it every time we sat down, but stopped the instant I said something.

"It's nothing. Really, Lucile," he said, trying to sound casual about it, which only left me more intent on following through.

"May I?" I said, kneeling in front of him. I took the hem of his pant's leg, lifting it just a bit. He nodded for me to continue.

"It looks worse than it is." He reached down and pulled the fabric the rest of the way up.

"Oh, Howard," I gasped. The injury was certainly not nothing. A bright red ribbon of a scar stretched across the kneecap. It was quite raised and looked inflamed and tender. "Does it hurt?"

"Not anymore. I promise." Though it was impossible to believe.

"Oh, you wouldn't tell me if it did." I couldn't take my eyes off of his knee. I could see the indentation where a piece of bone was missing and there were smaller scars all around it, evidence of flying shrapnel and the incisions needed to remove it. "You should keep honey on these."

"That's an old wive's tale," he said, pulling his pants back down, knowing I had learned that from my old, German great-grandmother.

"It is not," I replied, smiling softly, and looking down. An awkward silence followed and we both knew there were more questions to be asked and answered. I stayed seated on the ground at his feet.

"Were you scared?" I asked.

"Yes, but just until I realized it wasn't serious."

"Why did it take so long to heal?"

"It took several days just to get to Paris for the operation. Then it got infected while I was recovering." Howard was sent to convalesce in an old castle where it was cold, damp, and dirty instead of staying in a real hospital. There wasn't even enough food or proper toilets and then he got dysentery on top of it all.

"That's awful!" I said. Our little school of a hospital offered better care than Howard received.

"Most of France was destroyed, Lucile. It was chaos over there. So many men had it far worse than me." His words were completely diplomatic and absolutely sincere.

"I can't believe what you've been through." I shook my head, tearing up.

"Come here," he said, standing up and opening his arms. "My knee will be just fine. Don't keep thinking about the things that don't even matter anymore." We embraced.

"I knew you were hurt but I didn't know how badly. I didn't even know if you were alive Howard. It was horrible." I buried my face in his chest and really leaned into him, resting my body fully against his. I'd been standing on my own for so long.

"So, the not knowing was difficult for you too," he said. He kissed the top of my head and we stood there for several minutes, warmed by the sun, listening to the waves off the lake lapping at the sand beneath us. "We've got to get back, Lucile," Howard said, glancing at his watch. "We'll barely make it."

We had less than half an hour to traverse the width of the island and catch the last boat to Munising. We ran back along the paths to the dock as fast as Howard's knee allowed, arriving with minutes to spare, but quite winded and tired. We spent the short ferry ride in silence, snuggled close together at the back of the boat. Howard was leaving the next morning and we still hadn't discussed the one thing that had sustained us the most during our time apart, the thing that we'd almost lost to a German bomb and a rampant illness. Our future.

After that first night in Munising when he'd passed out in bed, Howard struggled with sleep. With everyone else's bedrooms on the second floor, he was free to roam about downstairs and despite his efforts to be quiet I laid awake with him, listening to his every move. I heard him open and close the icebox, lounge in the rocking chair in the parlor, and slip out the front door to sit on the porch. I wanted to join him but worried what the Dotys might think hearing us downstairs alone together and I never said anything come morning because I knew he would feel terrible for waking me. I finally gave in his last night there and crept down the stairs as softly as I could to check on him.

After searching each darkened room, I noticed the front door was slightly ajar. I could see his silhouette through the sheer café curtains in the window, backlit by the moon. He was pacing back and forth, stepping out of view before pivoting at each end of the porch to make another pass. He didn't look surprised when I appeared from the house, draped in Pa's wool dress coat, snagged from a hook in the vestibule.

"I'm sorry," he said the moment he saw me, though the pacing went uninterrupted.

"Trouble sleeping?"

"You should go back to bed, Lucile," he said. "This is just how it is for me now."

"How what is?"

"Nighttime. Sleep. It's not easy anymore."

"You haven't been back that long, Howard." I snuck past him against the railing and settled onto the giant swing filling the opposite end of the porch, before he could send me away.

"This isn't how I wanted our time to go," he said, still pacing. He spoke rapidly, his voice straining at the top of its range.

"What do you mean?" I said.

"I thought we could pick up where we left off. Revisit our plans. Make new ones. I didn't think it would be this hard."

"Howard, our plans are the same as they've always been." He stopped abruptly and glared at me.

"Lucile, I don't even know what kind of work I'll do!" he said loudly.

"Shhhh," I patted the seat next to me. He came and sat, but kept himself utterly separate.

"Where am I going to get a job? How am I going to support you?" he continued in a tight and pressured whisper. "It's not fair." He couldn't even look at me.

"No man should have to go through what you went through," I said.

"Not for me, for you!" he exclaimed. "Don't you understand? I'm not the same man you agreed to marry!"

"And I'm not the same woman," I said. I sat up and moved right next to him, face to face. "Do you love ME any less?" I demanded. My question silenced him. I'd never spoken to him so forcefully, with such resolve. I wasn't angry but I certainly wasn't going to give him permission to question our love. Not after everything we'd endured.

"Of course not." He was exhausted, tortured by his thoughts. "I'm sorry," he said. He slid all the way back onto the swing, out of words but still clearly on edge.

"Howard," I said. I waited until he looked at me. "I love you. More now than ever. It's just a fact and nothing..." I paused. "*Nothing* will ever change that." He took in a very deep breath and it trembled in his throat as he exhaled.

"I don't think you understand how much I counted on you while I was over there. How important it was to have something bigger than the war waiting for me at home." There were tears streaming down his face, but his words remained steady. "I saw what happened to the men who didn't have that—the endless rounds of dirty Janes in each village, drinking enough to pass out every night, charging out and over the top of those trenches into certain death."

"But you made it," I whispered. It was horrifying to think of him in such an awful place.

"Because of you." He reached into the pocket of his robe and handed me a tiny, leather bound book with a tattered green cover. "I carried this with me the whole time."

I opened the cover and found my own face staring back at me—it was the picture I gave him the day he left, taken by Howard himself. Parts of the image were worn away but there I was looking at him, through the camera, with a gentle smile and loving eyes. Behind the picture was an inscription on the first page of the book.

Notify—Miss Lucile Ball, Albion Michigan.

"I want you to have it."

"Oh Howard." It was a diary and listed everything that had

happened to him - written for me, whether he made it back or not.

Without saying another word, Howard tipped himself sideways and laid down across the swing, his head in my lap. He was quiet and still but I knew he wasn't sleeping. I stroked his hair and guided the porch swing back and forth by the very tips of my toes. We stayed there like that for an hour, watching as the fog engulfing the lakeshore gradually burned away in the wake of the rising sun. The lake was shimmering blue with shards of silver and white rolling across the surface as the new dawn light from the east caught the crest of each incoming wave. A haze of tender buds and green spring leaves hung in the trees scattered on the hill below the house and the forsythia surrounding the porch was aflame in golden yellow. Howard finally spoke to me about his desire for more schooling and a wish to defer marriage until graduation, when he could support us by himself. We decided I would continue to teach and save money to give us a good start once the rings went on. We talked about finding a little house of our own and filling it with children, at least four, but maybe more. By the time we got up and went inside a beautiful spring day had dawned and, once again, we were just a regular couple with a rich, full life ahead of us.

Howard left Munising later that morning. Shorty drove us to the Junction and we waited on a small grassy patch near the platform, hands intertwined, tired but glad for a few last moments together. When we heard the first train whistle in the distance becoming louder we didn't move, other than to draw closer. We had two more months apart before our next reunion and after all we'd been through it only seemed like something to celebrate, rather than lament. When the train pulled in there was less than a minute to say goodbye. We shared a brief hug and a kiss but the conductor was watching, anxious to gain even thirty extra seconds to pad his schedule and Howard was the only passenger boarding.

"I won't say goodbye. Not this time," I said.

"Our hearts would never allow it," he smiled and kissed me ever so sweetly on the cheek.

Howard turned over his ticket to the conductor before hoisting himself onto the train, disappearing into the car to take a seat. I waited for him to appear in the window and reached overhead to press an open palm against the glass next to him. He matched it with his own on the other side, just as the train began to move.

I watched and waved for a moment, but turned to leave before the train was even out of sight, confident there was no longer a need to steal a final glance of him in the distance. I knew where Howard was going and that he was safe. Our plans had been pulled out and dusted off, changed only a little, and certainly more valuable than ever. Thoughts of the war and the epidemic faded quickly once we were able to see into the future again and we picked up with life where we had left off, together and in love.

No more war, no more plague,
only the dazed silence that follows
the ceasing of the heavy guns;
noiseless houses with the shades drawn, empty streets,
the dead cold light of tomorrow.
Now there would be time for everything.

Katherine Anne Porter
Pale Horse, Pale Rider

Chapter 26

1933

"ARE YOU MRS. Howard Bridgman?" asked the police officer.

His badge showed he was from Auglaize County, just north of our home in Piqua, Ohio. Dr. Busler, the minister from Greene Street Methodist where Howard and I attended church, stood just behind him. He barely looked at me—not even a hint of good news on his face.

"Yes," I said. Auglaize was home to the town of St. Marys where Howard was duck hunting on Grand Lake that morning.

"Mrs. Bridgman, there's been an accident," the officer said.

"It's Howard, Lucile," Dr. Busler added.

"He's with Mac and the Miller boy," I told them. "What's going on?"

"I think it would be best if we came in Ma'am," the officer said. If Howard were okay I knew they would just tell me.

I pushed open the screen door and backed into the living room. A rush of chilly October air accompanied them in—it smelled of wood smoke and damp leaves. There was a group of pumpkins on the front porch, waiting to be carved with the children after supper. I had just gotten Esther and Martha off to school, my hands were sticky with maple syrup, and there were two baskets of laundry sitting on the dining room table that needed to be folded. My youngest, Richard, just three years old, clung to my leg and started to wail when the two large men crossed the threshold. He was still a bit afraid of strangers, but even his reaction was stronger than usual this time. My knees shook when I bent over to pick him up.

"Is it serious?" I asked. They paused and looked at each other before turning to face me. The officer was especially young and went pale in the time it took to come inside.

"We don't know Mrs. Bridgman. It could be," he said. Dr. Busler came and took Richard from me. It only made the poor boy cry harder, but I let him go anyway.

"Why don't you sit Lucile," he said. I gathered my arms across my waist without moving. I had only one thing to say to them.

"Where's Howard?" I demanded. "Where's my husband?"

Fourteen years had passed since Howard and I reunited in Munising and our life together had evolved into something wonderful and satisfying, though certainly not free from challenges.

After much careful thought, Howard enrolled in the YMCA training school in Chicago beginning in the fall of 1919, receiving assistance with tuition and books as a wounded and decorated soldier. I stayed on the farm at Mother's insistence, though I only lasted a few months before seeking other temporary teaching positions. The first was in Alma followed by a year and a half in Dowagiac—the latter of which allowed me to travel by train to Chicago for weekends with Howard. His school program was quite rigorous and in addition to class work and taking odd jobs for spending money, he had to work long hours as a park director in the rough stockyards district, just south of the city. It did him good to get reestablished on his own before taking on the responsibilities of a family and every time I saw him he seemed more and more himself—fit, confident, and relaxed. I must admit that I also relished those extra months of working and independence that I'd only just gotten a taste of in Munising.

With Howard's graduation in sight, we were finally married on February 4, 1922 at the farm with 32 guests in attendance. A simple morning ceremony in the parlor was followed by a lovely brunch, catered by the same ladies who served food at my parents' wedding. Vera was my Matron of Honor, already married and pregnant with her second child. Aunt Rose surprised us by filling the house with dozens of red and pink roses, shipped by special delivery from the West Coast. Howard and I took the train to Chicago that afternoon, spending our first night together as a married couple in his tiny two-room apartment. We stayed up late cleaning the kitchen cupboards for entertainment and instead of sleeping on a pile of cushions on the floor, Howard shared the twin bed with me for the first time.

Then, in August, we moved to Piqua, Ohio when Howard accepted a position there as the YMCA director. Nestled on the grassy banks of the Miami River it was a quaint little city of 15,000 with wide boulevards and a charming downtown square. We were able to purchase a tiny house near the river and I was five months pregnant with our first child the day we moved in. Walter Hugh was born right before Christmas and instantly became the center of our world. Howard worked harder than ever and while there was only a little money, I couldn't have been happier tending the house and raising our son. The babies kept coming and we gladly welcomed Esther, Martha, and Richard into the family—three more in just over four years.

It was Howard's work that took him to Grand Lake for an impromptu duck-hunting excursion with one of the Y's associate directors and a graduate of his Junior Leaders' Club who showed up the day before, asking for advice. This was a typical scenario for Howard since he couldn't turn anyone away who wanted his help and it provided a perfect excuse to leave the office. An irresistible combination.

"It'll give me a chance to see if it's worth taking a whole group up there next month," he explained as we were cleaning the kitchen the night before, long after supper was over and the children were bathed and in bed. It was a ritual we always did together and our only time alone as a couple every day.

"When do you have to get up?" I asked.

"Four-thirty."

"Don't wake the kids," I said, like he needed to be reminded to be quiet at such an early hour. Whenever I heard stories from the neighbor ladies I was always reminded that Howard was one of the most thoughtful husbands and involved fathers.

"You know I won't," he said calmly. He was rarely impatient or cross with me, even when I was tired and grumpy after a long day alone with the children.

"I'll get that," he told me, grabbing the bowl and whisk I'd collected to make a quick pancake batter for morning. "You go on up."

"I think I will," I said, dropping my apron on the counter. Howard abandoned the utensils and pulled me close for a hug and a kiss. He ran his hands up and down over all my curves, pausing briefly to knead the small of my back with his palm, knowing it always gave me trouble before bed. We were quite accustomed to being parents first and a couple second, content with the secret dance of intimacy that plays out in knowing glances, long embraces in the pantry, or a quick peck on the lips passing in the hall. I turned to leave but stopped in the doorway to issue one last reminder.

"Don't forget…"

"The cinnamon. I know," he chuckled, waving the whisk in the air to shoo me out of the room. "I'll be along in a minute." I was around the corner and halfway to the stairs when a most familiar, half-whisper caught up to me. "I love you, Lucile."

"Me too," I replied, not even sure if he heard me. Howard was so quiet when he came to bed and then again when he got up to leave that morning, that I never even heard him or had a chance to say goodbye.

Now, there I was trying to grasp the news that he was missing. Or, something even worse.

"The dock attendant reports they shoved off around 6:30," the officer said. He was crammed into the tiny, straight-backed Victorian chair from the farm that Mother used to sit in to knit. "A big squall moved in around seven this morning. We're hoping they went onshore to wait it out. The authorities in St. Marys are starting a search now."

"That was over an hour ago!" I gasped.

"The weather just isn't letting up, Ma'am," the officer replied.

"I know the police chief in St. Marys, Lucile. He's a good man," Dr. Busler said. "Someone will call when there's anything to report."

Someone, I thought. *Someone?* I needed to hear Howard's voice. It had to be him telling me everything was all right. Having barely sat down, I got up and crossed to the phone.

I dialed my neighbor and asked her to come watch Richard. She'd seen the patrol car in front of the house and was full of questions.

"Donna please, just come right over." I hung up without waiting for a response and went straight to the closet for my coat and purse. Vinton met me by the door, blocking my exit.

"You can't go up there," he told me. "You'll only be in the way." I threw my coat on over my dirty apron. "Let the search party do their job, Lucile." He didn't budge even as I reached around him for the doorknob. "There's nothing you can do." He said it slowly. Deliberately. His words nearly made my knees give out.

"Maybe not," I said. "But I won't just sit and wait." I glanced over at the wide-eyed police officer, watching the standoff, then back to Vinton. "If you two won't take me, then they will," I said, nodding at Donna and her husband Jim climbing the porch steps outside. "But that means I'll have to take my boy too." Not even my shaky voice belied my determination. Vinton sighed deeply, rubbed a hand down his face and signaled the officer. We left right away.

The light rain falling in Piqua gradually turned torrential as we drove north to St. Marys, the sky dark. The wipers on the cruiser barely cleared the windshield as we drew closer to the lake. Sitting in back, Donna and I held hands, silent. I stared out at the blur of road and trees as sheets of rain battered the window beside me. I forced myself to picture Howard standing on shore—water-soaked, glasses missing, wrapped in blankets—smiling sheepishly over the trouble he'd caused. The scene at Grand Lake was nothing like that when we arrived. There was no sign of him anywhere.

The tiny parking area beside the boat launch was overrun

with cars and trucks, parked every which way, spilling out onto the sides of the road leading up to it, many with empty boat trailers attached. A white Packard ambulance sat among them, its engine running. We pulled in as far as possible and Vinton jumped out before the cruiser even stopped, beating me out the door.

"You stay here," he said. "I'll check in with the police chief."

I got out too, but only went as far as it took to get a good view of the dock. It was crowded with eight or ten boats, another half dozen already launched and fanning out across the water in all directions. Groups of two and three men gathered behind a police officer handing out coils of rope. It took me a moment to realize that each expanse ended in a multi-pronged grappling hook that only had one use—dredging the bottom of the lake for bodies.

I began to shake uncontrollably, wrapping my arms around myself and buckling at the waist. Tears filled my eyes but I couldn't look away from the horror unfolding in front of me. Donna swooped in and guided me the opposite direction. As we zig-zagged in and around all of the cars it suddenly dawned on me that one of them was ours. I raced ahead looking over the roofs and hoods as best I could, guessing that Howard must have parked somewhere around the edges, arriving before dawn when the lot was surely empty. There were so many black Model A's that it took me a moment to find it, finally spotting Howard's green thermos flask laying on the dashboard.

I got in and closed the door, keeping my hands to myself, keenly aware he was the last to touch anything. A pair of shoes, a dry change of clothes, and a sandwich wrapped in waxed paper were neatly stacked on the floor in back. The metal cup from the top of the thermos sat empty on the seat next to me. I inhaled deeply. The car smelled like Barbasol and stale coffee. I reached up and pulled down the visor, cupping my hand underneath to catch the extra key Howard always stashed there. A small photograph fell into my lap. I stared at it, startled and slow to pick it up—a snapshot of our sweet, little Walter. Donna opened the passenger door and looked in on me.

"May I join you?" I didn't respond but she took my lack of protest as permission. We both sat there looking straight ahead at the tangle of trees in front of the car. I handed her the picture and she sighed deeply, deflating back into the seat. "Oh Lucile."

"I didn't know he kept it here." She passed the photo back to me and I smiled when I saw Walter again. "Look at that face. So precious."

"He was beautiful, Lucile. Such a good boy too." I nodded.

We had lost Walter to polio when he was only a toddler. His death devastated us both, but was especially debilitating for Howard who had only just started to leave thoughts of the war behind him, when our tragic loss struck. I slipped the photo back under the visor, then gripped the steering wheel as hard as I could, both hands balled into fists around it.

"This can't be happening." I began to rock back and forth in the seat, staring at the center of the wheel. "Why Donna? Why?" The sobs I was attempting to swallow finally came choking out. I tried not to scream but something between a moan and a whimper still escaped my lips. I rocked violently in place. Back and forth. Back and forth. Back and forth. Donna slid closer, but there was no comforting me.

"They're going to find him Lucile," Donna said. She tried to slip an arm around my shoulder, but I pulled away, rolled down the window, and pointed at the lake.

"Look at them Donna," I yelled. "They're not searching for men huddled on shore. He should have turned up by
now!" After losing Walter, I knew there really wasn't any order
to things.

Then, in the silence that follows such an outburst, in the
moment my dear friend paused, scrambling to think of something else to say that might stave off the truth, a faint but clear
voice pierced the air from a distance.

"We found one!"

Donna and I scrambled out of the car and ran to shore
along with every other person there. A lone fishing boat raced
for the dock, the whir of its tiny motor getting louder and
louder with each passing second. I shoved through the crush of
men lined up three and four deep and didn't stop until I found
Vinton and the police chief at the water's edge.

"Who is it?" I pleaded. "Is he alive?"

"We'll know in a minute," Vinton said.

The chief was busy and didn't address me, signaling two
of his officers to meet the boat, sending another one to get the
ambulance attendants and a stretcher. "Everyone stay back,"
he yelled into the crowd. "Give my men some space until we
know what we're dealing with here."

The boat came barreling up next to the dock at full speed
and the man in back didn't cut the motor until it ran aground.
"He's alive," one of the two rescuers shouted. The men onshore
swarmed the boat blocking my view, so I plunged into the lake
and around the other side just in time to see a pale, limp body
hoisted up and onto the stretcher. The Miller boy.

"No, no, no, no, no!" I heard some hysterical woman
chanting, not realizing it was my own panicked voice.

"Blankets! We need blankets!" the Chief yelled. Stan Miller

looked dead. He didn't move. His face and hands were blue, clothing stiff, his overcoat and boots missing altogether. I lunged for the sleeve of the rescuer sitting at the front of the boat.

"What about the other two?" He tried to pull away but I held tightly with both hands and gave a hard tug with each word. "Where's my husband," I pleaded, dissolving into sobs again. He relaxed his arm and really looked at me before answering.

"There isn't anyone else," he said. "The kid was the only one still with the boat."

I just stared at him, unable to let the words even begin to sink in. Still trying to hold on. "I'm sorry." He took his arm back and jumped out to follow the crowd to the ambulance. The men were all cheering and congratulating each other. Thrilled to find a lone survivor. The police chief came and talked to me as soon as the ambulance pulled away.

"I'm sorry to say it, but the kid says your husband tried to swim for shore Mrs. Bridgman." It took me a second to respond.

"No. He would have stayed with the boat. You always stay with the boat."

"The water out there is only seven or eight feet deep. He must have thought he could make it."

"That's not what you're supposed to do," I said. Even I knew that.

Irvin "Mac" Mackenzie, the other Y director on the trip, was pulled from the lake next. And then, Howard.

Having witnessed the rush to bring Stan ashore I knew they were both gone given how slowly the boats bearing their bodies returned. I refused to go home until I saw Howard for myself but both the police chief and Vinton were adamant that I couldn't see his body in such a state. After covering him with a dirty tarp from the back of someone's pickup they did allow me to pull up his pant leg and identify the scar on his knee as my proof. I was completely numb. No tears. No breakdown. No words for any of it. It took all my strength just to stay upright and keep breathing.

"The children will be home for lunch soon," Donna whispered, her arm around my waist. "We should go, so you can be with them."

The drive back to Piqua is a blur and I walked into the house to find some women from church folding laundry and fixing sandwiches in my kitchen, our family physician Dr. Kiser talking on the phone in the dining room, and Howard's YMCA director and another co-worker waiting on the couch. Like a row of dominos tumbling forward, the house fell silent room by room as I passed through from the back door. Donna stayed right with me and had to strip off my clothes and put me in the tub. She was there when I came out and made sure I looked as presentable as possible.

The girls walked in from school right as I came back downstairs. They stared at my wet hair and I had to rely on the heavy brass knob of the front door to keep from collapsing. No smile, no kiss, no greeting of any kind—just an empty shell of the mother who had sent them on their way less than four hours earlier.

"Mama, what's wrong?" Esther said. Both girls were stopped and silenced by the crowd of people milling about the house. Donna and Vinton hustled everyone into the kitchen, leaving the dining room empty in between, for privacy. I unlocked my knees and sank to the floor at the bottom of the stairs, just inside the front door.

"Your father was in an accident," I said plainly. The only way to keep from breaking down again was to banish all emotion.

"But he's duck hunting," Martha said.

"There was a storm and Daddy's boat tipped over." I made myself look at them but had to blur their faces with my eyes. I couldn't bear to watch as the next words I uttered changed their world so completely. "Daddy drowned."

"You mean he's dead?" Esther concluded, matter of factly.

"Yes." She was the same age as Howard when his own mother passed away. As tragic as that was, even he and his sisters had had some warning.

"Like Mary's nana?" Martha asked. Her best friend across the street had recently lost a grandmother and we all attended the funeral just weeks before.

"Yes. That's right." There was a long bit of silence and I could see them each working the news out in their minds. I don't think they realized before then that someone their father's age could even die. We'd told them a little about Walter, but he was hardly real, just a boy they saw in pictures.

"Do we have to go back to school?" Esther asked, standing and climbing halfway up the stairs.

"No, but I'll come check on you in a bit," I said before she disappeared around the corner. Martha stood to follow her sister but stared down at me first, tears tumbling down her cheeks.

"Are you sad Daddy's dead, Mama?" she asked in a shaky voice. Her question put a vice grip on my heart and it took everything in me to keep that wailing sound from spewing out again. I nodded and pulled my dear little girl down into a hug.

"But I didn't say goodbye," she said against my cheek.

"It's okay, sweetheart. Neither did I." She stayed there in my arms for a minute before pulling away. "Are you hungry?" I asked, brushing the tear-soaked pixie cut off her forehead.

"Not anymore," she said with a shrug.

"You're my brave girl, Martha Grace." She nodded and climbed up the stairs, pausing on the landing to give me a little seven-year old wave. She had the palest blue-grey eyes, just like her father's.

My mother, Aunt Rose, and brother Carleton arrived in Piqua that evening and I was so relieved to have them, as I could barely function. Mother's tendency to take over was finally helpful and Rose, as always, was most supportive. She held me and we cried together right there on the front porch after Mother went inside to tend to the children.

"What am I going to do?" I sobbed.

"You don't have to figure it all out today, Lucile," Rose said without hesitating and she didn't let go until that round of tears was exhausted. "You're going to be all right," she kept repeating. Rose had never once lied to me, but I just didn't believe her this time.

Carleton became my constant companion for the flurry of tasks and decisions that accompany a death and I blindly followed him wherever he took me. No matter what the decision—from picking a casket to planning the visitation—he always said the same thing when I looked to him for advice.

"Do what's best for you and the children." He was so careful to check all the paperwork and inquire about the costs and payment, the things I wasn't in the right mind to care about or keep track of, but would be so thankful for later.

The hardest decision of all was choosing where to bury Howard. I wondered if the children and I would even stay in Piqua so I picked Albion, though the thought of not being able to visit his grave whenever I wanted nearly sent me into a panic. Riverside Cemetery is perched on a gently sloped hill overlooking the Kalamazoo River and was where Walter was laid to rest with two empty plots next to him, one on either side. That and the fact that there were only good memories to recall of meeting, courting, and falling in love with Howard in Albion reassured me that it was the best decision. I didn't know how I could leave him there, but that was just the first of many impossibilities I would need to face alone.

I passed through those early days after the accident in a haze of grief and heartache so deep that I was lost to everyone. I saved whatever remnants of life I could muster for the children, but even those brief moments with them did little to relieve the debilitating despair. I couldn't sleep or eat and I cried so hard at night that the blood vessels around my eyes began to pop, leaving me looking battered. I moved the girls into our room since the idea of lying in the bed without Howard beside me was intolerable. Rose had to pick out clothes for the visitation and dress me and my father drove me to the funeral home an hour before it was set to begin, for a private viewing. I had thirty minutes to be with Howard before his parents and sisters joined me. Half an hour to say goodbye to the love of a lifetime.

"I would do anything to protect you from this," Father said as we paused in the lobby of the funeral home. The words came out slowly. The bitter confession of a helpless man. "Can I at least come in with you?" he pleaded. I shook my head no, but laid my face against him as we stood there. He was the only other man who loved me as completely as Howard did.

"Oh, Daddy." The thought of my husband, dead in the next room, hung on me like a lead cloak.

"My Lucy," Father whispered into my hair. I saw the funeral director waiting for me and went to pull away, but Father didn't let go. "I'll be right here," he said, before releasing me.

I couldn't turn to look at him. I followed the director into the visitation room. It was the largest they had, filled with chairs from wall to wall, except for a modest clearing surrounding the casket. I let his feet guide me as we moved all the way to the front. He opened the lid, but I averted my gaze, not wanting to risk seeing Howard until I was by myself.

"If there's nothing else, I'll leave you now," the director said. Even after hearing the door click shut, I just stood there. I don't know for how long. I was terrified of what my dearest Howard might look like after the awful death he'd suffered, full of so much struggle and fear. I finally lifted my eyes, shocked to even find him lying there. Asleep. Peaceful, in a way. Familiar, but not real.

I noticed immediately that his hair wasn't combed right and I walked up to gently fix it. My legs nearly went out from under me the second my hand brushed against his cold skin. I leaned forward, bracing myself on the edge of the casket and closed my eyes. The room was spinning. I barely had a grip. Full rows of flowers fanned out along either side and the sickening sweet smell of lilies and embalming fluid almost made me gag.

"Oh Howard," I groaned, waves of confusion and disbelief rolling over me.

Why aren't you getting up? The children can't see you like this. Don't leave us Howard. I can't do this without you. Please wake up. This can't be happening.

"I still need you with me, Howard. The children need you," I whispered over his body. "I'm not ready to say goodbye."

I held Howard's hand. I kissed his face over and over again. As I sobbed with my head on his chest, all thoughts dissolved in the bottomless sorrow that enveloped me. The deepest pain. The purest love.

I will never truly know how the children and I got through the visitation. I spoke to hundreds of people and only remember one conversation from the entire evening. It happened near the end, when the crowd had dwindled to only family and our closest friends and Vinton escorted a couple over to where I was sitting. I had noticed them earlier, coats on, standing in the same corner of the room the whole time as dozens of other mourners came and went.

"Lucile, these are the Millers," Vinton said. I knew the name, but I was quite sure I'd never met them before. "Stan's parents," he added. I felt every drop of blood drain from my face. "They were hoping to speak to you."

"If this is a good time, Mrs. Bridgman," Mr. Miller stammered.

"Certainly," I said, but wondered if there would ever be a good time for this conversation, necessary as it was. Vinton pulled a chair over for Mrs. Miller who looked to be in as bad of shape as me. "How is Stan?" I asked. His mother started to weep into a handkerchief.

"He's going to be fine. He really wanted to be here to pay his respects, but he didn't want to upset you," Mr. Miller explained. I reached out and touched his wife's knee, looking at her straight on, mother to mother.

"I'm happy to know your boy is all right and Howard would be too." My voice broke and she took my hand and didn't let go.

"I'm so sorry Mrs. Bridgman. Your husband did so much for Stan," she said. I was instantly flooded with the tears I'd held back all night and it took several moments for each of us to compose ourselves and continue.

"Stanley made us promise to tell you something," Mr. Miller said.

"What?" Their son was the last person to see Howard alive.

"He's wracked with guilt but wants you to know what really happened." He paused. His wife encouraged him with a nod. "They saw the storm blowing in. Your husband suggested they turn back. Stan says there would have been time to get to shore if they'd only listened to him."

And, just like that, I was saved from a lifetime of not knowing.

Howard *was* the safe leader everyone knew him to be. He *did* try to keep a dangerous situation from developing. Then, once they were in trouble, he broke the biggest rule of all. He left the boat and went for help. He felt responsible for not insisting they turn around—trying to fix his own mistake. I took a full, deep breath for the first time in days.

"It was a terrible, terrible accident," I said. "There's no one to blame." With all of Howard's trips and travels—not the least of which was going to war—I knew there was no denying his adventuresome spirit. "He could have made them turn around if he was really that worried. You have to make Stanley understand that. I'll tell him myself if that's what it takes." The

Millers just stared at me like I was speaking to them in a foreign language, as if they'd prepared for a meltdown, a flurry of accusations and rage. No wonder they'd kept their coats on the entire time.

There wasn't an empty seat at the church service the next morning and twenty-five cars made the 195-mile trip to Michigan. My darkest moment came as I watched Howard's casket lowered into the ground, Walter's grave marker visible over the pile of freshly turned dirt. My father and Aunt Rose held me up from either side and the girls stood in front, Richard in Mother's arms beside us. Muffled sobs came at me from every direction and as much as I wanted to wail over what was happening, I was determined not to let the children see me break down. Visions of an escape did flash across my mind when I heard the first shovels of dirt dropping onto the coffin. I pictured walking all the way to St. Marys and throwing myself to the bottom of the same dark, churning lake where he died, but there were three reasons not to. The children were the only things left to convince me that my life had not ended as surely as my beloved Howard's.

Aunt Rose hosted a reception in her home for all the travelers and dozens of local folks who wished to pay their respects. There were professors from the college, the owner of the hardware store where Howard had worked, the eighty-year old cook from his fraternity house—these were people who knew the same man I fell in love with. After the appropriate sympathies were expressed several of them started telling stories about Howard from our college days and they spoke highly of his intelligence, good humor, and moxie. Their genuine fondness of him and the warmth of the memories they shared brought a smile to my face when I didn't think that was even possible.

It was wonderful to see and hear that Howard had impressed so many people and I hoped that one day I could think about him like they did, only remembering the good things, without feeling so terribly lost and alone.

The drive back to Piqua was exhausting and I couldn't even begin to deal with the kettle of vultures waiting at the house to inquire about buying Howard's sport coat, the cameras, or our car. I would need the money soon enough, but I was done making decisions by then. The children and I waited as our driver Mr. White chased them off the porch and down the street yelling just what he'd do if he heard they came back. I took Esther, Martha, and Richard inside and put them to bed myself for the first time in over a week. It was just one of many routines that had to change and I thought it best for all of us to get on with it as quickly as possible. Once I was sure the children were soundly asleep I went into the basement to scream and sob into a pillow. It took an hour or more to get it all out. It would take years to uncover the endless ways we would miss Howard as a husband and a father, but that first night after the funeral, was one of the hardest.

For every person that brought food to the house or a basket of sewing for me to earn a little money, for all the boys Howard worked with who came to play with the children or his colleagues from the Y who maintained the house and shoveled the walks, there were also some visitors who showed up only to take advantage. There was a woman who professed to be a friend that came with the express purpose of informing me I would not be able to continue with any of our couple friendships now that I was widowed. I knew that already, but resented her approach and especially her thin, helpful facade. Several different salesmen arrived offering me work, all with the same vile notion that given my circumstances people would buy anything I had to sell. I told each one, in no uncertain words, that I could never do that to my friends and neighbors, when the people of Piqua had been so good to us for so many years. The money they promised was hard to turn down but I couldn't have lived with myself if I'd given in to the growing desperation.

My financial circumstances turned quite grim come winter. The YMCA had been most generous to give me two months of Howard's salary, but I used it towards funeral expenses and still owed over a hundred dollars, with no way to pay. I took as many substitute-teaching jobs as I could but they did not come often and at only $5 per day, plus a dollar to have someone watch Richard, there wasn't even enough to keep the pantry full. I was relying much too much on gifts of food showing up and knew it couldn't continue much longer, so I had no choice but to cash the Liberty Bond I'd bought in Howard's name during the war, five years shy of maturity. I did consider selling the Croix de Guerre Medal of Honor, awarded to Howard by the French government for acts of heroism, but had to draw the line somewhere. There were calls every day from bill collectors and even ones who were sympathetic to my situation at first, were becoming impatient and more threatening each time I asked for another extension. I tried to leave what little savings we had accumulated untouched, to spend on the children that first Christmas, but the heating bill had to get paid or risk being cut off. We spent the children's entire school break with my family since there was no way for me to trim a tree or roast a turkey on my own. And for all that time I continued to lose weight and couldn't sleep most nights, often reading until two a.m. or later. Missing Howard was slowly breaking me, with no end in sight.

All of that changed one day in February when my doorbell rang and I answered it to find two members of the American Legion Auxiliary on the stoop, a man and a woman.

"Mrs. Bridgman?" the woman asked. I nodded.

"This is for you," she said, handing me a bag of groceries. It was full and heavy and I tried to sneak a glance at the contents before politely setting it to the side. The Legion helped families of deceased soldiers and I had considered contacting them for assistance, but presumed they only supported those who'd lost a man in battle.

"We were sorry to hear about your husband's death," the man said. "May we speak to you about our services?" They were both smiling and so pleasant.

"Yes, please come in." It was early afternoon and the girls were in school and Richard was down for a nap. I offered them tea or coffee but they declined, instead settling quickly onto the edge of the sofa.

"Mrs. Bridgman I'll get straight to the reason for our visit and I hope you won't take offense," the man said as soon as I joined them. "We've come to discuss the welfare of your children."

"My children?"

"Now that their father is deceased," he added.

"With everything that's happened, we know it will be a struggle for you to take care of them properly," the woman said. "We wondered if you've considered giving your children up, at least for the time being, while you put your life back together. Find a job. That sort of thing." She was the kind of woman who could actually say such horrible things without compromising the smile on her face or the lilt in her voice.

"What? No." I started to tremble uncontrollably. My mouth dried up and it became hard for me to even speak.

"While it may seem like you're doing all right now, we've seen situations less serious than yours deteriorate very quickly," the man said.

"No one means for the children to suffer of course," said the woman. "Especially a good mother like you." Her shameless attempt at a compliment hung in the air and I stared at her. Enraged. Terrified. It sickened me to have been so easily fooled, enticed by a bag of food and a pair of bright smiles.

"You don't know me or my children," I said, being careful to look them each directly in the eyes before standing and walking to the door. "You should leave now," I told them, opening it. They remained seated and shared a knowing glance. Perhaps they were used to some parents putting up a good fight before giving in. The woman continued with her pitch.

"We have a lovely facility up in Otter Lake, Michigan. The children there live in smaller cottages with a dorm mother. It's not the institutional kind of place you're probably imagining. At least come take a look," she suggested, her face still beaming like she was asking me to try a new face cream at no charge.

"I'm sure you wouldn't want me to call the police." I kept my eyes fixed on her until that cheery gaze finally dropped away, prepared to throw her out myself if she didn't move. With raised eyebrows and pursed lips, she shook her head at me and stood up. The man followed her to the door. He stopped beside me, holding out a business card, which I snatched and tore in half several times before tossing it at him like confetti. He smirked and chuckled right in my face.

"I know you're grieving Mrs. Bridgman, but don't be foolish," he said, depositing another card on the table before walking out.

"Get out!" I shrieked, grabbing it, along with the bag of food, and throwing it all onto the porch. The crash startled them and they tripped down the last few steps to the sidewalk, not a smile left between them.

"I wouldn't let the likes of you watch my children long enough to run to the corner store!" I slammed the door and locked it, then ran to the back of the house to do the same there, my hands trembling so hard I could barely get the chain lock lined up in its track. I returned to the living room and stood guard in the front window, just to make sure they were really gone.

After a half hour of pacing, I collapsed in a chair. Even though I'd uttered the words "I can't do this," any number of times, I didn't mean it. Not really. To learn there were people out there who actually thought I couldn't care for my own children was unimaginable. Horrifying. I desperately wanted to tell someone—my family, Donna next door, Dr. Busler—but the shame of those people even crossing the threshold of my own home prevented me. Certainly, nobody I knew would ever encourage me to consider the Legion workers' offer, but what if there was a pause in the conversation after I described what happened. A hesitation. A question in their own minds rising up.

Is this what everyone thinks?

Living on handouts. No job. No plan for the future. It certainly wasn't an impossible conclusion. Howard's death left me feeling like I'd lost everything, but the visit by the Legion workers showed me that there was much more at stake than I ever realized.

It was sitting there in that chair, bathed in pinholes of light filtered through lace curtains, when my vision of the future shifted ever so slightly, for the first time since the accident. Until then, it had always included Howard. Always. But in that moment, I could finally see that I had to move forward without him there, living in the present with our children, with what we had left. Undeterred by "what-ifs" or what might have been had he lived. And I knew, in the deepest way possible, that that is what Howard would want too, even though it meant I had to do it alone, without him by my side, but always still in my heart.

Slowly, deliberately—I stood up, took a deep breath, and crossed to the front door. As much as it galled me, I went out on that porch and gathered up every last bit of food—a can of powdered milk, a pound of butter, potatoes, onions, some carrots—none of it worse for being tossed around. There was a piece of leftover roast in the refrigerator and I decided to make pasties for dinner that night. I hadn't made them in years but they are large and filling and I knew the children would love them.

Then, I would see about tomorrow.

Author's Note

2018

LUCILE BALL BRIDGMAN died April 4, 1979.

Grandma Bridgie, as I called her, never returned from the hospital following a routine gall bladder surgery. My family gathered several days later, at her cozy bungalow on Nicklin Avenue in Piqua, after the funeral. The house was ringed in muted shades of purple and green, the sweet smell of spring lilacs greeting us as we climbed the porch steps.

The tiny rooms inside were full and loud, as much of a reunion as a remembrance. Each of the grandchildren took turns going upstairs to claim one of Grandma's handmade quilts from the linen closet and we all drew numbers to distribute the thicket of houseplants lining the windows of the back porch. It was a gathering that she would have loved, happy to sit in the broken-down easy chair by the front window, hearing aids turned low against the din of over two dozen people, a smile on her face the entire time. By then, she had seen twenty-eight years of teaching, celebrated all of her children's college graduations and marriages, welcomed eleven healthy grandchildren, and even enjoyed several trips abroad. Lucile never remarried, but certainly made the most of life without her beloved Howard.

My mother and aunt were the ones to find the box in the basement, left by Lucile. Filled with sepia prints of her and Howard, love letters postmarked from France, the diary he carried into battle, a Red Cross armband, and a gauze mask from the epidemic—it was one of countless musty, tattered cartons that could have just as easily ended up in the trash. Instead, it received a final cursory inspection and ended up being our family's greatest inheritance.

The treasures inside told the unspoken story of a woman we recognized but barely knew. Described a simple but abiding love affair tested by epic circumstances. And, revealed how one woman managed to persevere even when faced with unexpected challenges and tremendous loss. While she never took the opportunity to share many of her experiences with us directly, Grandma Bridgie left an amazing legacy in the end, the greatest of which was her life's example of bravery, resilience, and the power of love.

Lucile herself wrote the following on the 36th anniversary of Howard's death:

"In retrospect, I realize that I have traveled a far different path
living my own busy, frustrating, adventuresome,
often satisfying and pleasurable life
that has come with more than my share of loss and sorrow,
but also with tremendous love.
And it is the love that has always seen me through."

Acknowledgements

FIRST, I WISH to thank my husband Norm, for his infinite support and years-long interest in this book, as it has slowly evolved from a wish to a reality. Thank you also for your thoughtful presence and careful attention as the book's editor. You have literally touched every page and it wouldn't be the story that it is without you.

I also want to thank my mother, Martha Bridgman Stone, who was the first to discover and piece together this story from the box in Lucile's basement. Initially, we planned to work on the book together, but I took it on as my own after her sudden death in 1995. My mother's energy and presence have remained a part of this project throughout the entire journey to publication and I know she would be thrilled beyond belief to hold a copy of it in her hand.

Thank you to the Munising Schools Public Library and the Alger County Historical Society for their assistance with my research on the epidemic.

To the generous writers at Red Oak Writing studio in Milwaukee, WI. Your feedback and support during our roundtable discussions gave me the first inkling that maybe I really was a writer and could actually weave this personal, family story into an interesting and compelling read.

Thanks to all my beta readers who selflessly gave of their time to not only read my manuscript, but provide their honest feedback and impressions.

Finally, I wish to acknowledge the many courageous people who worked tirelessly, and at great personal risk, to lessen the suffering and death wrought by the epidemic, especially in Munising. It is with tremendous respect and admiration that I share their story.

Michael Stone is a writer and social worker who lives in Evanston, IL.

Additional References:

Excerpt from "Pale Horse, Pale Rider" from PALE HORSE, PALE RIDER: THREE SHORT NOVELS by Katherine Anne Porter. Copyright 1937 by Katherine Anne Porter. Copyright © Renewed in 1965 by Katherine Anne Porter. Reprinted by permission of Houghton Mifflin Harcourt Publishing Company. All rights reserved.

Symon, Charles A., editor. Alger County: A Centennial History, 1885-1985. Munising, MI: Alger County Historical Society, 1986.

The Munising News. August 16, 1918 – May 9, 1919.

Lucile on the shore of Lake Superior, 1918

CPSIA information can be obtained
at www.ICGtesting.com
Printed in the USA
LVHW032030100321
681107LV00003BA/773